DALE STOHRE

FIRESTORM

Firestorm
Author: Dale Stohre
Editor: Griffin Mill
Cover Design and Interior Layout: Michael Nicloy

ISBN-13: 978-1-957351-74-2

PUBLISHED BY NICO 11 PUBLISHING & DESIGN | MUKWONAGO, WISCONSIN
MICHAEL NICLOY, PUBLISHER | WWW.NICO11PUBLISHING.COM
QUANTITY AND WHOLESALE ORDER REQUESTS MAY BE EMAILED TO:
MIKE@NICO11PUBLISHING.COM OR BE MADE BY PHONE: 217.779.9677

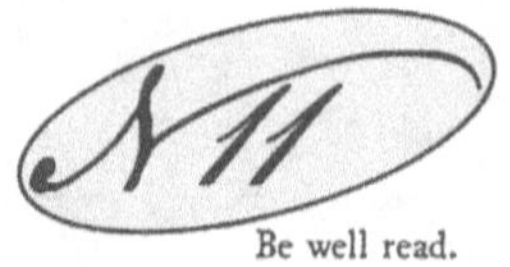

Printed in The United States of America

To you

—especially the children—

who have endured or are enduring
the cruelty of war,
neglect or abuse,
condemnation or indifference:

You are loved;
you are not forgotten;
you are more wonderful
than you know.

"Be strong and courageous …"

Joshua 1:9

FIRESTORM

PROLOGUE

We begin in a graveyard. It's quiet here; a hundred tombstones, maybe more. Most lean at odd angles, eroded with time and carrying names and dates barely legible. Some lay where they fell, twenty, sixty, or a hundred years ago. Few have living descendants to remember them.

A rutted gravel road passes by—the only road for miles in any direction. Some winters, it's impassible; the snow can drift shoulder-high and more, along this windswept knoll miles from any town, amid the endless undulation of the Great Plains.

Oaks and maples a century old guard the graves of settlers who stamped the indelible mark of white culture over the gentler traces of Indigenous nations—Cheyenne, Lakota, Comanche, and more—who preceded them. Settlers did not come in great numbers. This land, best suited for wide-ranging cattle, stretches beyond the horizon, encompassing nineteen thousand square miles between the Platte and Niobrara Rivers. There are no cities, and counties may have only one town, thirty miles from its neighbors across the rolling sea of grass known as the Sand Hills.

Good people are interred here—in the middle of nowhere, it is said. Their graves are of no interest to the world, and their kin had every reason to expect this place to remain peaceful, sacred, and obscure. For more than a century it did. But two graves cradle a mother and daughter, side-by-side among the graves of their neighbors, overlooking a modest spring-fed stream that feeds into another stream, then another. Its water joins the North Platte River, which carries it to the Missouri, then the Mississippi.

Hardly anyone visits this field of tombstones. One who does is approaching now.

Chad Harris, his twelve-year-old son Matthew riding shotgun, pulls a trailer burdened with lawn mowers, gas-powered string trimmers, rakes, and shovels into this quiet, isolated cemetery. Their big Toyota four-by-four is caked with Nebraska mud, thanks to a thunderstorm the night before. It eases up the road between headstones that mark life and death on the prairie.

Twice a month, Chad comes to maintain this hallowed ground. It's a Saturday morning tradition. It takes perhaps two hours if he does it himself, but it will take him three today, since he will mentor his son in the care of this sanctuary.

"Dad, I see tire tracks across the grass. Somebody's been here recently."

"Maybe someone's family, or maybe just another tourist."

Matthew sees a paper cup, straw still held by the plastic lid, resting against a headstone. Not far away, a paper bag with a fast food logo drifts toward the fence in the light breeze.

"That's disgusting. Why don't we just lock the gate and keep people like that away?"

"I know, Matt. It's rude. But some people really need to see this place. It's not just our history here."

Chad remembers a spring day in 1978 when a man he once knew, a local boy who had made a name for himself, lay his loved ones to rest among their ancestors. The moment was captured by a herd of journalists who reported on those who attended, the color of the caskets and the dignity with which the survivor carried his grief. He shed, they observed, not a single tear. This hillside would be burdened again, when his rise to national stature drew the curious to this piece of his earlier life, not to honor the dead as much as to add a few snapshots to their scrapbook or another clip for their travel video: Yosemite, Mt. Rushmore, *that Cemetery*.

Some say that you can't get there from here. They hope you will believe them, though if you persist, you may find it. Distances on the Great Plains are exaggerated by urban standards; many who set out for the cemetery turn back short of their goal, convinced that nothing of value could be that far from civilization on a road that poorly maintained.

Indeed, the dusty, seventeen-mile trek chills the enthusiasm of those used to diversions within sight of an Interstate. A gravel road marked only by a number turns north, and for the first few miles seems promising enough. But beyond the last of the few ranches in this sparsely populated country, the road languishes. Its rutted washboard surface is meager improvement over the trail that once carried horse-drawn wagons between cattle ranches and towns to the south and east. But the impatience of the time-conscious preserves for the few who persevere a memory worth the effort.

⁜

The equipment is rolled off the trailer. Before Chad starts the mower, he pauses, steps off the machine, and turns toward his son. "There's something I want to show you."

They walk toward the high point at the center of the cemetery. They find two matching headstones. Matthew reads the dates: Kathryn Rossberg Eastland 1947-1978 … Monica Eastland 1966-1978.

"They both died in 1978—and this Monica was only twelve? That's my age."

Chad nods. "Yeah, Matt. They died in a plane crash."

"'Eastland' … Wait—are they related to the president?"

"They are, Son. His first wife and daughter."

"They lived around here?"

"Whitman, originally."

It took Matthew a moment to connect the dots. "Then … did you know them?"

"I graduated with Kathryn."

"You were friends?"

Chad pauses, haunted by what could have been. Chad knew that if he were honest, he would be revealing to his son the deepest loss of his life. But his son was becoming a man; perhaps this was the time to tell the truth. Chat took a deep breath, and said, "She was my fiancé."

Matthew misses the cue: *I'd rather not talk about this*—"So if she married someone else, what happened, you know, to her and you?"

"Let's just say, Matt, that she chose a more glamorous life than a cattle rancher could offer."

⁜

Those who call these lands "home" would put up a fence—a wall if they could—to restore the tranquility lost when people suddenly cared about their cemetery. *Let our dead rest. There are no gift shops or restaurants or hotels out here. We're tired of casual tourists asking directions. Tired of your pleas for help when you get lost this far from what you call civilization. Tired of you tourists who stop, point your lens at the cemetery, and drive away. This is not a tourist attraction! This is sacred ground. So don't come.*

They won't say that. They are far too gracious to say that—but still, they're tired of being treated like a human zoo.

The hillside is quiet now. The traffic of the merely curious (who seek whatever people seek on ground cursed by publicity) has faded, returning this hallowed ground to its true purpose: the occasional visits of those who call the Sand Hills home. The grass is growing again, erasing the paths converging on the granite headstones of a mother and daughter, whose lives of distinction ended far too soon, denied the privilege of living, dying, and being interred in peace.

CHAPTER ONE

SPRING

Seven hundred miles to the northeast, the grass was not yet growing. Ice still held Madeline Island in its grip. The residents of La Pointe—the only village on the only inhabited of the Apostle Islands, were still shoveling an early spring snowfall, when the visitors came.

Frank Cooper held the steering wheel in a death grip. He was glad to be driving; having something to do masked his nervousness. His colleague in the passenger seat, having nowhere to put his anxiety, was squeezing the Wisconsin highway map (he preferred them large, foldable, and not digital) into a wad in his fist.

"I don't believe people actually do this." Cooper broke the silence, his voice betraying the tension as he steered the rented sedan around another barricade marking another pool of water. Their car—a poor choice, they were discovering— moved cautiously across the only"road" to the island, two-miles of deteriorating ice marked by a line of discarded Christmas trees, and better suited for a Jeep. It stretched from the Wisconsin mainland to an island with a history encompassing a millennium.

His partner, "D.C." Barker, agreed, as he stared straight ahead. "I don't like this. Not at all."

It was a Tuesday in March, 2000, late in the morning but early in the insanity that marked an election year. A heavy overcast was shedding its moisture in a moderate snowfall, driven by gusty winds across ice that was thinning, taking on the darker, ominous hue of "black ice" as it surrendered to the encroachment of spring. The car's two occupants were clearly ill-at-ease knowing that only a slowly-disappearing layer of frozen bay separated their vehicle from 160 feet of very cold water.

Their instructions for this trip had been issued a thousand miles to the east, by people who clearly did not appreciate what they were asking.

Barker spoke again. "I enjoyed this little adventure, until about fifteen minutes ago."

"Yeah. Right."

"Finally, we get out of the city and see the real world. I mean, real open country. Real farms. Real small towns. Real people."

"Yeah," Cooper added. "And real thin ice."

The trip had promised the two city dwellers a refreshing change of pace that ended abruptly when, entering the village of Bayfield from the south on State Route 13, they saw the ice road, their route across the frozen bay. What had been casually mentioned in their itinerary was now an unsettling reality for two men who preferred roads that were well-paved, lined with tall buildings and built on solid ground.

They winced at the sound of the front tires, then the rear, pounding across another crack in the ice. Barker recalled an encounter barely five minutes before. "That guy in the grocery store probably thinks we're a couple of wimps." The two men had driven per instructions to what in summer was Bayfield's public swimming beach, and in winter the approach to the ice road. They were met by a pair of crude signs nailed to a post where the pavement gave way to fifty yards of frozen sand. One, clearly intended for this time of year, stated: "Ice Road Unsafe." The other, no doubt with warmer months in mind—or was it?— warned "No Lifeguard On Duty."

Cooper put the car in reverse, and retreated to the grocery store on Rittenhouse Avenue. When they inquired about the sign describing their intended route as "unsafe," the grocer eyed the two urban dwellers, snorted, and said, "Of course. An ice road is *never* 'safe.' Just follow somebody. You'll be fine."

They were hardly reassured, but orders were orders. They returned to the beach and waited. A pickup arrived, drove across the sand, and ventured out onto the frozen bay.

"What d'ya think, Barker?"

"I think he's a local."

"I think he's *nuts*," Frank replied. Barker, however, saw their one chance to reach the island disappearing in the blowing snow

"I also think we should follow that nut. He might know where's he's going."

"Okay. But I'm staying way back."

Following at what they hoped was a safe distance, Cooper carefully steered their car in the same tracks that guided the truck, trying not to go too fast, yet not wanting to lose the taillights of their unwitting guide in the clouds of blowing snow.

They were well trained and highly disciplined, in a profession that often put them in harm's way. But with every bump they were a little more unnerved. And they were overdressed for this time and place. Their well-tailored suits (each concealing a shoulder-holstered handgun) and well-polished shoes would prove highly impractical in the snowbanks that lined the village streets. By day's end, they would not only feel conspicuous as the only people in suits to grace the island in over a month, but miserable as well, their expensively-shod feet thoroughly soaked with melting snow.

No one paid much attention to them at first, and that was better for everyone concerned. The few who did were puzzled by two obviously urban males, one in his 30s, the other in his late-40s. This was months before the tourist season, and they had no apparent agenda except to look, closely, at everything. The handful of residents picking up their mail or buying staples in the small grocery store wondered why so much attention was being paid not to the lake, the galleries and shops (which would remain closed until May), or the other islands that formed much of the horizon. Instead, the strangers took notes and photos, documenting the telephone system. The number of hotel rooms. The capacity of the ferries that connected La Pointe to the mainland during warmer weather. Its police and medical resources—which were distressingly few.

The island was undergoing even more scrutiny than the locals perceived. Their notes included accessibility for helicopters. The proximity to airports capable of handling very large aircraft. And the ability of this small community to provide safety and privacy for a very unusual family of four and their sizable entourage.

The first person to notice was Alice, manager of the modest two-story motel that accommodated the island's few winter guests. They were courteous, not interested in small talk, and evasive. There was confusion even over their names at the motel's small registration desk: I believe you have a reservation for Jim Smith? No. Robert Jones? No. John Smith? Oh—yes.

Alice thought it strange, and said so to her afternoon coffee companion, who told her sister-in-law who told her husband … and by the time the strangers left the next day, they were being watched inquisitively, and they knew it.

Whatever discomfort the visit had caused the strangers, it had become a minor embarrassment for at least one islander. By the time they'd left, the island's only year-around bar was the scene of lively speculation.

"Developers?"

"Yeah, probably. Developers looking for land, I'm thinking."

"I heard someone in Bayfield saying that some rich guy from Minneapolis wants to build a resort on the east end of the island."

"No. Gotta be reporters, doing another story on "Island life in the winter.""

"*What* 'life?'" The room convulsed in laughter.

"You know, it could be organized crime."

"'Organized crime?' Where did that idea come from?"

"Well, they really checked out the airport. Especially liked the fact that the runway is lit at night. I bet they want to run drugs or something in from Canada. "

"Canada?" More than one bar patron scoffed. "Don't be ridiculous."

Alice said, "They booked only one room at the motel …"

Small town conversation in the winter could be imaginative, and in this case wrong on all counts. Police Chief Albert Benson suspected that it was, and confidently assured the islanders leaning against the bar that he had ways of finding out. "Just give me until lunch tomorrow."

"Gonna use your 'connections' again, Al?"

Benson stilled the hearty laughter with a quiet, confident, "Just like always."

It was not just like always. The two visitors simply vanished. The first step was easy; he traced the rented car with Minnesota plates to a rental agency at the Duluth airport. But there, the trail abruptly ended. The names on the motel registry didn't match any names used to secure the car, nor any listed on passenger manifests at the Northwest Airlines ticket counter. Nor were there any traceable private charters in or out. The visitors left nothing: no footprints, no fingerprints, no paper trail. And Albert Benson was forced to endure a merciless chorus of good-natured jokes at lunch the next day. He was more than embarrassed. He was frustrated, and not a little worried. He was paid to worry about intrusions into life on his island.

CHAPTER TWO

THE COMEBACK KID

On an early spring morning, the faintest hint of dawn penetrated the low-hanging clouds. One could barely hear the hum of a vehicle carrying its passenger to work on the mainland, three miles across the frozen bay. The only other sound was that of footsteps on the crusted snow and ice.

A woman watched from the shore. She wondered why this man, raised, trained, and employed in a great American city, loved this remote place so much. Especially with winter still holding its grip on all she could see.

The footsteps were unhurried. Mark Neale was where he wanted to be. A visitor here since childhood, he found respite from the hellish pace of promoting his livelihood: a series of books dissecting American presidencies, past and present. It was his passion to create well-crafted critiques of the brutal and soul-crushing world of national politics, a world that surrounds the District of Columbia townhouse he shared with Debra, his wife of eighteen years, and Tony, their son.

Awakened at 5:00 a.m., he made the first pot of coffee, slipped into warm clothes, and waited for Debra to join him. They left their modest dwelling half the size of their townhouse in the nation's capital, drove two miles into La Pointe, and parked. Mark walked out on the expanse of ice that stretched to the hills on the opposite shore. Debra watched, coffee in hand, preferring solid ground under her feet.

It was an idea birthed in the predawn silence that roused him from slumber. He didn't begrudge the busyness of his mind in the early hours—on the contrary, he looked forward to such times for unhurried refinement of the raw material that feeds the labor he loves.

For a year now, he had been studying the current occupant of the Oval Office. Mark Neale liked this president, and knew that his scholarly detachment was compromised as a result. He would like very much to see the incumbent reelected. But hopefully, his writing would mask any marks of unseemly bias.

The sound of waves on the sand would remain stilled by the grip of winter for another month. Until then, he would be thankful to experience such stark beauty. *The heavens declare the glory of God,* he mused. Perhaps that ancient poet had been looking at the same early morning sky.

Soon, people would awaken, and he will set aside this refuge for more visible duties. But times like this were building reserves for the accelerated pace of the months ahead. On this late-winter morning, he could not imagine what those duties would entail.

⁜

It's almost automatic: sitting presidents want to keep their job. The first half of a presidential term may be policy-driven, but after mid-term elections campaigning begins in earnest, and by election year, it dominates. The president's party is stacked with loyalists who lead fundraising and campaign logistics. An officially independent re-election committee begins sucking in communications and media gurus, strategists, consultants, pollsters, even cabinet secretaries, like a black hole absorbing nearby stars … and in a strange metamorphosis, the White House increasingly serves the campaign. White House thinking and planning is led by the president's chief of staff, and four more years becomes their primary job.

Few people look forward to this process, nor do they welcome the prospect of wearing two more-than-full-time hats. But inevitably, that is what they wear. They may want to be public servants, but their highest priority and job security is to serve the man behind the Resolute Desk. Politics in all its glory.

Earlier that winter, at precisely 7:15 on a February morning, President Robert Alan Eastland began his day with coffee, pastries, and his brain trust. This was year four of Eastland's first term, and his decision to seek a second would be, they assumed, affirmed by the party faithful in the primaries. In fact, his Republican Party offered virtually no opposition.

The party's convention was half a year away, to be held at McCormick Place in Chicago. But the caucuses, straw polls, and primaries were breaking upon the political establishment like a tsunami. The parties were prepared as much as humans can be prepared for an inhuman gauntlet, but outcomes were far from assured. The general election would not be easy: defeating G. Edward Brady, Democratic Senator from New York.

Peter Scott, Chief of Staff, began the briefing. "Good morning, everyone. First of all, we got our budget deal. Congress will claim victory or claim we are politicizing important national issues, blah, blah, whatever. But by noon tomorrow, it's over."

"How much did we give up?" It was Richard Gray, the vice president.

Scott turned to the man on his right. "Terrence?"

Budget Director McCutcheon spoke. "Not a thing. We built some sacrificial lambs into our proposal—feel-good initiatives that got us some mileage just for proposing them, and by giving them up in haggling with the Hill we got what we wanted in the first place. Plus, we can blame a stingy Congress for killing them. We win, people."

Scott turned to his left. "Brad—any interesting numbers?"

Brad Peyton was their pollster. "Our opponent has scored big in the Northeast with his photo ops at the municipal worker's strike in Boston. Labor types love Brady and frankly, they always will."

"So, we can forget the AFL-CIO endorsement … again." Once again, it was Vice President Gray, Eastland's rival four years earlier in the last round of primaries. His pleasure at being in the Oval Office was muted by the pain of being on the wrong side of the desk.

Everyone chuckled. Peyton replied, "And the Teamsters, and the NEA, and the Fraternal Order of Widget Makers, and anyone else with a union card."

"And," the vice president added, "anyone who's a registered Democrat."

"Not necessarily. 'Meltdown,' remember?" Peyton was referring to his favorite analogy, one he proudly insisted was original—that America's social ferment acted like heat, melting once-solid political alignments and creating a more fluid political landscape. Peyton continued: "And here's Brady's problem. Labor support for a Democrat is ambiguous because labor is ambiguous. The 'working class' votes Democratic because Democrats are usually kind to labor, protecting them from the evil fat cats of the corporate boardroom."

The president smiled. "In other words, our most generous contributors."

"May they all live long and prosper." Peyton paused, then added, "I'm just glad we're not facing Governor Marsh. Whoever runs against him would really have to earn it."

Gray winced. He had ambitions to succeed the man he now served and knew that Frederick Marsh's growing popularity would be hard to beat.

The pollster resumed his assessment. "What makes labor's connection to the Dems ambiguous is that most card-carrying hard-hats are also pretty conservative—unlike much of the rest of the party. But there's more. Especially on social issues, Brady is all over the map."

The polls and pundits were already keeping the news channels and talking heads busy, predicting the outcome in November. With near unanimity, they were predicting that Robert Alan Eastland would win his party's nomination, and re-election, by trouncing Brady in November. Brady had lost to Eastland three years earlier and was spoiling for a rematch.

He'd devoted those years to convincing the Democratic faithful that this time, he was ready and able to win. Brady didn't avoid the fact that he'd lost. His speeches, press releases, and an autobiography created an attractive legend that often plays well in American politics—humbled and bruised, having learned profound lessons in defeat, he remains undaunted, ready to rise from the ashes. The Comeback Kid.

It played well with the party faithful. But not with the political talking class. The columnists, commentators, and participants on the political talk shows on CNN, FOX, and the shrinking but still influential print media, were cold and heartless. Nice try, Brady, but you'll be a two-time loser to Eastland. Slam dunk. A done deal. Best chance the Democrats have will be four years hence, when Brady's likely running mate, former Wisconsin governor Frederick Marsh, steps up to the plate. Marsh, in fact, should be the Democratic candidate *this* time. The best and brightest. The rising star. The future.

A phone buzzed on a side table. It belonged to Ellen McCay, the president's press secretary. Scott glared at her for allowing the intrusive gadget to interrupt a conversation in the Oval Office. She wasn't embarrassed; she knew that only the deputy press secretary had the number. It was their private "hot line," and it awakened only when in some part of the political universe, the sky was falling. "Excuse me, but I need to take this call."

Scott was furious. "McCay, not now!"

"Peter, when this phone goes off, we need me to take this call." She got up and left the room.

Ninety seconds later, a visibly shaken press secretary returned.

"Brady's dead."

All eyes on the suddenly silent room turned to her. "His plane went down twenty minutes ago in upstate New York. Lost an engine taking off from Albany; not enough runway to stop. No official word yet, but my source was an eyewitness—a reporter for the *Times* who is right now thanking God that he missed the plane. Says there is no possibility of survivors."

Everyone in the room processed this in different ways. There was the human calculation: real persons, many of whom were not just names but acquaintances, now bereaved by several dozen families. Also lost: one candidate; the head of one campaign staff; several nationally-prominent journalists … and two of the nation's finest, known to the occupants of this office: Secret Service agents detailed to protect every serious presidential candidate.

Virtually everything they had been talking about was now more or less irrelevant. Marsh is now the front-runner, and the future is now. Further, he'll command a huge sympathy vote. Within hours Washington's attention will shift to Frederick Marsh, who will evolve into a formidable opponent.

But this is an opponent Eastland cannot—yet—attack. Politics is tough, but to simply continue attack ads and insert "Marsh" where "Brady" had been would be seen as a very un-American kind of "piling on."

For the immediate future, Eastland would be nothing but a kind, sensitive soul for the nation, leading its grief, offering highly-visible sympathy for those bereaved, ordering a full investigation by the appropriate agencies, and praising the man he had just been savaging.

There would be many funerals to attend, a "cease-fire" in the campaign, and a carefully orchestrated rebuilding of momentum. But this morning, the immediate task was to write two statements. One would call for calm until there was official word on the fate of the plane's occupants, and a plea that all Americans join the president in prayers for all involved. Then there would be a second statement expressing the president's "profound sorrow at this terrible loss to our nation."

And there would be a third step: starting immediately, but far from public view, a rewritten campaign strategy against their new opponent.

CHAPTER THREE

TWO SQUARE MILES

It began with a dispute over wood pulp.

"It's about jobs, Malone. Real people. Trees don't vote."

The President of the United States leaned back in his leather chair, eyes focused on nothing, while the verbal battle between Terrence McCutcheon, Eastland's budget genius, and Interior Secretary Tom Malone raged across the desk.

The morning had begun, as usual, with the latest assessment by Brad Peyton. "Marsh is like Brady in one respect: he hasn't won the hearts of all the faithful in his party. He's inherited Brady's Labor endorsement for the same reason Brady did—he's less offensive to them than we are. But they don't necessarily like being in bed with environmentalists, civil-rights advocates, abortion advocates, gay rights groups. Marsh is suspect to lots of special interest groups on the left edge who would prefer a more purely liberal candidate."

Gray interjected: "Yeah. Didn't he make welfare cuts in his home state? That would worry minorities. He opposes strike replacement workers, but if he also opposes minimum wage hikes, he's suspect to labor."

Peyton lit up; it was time to float his latest analytical trial balloon. "And here's where it gets interesting. He is, my friends, particularly vulnerable on environmental stuff."

The vice president's endorsement evaporated. "Vulnerable? That's his favorite issue. He plays it like a violin."

"Precisely! Find a weakness there, where everyone thinks he's solid, and he makes a very large target. And I guarantee you that he has a weakness there. His home state has both environmentalists and industry. Timber. Iron. Shipping. Manufacturing. Big-time agribusiness. There's no way he's pleased all sides. Just pick a place where he's sided with the exploiters and ravagers of Mother Earth—"

Gray completed the thought. "And he loses Green votes."

Press Secretary McCay spoke. "Gotta be something out there. Any nuclear power in Wisconsin?"

"Clean as a whistle."

"What about fossil fuel power plants?"

Scott was annoyed. "McCay, you're always wondering about someone's power plants. Got a problem with electricity?"

"It's an environmental issue, isn't it?"

"Maybe, but that's a no-win issue for us, too. Too complex. Too ambiguous. We don't need a 'quagmire' issue."

This time, it was the president, wrapping up the meeting with instructions for his chief of staff: "Scotty—find me something we can use. And I like the idea of finding it in his own back yard."

⁜

Later that morning Peter Scott did find something, but not where anyone expected.

As often happens when prospecting for political gold, one thing leads to another … all that is required was an open and somewhat mischievous mind. Scott placed a call to the secretary of commerce.

"Wisconsin? Nothing major—wait a minute. Seems there was a standoff a couple years back between a railroad and some Native Americans about transporting hazardous chemicals across their reservation … I'll get back to you in an hour."

That afternoon, the campaign's brain trust reconvened, now with a weakness to exploit thanks to the secretary of commerce. Of course, if this particular weakness proved unprofitable, they were confident they could find (or create) another one.

In the end it was neither railroads nor hazardous chemicals. But it involved northern Wisconsin's Indigenous community, and the shrinking acreage of unspoiled timberland. The question was simple: *On which side will we find the most votes?*

"Believe it or not, Mr. McCutcheon," It was Tom Malone, Secretary of the Interior and the only Democrat in the Cabinet. "Some of those 'real people'—who vote, by the way—happen to like those trees you're so eager to turn into beer cartons, and they'd like them to stay right where they are."

"Two square miles of undeveloped land?" McCutcheon was dismissive. "Most of it, according to the report, is bog and scrub brush."

"No, just *some*. Most is birch and poplar, and of not insignificant commercial value to a pulp-hungry paper industry and job-hungry loggers."

McCay looked at the briefing paper in her hand. "And someone wants to buy it?"

Malone shook his head. "Not buy; *lease*. It belongs to the State of Wisconsin, which has been approached by private contractors about logging rights. And the Badger State would gladly sign the contracts and collect the royalties, were it not for the neighbors."

"Who are …"

"Among others, the Red Cliff Band of Ojibwa. They've been engaged in a long-standing dispute over a Nineteenth-Century treaty which they insist gives them jurisdiction over the land in question."

Peter Scott was dismissive. "As national issues go, this is insignificant."

Malone took off his reading glasses, leaned forward, looking past Scott and toward the president, the one more likely to listen. "But it has considerable *symbolic* importance. To those who live in Wisconsin, it's not just trees or jobs. It's another clash between two cultures."

Secretary Malone continued. "To the Ojibwa the land is sacred. Further, clear-cut land is no longer suitable for hunting, one of their ancient traditions protected by the treaty."

McCutcheon interrupted. "*Allegedly* protected."

Malone continued. "As you wish, 'allegedly.' But like virtually all Native Americans, the Red Cliff folk are tired of finding what they firmly believed were solemn treaties between sovereign nations, in their eyes—broken by us with impunity."

Malone and McCutcheon were a political odd couple in a classic Washington turf fight. Eastland's budget director was a brilliant bean-counter, savvy communicator, the Chief Executive's fiscal attack dog, and he loved the role.

Malone's presence only surprised those unfamiliar with this president's strategy. They despised each other's politics—no problem for the president, but more of a problem to Malone, when he had to advocate for the president's policies that were also counter to his own convictions—which they usually were. Eastland offered him the job because Malone broadened the political appeal of his Cabinet. Malone accepted because he believed that it was the only way to protect the environmental policies he helped craft as a congressman three decades earlier. A '60s-style liberal trying to protect a crumbling environmental vision as well as a forest, versus a confident, ambitious representative of the new power base in town.

And if any of them were candid, it was not about trees or jobs, but re-election.

"I'm tired of talking without results, people." The president was noticeably irritated. "Malone, your multicultural sensitivities are heartwarming. Are there any votes up there?"

"Malone," it was Scott this time. "With all due respect, I personally don't care a hen's tooth for your little trees. If you want to protect the north woods, make it politically interesting to me and I'll listen."

Malone was mildly surprised; only because the truth is rarely told so directly in a building where most conversations were recorded for posterity. But he made it politically interesting, crafting a new presidential strategy along the way.

"Then I suggest, Mr. Scott, that we can box our opponent in on this one, if we seize the initiative. Remember: Marsh has a track record, and it's ambiguous. We can stand for preservation of this unique national resource. Marsh will have to respond. But for him, it's a no-win, because we can blast him for hypocrisy right in his own back yard. We can also score points with Native Americans. But Marsh can't win."

Win/lose. It was Scott's language. Music to his ears.

CHAPTER FOUR

GRAND SLAM

So, who do we know on the Hill?" Vice President Gray knew that well-placed allies would be crucial.

Gray answered his own question. "There's Crandall. She represents that area."

The president waved it off. "No. That a Republican got elected in that part of Wisconsin is a minor miracle. She won't touch this one. Political suicide."

Press Secretary McCay decided to buck her boss. "But the Congressperson is our most loyal ally up there, and she'd love to undermine her ex-governor—right, Brad?"

The pollster responded: "True. But she's not stupid. Besides, we'll need her in the fall, and in the next Congressional term. Get Crandall embroiled in a divisive issue and lose the only friendly vote in the region? The cost/benefit ratio stinks."

"Malone," Scott interjected, addressing the secretary of the interior. "I think you need to conduct a fact-finding trip to Wisconsin. And what you'll find is the fact that our opponent has failed to show leadership in an important matter affecting his state."

The cost/benefit ratio was improving, but only slightly. McCay sarcastically calculated the possibilities. "That should be good for a sound bite on NBC, and maybe a bit of regional coverage. Who knows? If we get lucky, the *Post* might do a social consciousness piece on Native American rights. Boy, that'll win us a lot."

The president countered with a more positive assessment. "But at least we'll lose precious little, since Malone is suspected by environmentalists as a traitor for joining the cabinet and has little political capital up north anyway. And if you're a loyal and principled public servant, Mr. Secretary, you may actually do some good."

For the first time, Malone smiled (which worried Scott and Eastland). "I'll begin making plans, Peter."

Of course he would. He'd be a loyal team player. He'd also make sure he got some press as well. It didn't hurt if potential clients saw this consultant-to-be visibly serving the President.

But the president's mind was working too, and Eastland would soon upstage Malone.

The verbal battle over the fate of a few acres of land triggered an all-too-distant memory in Eastland's mind. The last two decades of his life had been consumed by pursuing a prize that now felt more like a prison. He had grown up in a land with wide horizons. He wanted to feel again what had given him pleasure before the pursuit of power became his mistress: the wind on his face, soft ground under his feet, the silence of open country. And, distance from the insanity of power and those who sought their piece of it—including himself. Even for just a few glorious days, he needed to get as far from the Beltway as possible.

Never one to miss turning a crisis into an opportunity, he instinctively saw potential for some innocent R & R—and more. Eastland fancied himself as an above-average political strategist. Not the kind who thought through a chess-like progression of steps; rather, he saw himself as the occasional-flash-of-genius type, who doesn't need to hit a succession of singles because given enough time, he'll stroke a grand slam.

Eastland saw a grand slam in Wisconsin.

"You know, if we finesse this, it could soften the hostility of Native Americans toward us, and mute some critics in the minority community." The president leaned forward, stabbing his finger in the air toward his chief of staff.

"But the greater political paydirt lies elsewhere. Unlike your preference for win/lose strategies, my dear Scotty, I don't expect to entice Marsh's constituencies to switch sides en masse. But we can chip away at their support and fragment his base while they argue with each other about Marsh's ideological purity."

The green crowd may have liked Malone, but they did not like the president, who had pushed numerous business-friendly initiatives, and by executive order erased volumes of regulatory burden. His off-handed comment at a press conference: "Democrats love red tape. In fact, it's their cruel gift to the businesses that make America the powerhouse it is in spite of the regulatory burden they face. But we're for turning the American economic engine free to soar! That's why we're for bureaucratic *green* tape!" Green Tape mushroomed into a slogan that won him praise from the corporate boardrooms, grudging respect from economists—and near hysteria from the environmental lobby.

Eastland knew his opponent. Ostensibly an environmentalist, Marsh was governor when the legislature rolled back restrictions on timber production. It was a narrow window, but a window nonetheless. So why not vacation right in the ex-governor's back yard, and express your presidential horror at his insensitivity to Native peoples and the destruction of the nation's virgin wilderness?

That was the rationalization. It was fairly thin, and fraught with risks. Eastland didn't care. In his heart, he just wanted to get away from anything resembling cabinet meetings, phone calls to placate stubborn senators, even the Oval Office itself. The president looked toward his chief of staff and announced: "I'm going fishing."

CHAPTER FIVE

A FEW DAYS OF FRESH AIR

There was silence as the others in the Oval Office tried to decipher what they thought was just a metaphor for … something. The president looked around the room and continued: "I'm going on vacation. Where, you ask?" (They hadn't.) "To Wisconsin."

His press secretary, who wasn't afraid to challenger her boss, said gravely, "Sir, I suggest that we remain focused—"

"I'm dead serious. I really do want to take some time off before this place drives me over the edge. A few days of fresh air would do us all some good. And while I'm at it, I can see first-hand what all the commotion is about. And get in some fishing. And here's the frosting on the cake: Let's do this fishing over the Fourth of July."

McCay frowned. Eastland instinctively looked her way; if anyone would see a problem, his press secretary was usually the first to verbalize it. "What's wrong, Madam Secretary?"

"Mr. President: Don't presidents always stay in Washington on the Fourth of July?"

Eastland sighed. "Do they?"

"Mostly," Secretary Malone interjected. "But not always. I'm not sure Washington ever did, and I know that Roosevelt once spent the Fourth in the Bahamas."

"But I still think it's a bad look, Mr. President," McCay countered.

"Okay, okay. Then we'll come home on the morning of the Fourth. Satisfied, Ellen?"

"Yes, Mr. President."

Malone couldn't resist one more poke at the embarrassed press secretary: "By the way, in 1926, Coolidge spent the Fourth fishing, in Wisconsin."

The president smiled. "Well then, we have precedent! Peter: make the arrangements."

Eager to re-enter the president's good graces, McCay offered, "Actually, there may be some advantage here. Talk the destination into having their fireworks on the third, fly home on the Fourth, make the destination and tradition happy. Not a bad look, actually."

"Thank you, Madam Press Secretary." And with that, a smiling Eastland stood up and walked out of the room, the fate of the virgin timber still unresolved.

⁜

Robert Alan Eastland's attack on the bureaucracy and Washington "insiders" had, of course, been orchestrated by the other power broker in the Oval Office, for this and other power struggles that filled much of the president's days.

Among Washington insiders, Peter Scott was respected by some, feared by most, and liked by none. He was a shrewd, instinctive street fighter with a lust for power, a "wonder boy" who as campaign manager engineered Eastland's run for Congress, as a senior aide crafted a formidable legislative record—and as chief of staff to the president, was laying a fail-safe strategy for earning a second term.

He cut an imposing swath when he walked, usually briskly, through a room. His frame was as solid as it was large; he was legendary for intense workout sessions in the White House gym. He drove himself mercilessly to sustain the body of what once had been an above-average college football player and, following college, a member of the military's elite Green Berets. And he drove others with the same intensity.

When he entered an office, he would open the door suddenly, trying to catch someone being less than wholehearted in their labors. A lack of diligence is rare in the White House, and Scott's presence tended to heighten one's concentration. He enjoyed shaking up the troops once in a while. *Someday*, he occasionally fantasized, *I'd like to just stand there by someone's desk watching them work, to see how long before they collapsed out of sheer terror.*

Scott sported trademark close-cropped hair, rimless glasses, and cold, expressionless eyes. Only he knew the risks he had taken and the prices paid to bring Eastland to the White House. He was determined to make these investments continue to pay off.

Still, it was a rare event when Peter Scott couldn't dissuade the president, and this was one of them. An exhaustive study would need to find the best location for the president's last extended break before the brutality of the campaign. He placed a call to a veteran of the Secret Service.

"Barker? Scott. The president's taking a vacation this summer, and I need a discrete look at the area."

"Okay, where? Sounds like this won't be Camp David."

"Somewhere around Bayfield, Wisconsin. Actually, there's an island nearby that looks even better. More seclusion. Might be easier to secure."

"Where's Bayfield?"

"Look it up."

"As we speak; I'm bringing it up—Bay Field, or Bayfield?"

"Figure it out."

"Found it. You have got to be kidding."

"Do I sound like I'm kidding, Barker? Check it out."

"But there's next to nothing up there."

"There's not supposed to be. POTUS wants to get away from it all."

"Looks like he'll succeed."

"All he thinks he needs is a decent hotel or B & B. That's a pipe dream. We need something substantial, and not just for the Eastlands. It needs a degree of remoteness, so check the island first. But there'll have to be adequate facilities for the rest of the traveling circus, and we need to make sure no one, especially the press, has to sleep in their cars. Maybe Bayfield has capacity for overflow. We need to keep everyone happy at least until November. It's supposedly a tourist area; gotta be something suitable."

"Yeah. And where will *we* sleep? In tents?"

CHAPTER SIX

INTRODUCTIONS

Albert Benson was an ex-Baltimore cop, a burned out veteran who needed a change of scenery. Not that he wanted one. From childhood, "Al" Benson was proud to say that his dad was "a cop and a good one." He followed his father into law enforcement, proud to serve the city in which he was born and raised. But Albert had inherited from his father a contempt for anyone too poor and dark-skinned to be, in his mind, trusted. Most of the time, he stayed between the guardrails. But he'd hurt some unfortunate fellow Baltimore citizens over the years, and was warned that one more infraction …

He understood that he had gone too far. Too far, in fact, for his wife, who left him, saying that she never wanted to see him or his anger again.

Losing Rita was a crushing blow. It made him a more restrained officer, for awhile. But one suspect made the mistake of pushing back, and the old Officer Benson resurfaced. This time the city put him on desk duty, until the reports had been processed, a lawsuit against the city and police department of Baltimore and Officer Benson was in the news, and this lifetime officer of the law was relieved of his duties, his beloved badge, and his service weapon. He was now an *ex*-Baltimore cop.

But he was still a cop. He shopped his services nationwide, seeking a new life a long way from Maryland. Madeline Island took a chance on him. They offered him a safe place to land and lick his wounds. It did that, and even restored some faith in humanity. The people of Madeline Island welcomed him, and within weeks, he was a common and welcome sight in the local watering holes. Being a cop again felt good, although being the only officer was a new and uncomfortable experience, especially in the busy summer season, when the Island's two hundred residents are surrounded by hundreds more: campers, golfers, and weekenders, clogging the streets, shops, beaches, and cottages, all too often drinking too much and spoiling too many perfect summer days for too many people.

And his hope of leaving urban issues behind was threatened by the mysterious visit of two strangers in suits. Had he known that they were Secret Service, he may have raised a host of questions that would not be readily answered. But he would soon learn that the urban world he'd left behind was about to follow him to Wisconsin.

There was one intrusion into the village's serenity that winter that didn't worry Albert Benson. Across the room in the pub, removed from the patrons nursing their brews at the bar, two men and a teen-aged boy sat at a table, engrossed in conversation. One of these men: medium height, frail build, graying hair above a receding hairline, was a widower nearing the age of eighty. His gentle eyes matched a soft-spoken, thoughtful demeanor. Across the table was a younger man, slightly taller, a trim, not-quite-athletic build. He looked through eyes much like his companion and made no secret of the bond between them. Next to him, a sixteen-year-old boy dressed in cutoffs and a T-shirt with his favorite band in bold print on the front, their tour schedule on the back. If one were to guess they were father, son and grandson, they would be right.

Franklin Neale hoped that this island could become his year-round home, keeping a commitment to himself he had made decades before. With his wife Carolyn, he purchased the modest turn-of-the-century cottage on Madeline Island in 1970. In 1990, his son Mark helped expand and winterize the property thanks to writing a second best-seller that gave him a degree of notoriety and the accompanying disposable cash. Carolyn was gone; a stroke took her five years later. But for Franklin, the cottage became his home.

For Tony, Mark's son, it was Spring Break. At his father's invitation, and bribed with the promise of "really great" pancakes, Tony sat across from his father and grandfather, hoping to learn more about the community that had won the hearts of two generations of Neales.

Tony was curious. "So the serious dude in the olive jacket's the police chief?"

"Yes," Franklin said. "I'll introduce you to him, but I don't think Albert wants to be sociable at the moment. And the man next to him—"

"The guy giving him such a hard time?"

"That's Jerry Mills. Quite a guy."

"Why?"

"Jerry's a bit boisterous," Franklin said. "Drinks way too much. People know he can get out of control, but no one bothers him; it's just a given. Jerry's been labeled the town drunk, trying to figure it out himself. Fortunately, La Pointe has a tradition of taking care of those who are at risk of a crash-and-burn. Pretty patient, loving people."

"Alcohol?" Mark asked.

"Alcohol."

Tony looked out the window. He knew that as the new guy he'd get more than his share of curious glances. *Wish I could take notes while Dad and Grandpa talk,* he mused. In these early days here, he was a sponge, eager to soak up as much information as he could, from sources he trusted.

"Okay—the guy in uniform. Another cop?"

His grandfather answers. "As of just a few weeks ago, yes. That's Wade Sanders. New part-time officer here."

"Looks Native American," Mark added.

"Right. From Red Cliff. Tony—would you believe he's the tribe's Chief? Super guy. Has to be to have credibility with both communities."

Tony saw a solitary figure watching but not participating in the conversation at the bar. The man was bearded, dressed in gray coveralls, with a salt-and-pepper mane under a worn baseball cap. "Who's the ponytail?" It was a casual question, but the response was not. His grandfather didn't look up, and said, "Don't let him know you've noticed him."

Tony looked back at his father, then folded his hands around the coffee mug. Looking at the pine table, darkly stained and covered with numerous coats of polyurethane, Tony softly said, "This ought to be interesting."

"The ponytail," Franklin said, almost in a whisper, "belongs to Michael Erickson, who will test your belief that God loves all God's children."

"I'm listening."

"Michael is one of the most mysterious and at times frightening men you will ever meet. I see him occasionally, on his rare trips into town. But getting to know him is something neither I nor anyone in the last decade has accomplished. He lives alone, in a pretty well-built but spartan place back in the woods, where he makes some of the best custom furniture you will ever see. What he does with his hands is legendary, and worth his very high prices. But—" The elder Neale started to say more but stopped, and simply shook his head, seeming unable to complete a thought. Tony looked up expectantly, "Yes?"

"I don't know, Tony. I know his mother died fairly young and his father, who's been dead for nearly twenty years, was antisocial and volatile. I wouldn't put Michael in the same category as his father, but there's something disturbing about him. Vietnam veteran, that I know. Beyond that … ." He just shook his head.

Back at the bar, a far different conversation continued between the Police Chief and Henry Selkirk, who as Town Board chairman shared the chief's concern about two recent, very curious, visitors. "Personally, Chief, I don't like it when people show up and we don't know what they want."

"All the more reason, Henry, why I'm glad we added a part-timer to the roster. More and more intrusions by outsiders, and I'm not comfortable when I don't have any backup."

CHAPTER SEVEN

SCOTT, BATES, AND THE SHORT-TIMER'S CLUB

It was time to inform the press. But not all of them.

"Gary? Peter Scott … yeah. Thanks for the piece on Sunday. Nice to get some positive press once in a while—ah, off the record for the moment?"

"Off the record." It was Gary Bates, White House correspondent for the *Washington Post,* one of Scott's discrete contacts in the press corps.

"This is on background for a while, but you'll be the first to report it."

"Deal. What's the big secret?"

"The president is taking a fishing vacation to Wisconsin this summer."

"That's your big secret."

"While he's there, you'll find him shocked and disturbed at his Democratic opponent's deplorable failure of leadership as governor."

"I'm listening."

"Just pack your bags and bring your insect repellent. And don't let Malone out of your sight. Whatever you hear, you'll hear it from him first. Fourth of July weekend."

Scott hung up without saying good-bye. Bates would make his own travel plans directly, bypassing the newspaper's travel office. He suspected, correctly, that when his travel plans come through the usual channels, they are fed to other journalists who in turn suspect, correctly, that Bates has connections inside the White House, and often knows ahead of time where and when stories would break. He placed one in-house call, to his Editor in Chief Archibald Perkins—who was sensitive about his somewhat archaic name and has threatened to fire anyone who calls him Archie.

"Perkins."

"Perky? Gary. Just got a call from 'Background'. Seems POTUS is going on a fishing vacation in Wisconsin this summer. Mind if I go along?"

"White House correspondents don't get vacations, Bates. Besides, I hate your favorite acronym for The President Of The United States. Just call him the Prez, or something else, Okay? POTUS sounds like a disease."

Bates ignored the innocuous jab. "From what I hear, it'll be no vacation. You may have heard there's an election this fall? I suspect there'll be news in the north woods. And at the moment we're the only members of the Fourth Estate who know."

"I assume you know what this 'news' is."

"Not a clue. Well, I have one clue; something involving Tom Malone."

"Let's see: Tom Malone: life-long bureaucrat past his prime, cabinet official who's probably out of favor with the White House again, and most likely a member of the short-timer's club. My heart isn't palpitating yet."

"Well, if you want me to stay in D.C. and cover the goings-on at a largely empty White House this July Fourth while the rest of the world is setting up their little laptops in Wisconsin—hey, I understand perfectly, Perky." Bates and Perkins shared a caustic humor that masked a mutual respect. Their interpersonal chemistry had served them both well, helping them achieve and hold positions near the top of their profession. And it was almost always, at least over the phone, traded back and forth by two men trying to out-insult each other while grinning from ear to ear.

"Right now I'm thinking: 'Gee, Bates is being sarcastic with his boss again.' And I'm also thinking: 'Maybe I should fire the little smart-mouth.'"

Bates, unworried about job security, exaggerated the emphases on a few carefully chosen words. "No, you're supposed to think: 'Wow! That little *genius* is once again onto something truly newsworthy about which no one else in our entire industry has a clue yet so I'd better give him *generous* access to the *Post's* stash of credit cards so he can make travel plans.'"

"Gonna check out the female population in Wisconsin while you're up there?"

"I take that as a green light."

"You know the drill: independent travel agency; nothing in writing until necessary; all the rest. Go ahead and make reservations."

"Thanks. By the way, I already did. First class."

⁜

One of Scott's calls was to the press secretary.

"McCay."

"Ellen, since we're going to Wisconsin, we need to make sure that Mr. Malone is included prominently in the published itinerary."

"So we do have to take that fossil along?"

"Yes. In fact, he'll have a role to play once we get there. A visible secretary of the interior might win us some environmental votes."

"Don't count on it, Mr. Scott."

"I know. But he'll be on the clock and not on vacation, so he can do some of the president's speaking for him." Scott knew that some on-camera time would suit the secretary, who was chronically out of favor with the president, just fine.

McCay relented. "Well … It might get one annoying monkey off my back, if it dampens speculation that Malone will be gone once the election is over."

Speculation that was probably correct. Scott grinned as he hung up the phone. *Malone you old fool, enjoy this. It'll be your last moment of glory. Come January, you're retired.*

⁑

The vacation site had to meet parameters far more than most families worry about. And "worry" describes the dominant mindset. In reality, presidents take working vacations, involving infrastructure for 70 or so phone lines, foolproof security, a nearby airport suitable for a 747, about two hundred hotel rooms, and, for the president, a host of refined creature comforts (apparently the Constitution forbids presidential backpacking). Above all: the location must be politically advantageous. Northern Wisconsin might not give Eastland thousands of votes in return, but its long Native American history and environmental sensitivity dovetailed nicely with Eastland's need to soften his image.

The discrete study was followed by a decision long before any public announcements. Even the lucky community wouldn't know that it had won the presidential sweepstakes for a while. This was understandable. Security concerns made the president's plans best kept under wraps as long as possible.

However, logistics demand some local involvement, and a lucky Wisconsin congresswoman was quietly visited by White House staffers who sought, not permission (no congressperson in their right mind would decline a presidential visit to their district), but cooperation, including contacts in or near the destination that could be trusted to keep their mouths shut.

CHAPTER EIGHT

THE ROOKIE

Think we should have waited another week, John?"

"Nah. This teeny bit of ice won't stop us."

The captain knew the abilities of both his vessel and himself, but still winced every time the steel of the ferry met another chunk of frozen water.

"That's what they said on the *Titanic*."

While White House staffers were dreaming of balmy summer days, the people of northern Wisconsin were debating when the ice would release its grip on the lakes. The days were getting steadily longer (and occasionally warmer); the snow was retreating and Spring was teasing winter-weary residents with occasional glimpses of things to come. The first robin. The first outdoor walk without a winter coat. The first day to wash your car in the driveway.

The car ferry Island Queen, packed rail-to-rail with passengers, shuddered to a stop. For the fourth time of the afternoon, Captain John Ward eased his vessel back down the narrow trail he'd just cut, for another run at the stubborn sheet of ice that separated Madeline Island from the mainland.

A week earlier and twenty inches thick, it had been a highway carrying the intrepid islanders back and forth. It had been a good ice road as ice roads go: nearly two months of more or less reliable crossing, marred by the occasional detour around a crack or a pressure ridge. Those detours had become more frequent. The approaches typically melted first, as the sun warmed the shallow bottom along the shore, making transit more and more uncertain.

Some islanders, wary of black ice, quit driving several days earlier. But the bolder drivers persisted, until a heavily-laden plumber's truck dropped a tire through the ice. By the time they'd readied a tow chain to free the stricken vehicle, it was disappearing backwards into forty feet of water, with the owner wondering how he'd explain to his insurance company that his truck had sunk. It was time for the "windsled": part boat, part sled, part carnival ride that carries people, groceries, packages and mail during the in-between period of decaying ice.

And now, the traditional first ferry of the season. Free passage. It's an on-deck party—bring a cooler of refreshments. Half the population of Madeline Island was aboard, watching the skipper and *The Queen* work their magic.

Even thin ice is strong in quantity, overmatching the ferry's six hundred horsepower. So the strategy is simple: when the ice stops the boat, back her up, hit the throttle, and ram ahead until she stops again, then repeat.

⁜

"I owe a fortune in college loans for this?" A shivering Samantha Wells stood at the Bayfield dock, watching the ferry's slow progress. A rookie in her first full week as a reporter for a Duluth TV station, she was there to cover the season's first ferry.

"Once again, we stand around and wait," quipped Freddie Adams, aka "Strobe," the station's most experienced cameraman, leaning on the tripod. "You'll get used to it."

"I'll never get used to cold and wet feet."

"Where you from?"

"San Diego."

"Nope—you'll never get used to it. Great business, right?"

"So far, I've stood in a blizzard covering junior high ski jumping, gotten lost in fog trying to find the grand opening of a health club, and nearly broke my neck on an icy sidewalk. Even the sidewalks here are lethal. I hope there's more to my journalistic career than this."

Strobe smiled. "Sam, don't worry. Frankly, I think you're good. Just be patient. You'll get your break."

So they waited, hoping to interview a passenger or two and the ferry's captain, make a few on-camera comments, and head home with footage that may, or may not, merit sixty seconds on the evening news.

A formation of geese flew noisily overhead, northbound. Samantha had an idea. "Strobe: get some footage." He pointed the camera up, zoomed in, and shot fifteen seconds' worth.

"Okay, let's do the intro." In a few minutes, Reporter Wells was smiling into Strobe's camera, microphone in hand.

"To the people of this region, spring is a mixed blessing. It heralds the beginning of the months in which many here earn their living. It also means the end of the tranquility that began in November, when the tourists had largely gone home and locals could enjoy the peace that rooted them here in the first place.

"This region's history dates back centuries. Indigenous peoples were here after the glaciers gave way to the greatest of fresh-water lakes, teeming with fish and wildlife." Samantha turned away from the camera, her eyes and hand dramatically sweeping the horizon. "But for the Anishinaabe, this was always more: it was and is a sacred place."

Adams was impressed. *She may be new, but she's done her homework. I live here and didn't know that.* He and Samantha would back the next words with footage of the well-preserved buildings in the picturesque village behind them.

"Toward the end of the 19th Century, newcomers arrived: people who came not to work, but to rest. They dotted the hills around Bayfield and the islands with summer homes ranging from simple to elegant.

"And no wonder. The beauty is stunning; the fishing excellent, the sailing some of the nation's finest—and with the islands, seclusion is available to those who seek it. These islands are a beloved destination for boaters, day hikers, and campers."

At best only a portion of her work would be deemed worthy of airtime. But yes, she'd done her homework.

"Today's first run of the season by the Island Queen, one of four ferries that serve this community, marks not only a change of pace for the island's people, but it's the signal for others from the upper Midwest and beyond to return, like migrating geese, to their summer paradise. This is Samantha Wells, reporting from Bayfield, Wisconsin."

CHAPTER NINE

WALTER, MAGGIE, AND MICHAEL

Walter Kolquist, bank president and perennial Republican activist, closed the door on the good-natured scorn of his staff. This former Bayfield mayor had once again succumbed to spring fever as he had every year anyone could remember, by bringing his putter to the office. He arranged his office floor to practice for what he might soon be doing outdoors. He didn't know that Bonnie Heller, his secretary, and Kevin Clark, loan officer, bet on which day the putter would make its annual visit, carried by a blushing CEO to a chorus of jokes about his inability to wait any longer—which was precisely the case. This year, Bonnie Heller won the bet.

She also interrupted his first practice. "Mr. Kolquist? Sorry to interrupt," (she wasn't) "but Congresswoman Crandall's on the line." He was tempted to have Bonnie take a message. Putting was vastly more satisfying than this conversation would be. *Maggie Crandall again? The woman I helped elect against all odds needs another favor?*

Electing Crandall was hard, but immensely satisfying. Most pundits predicted a humiliation for anyone from that party challenging an airtight Democratic stronghold. She won anyway, winning Kolquist immense satisfaction, even if she could talk you to death. He sighed and picked up the phone.

"Hello, Congressman Crandall." He used the masculine form intentionally, confident that she'd be so eager to talk that she wouldn't notice.

"Walt! Glad I caught you. Got a minute?"

She didn't wait for his answer, but plowed ahead, talking up a rider that would ease loan fee restrictions she'd buried in a larger bill. To her, he was simply an empty vessel waiting to be filled. "That will feel good, won't it?"

Again, not waiting for a response. *Does she ever stop to breathe?* Kolquist mused.

"So how does the tourist season look this year?" This time, she awaited his response. *She does breathe,* he thought.

Her big defect in Kolquist's mind was that while she could mesmerize when she talked, she never really listened. While you talk, she is framing her reply. Reply framed, she'd simply start talking, forcefully and fast.

"Actually I'm pretty optimistic, Maggie. At the Chamber lunch yesterday, we heard—"

Apparently, the congresswoman had inhaled, and now interrupted him with a bombshell.

"I need your promise of absolute confidentiality about this. Agreed?"

"Agreed." (What choice did he have?)

"President Eastland may come to the Apostle Islands for a vacation this summer."

Kolquist went white. "Why?"

"Are you ready for this? He wants to go fishing."

"If he's fishing for votes, there aren't a lot of those up here to catch."

Crandall apparently didn't hear Kolquist's appraisal. "Nothing's definite, but it looks good, and I need your help in making arrangements."

"Of course. But—"

"But you cannot breathe a word of this to anyone, at least not yet. If word gets out, the whole thing's off, and you'll be seen as the one who drove the president away." She'd also have egg on her Republican face at the next election. "We both need this one. Don't screw up."

Congresswoman Crandall rattled off what to expect: a visit from an advance team, the need for a few key local officials in the loop. She also promised that a certain bank executive would have his choice of public appearances with the president.

The putter slipped from his limp hand, banging on the brass wastebasket, and startling his secretary. He never heard it. His mind was reeling with possibilities for enhancing his hometown … and perhaps making this Democratic kingdom a little more tolerable for Republicans. Plus, the possibility of meeting his party's standard-bearer face to face would be a refreshing distraction.

Walter Kolquist faced a delicate dance: to build support for an event of a lifetime, without telling anyone what it actually was.

"Bonnie: bring the Rolodex. And hold my calls. I've got some calls I need to make."

However, not everyone was thrilled.

CHAPTER TEN

THE DISSENTERS

There are two churches on Madeline Island. St. Joseph's serves the Catholic faithful, and at St. John's, a largely Protestant crowd fills the pews. Two traditions, two clergy, serving one community.

Father Tom Groppi heard the news first, from a parishioner who was active in Republican politics and unable to keep a secret. Father Tom called Rev. Shelly Griggs, his island colleague, whom he knew could be trusted with news that he knew would impact them sooner or later. Her initial response was not what he'd hoped for.

"Wow. Very cool. That will put the island on the map."

"That's what I'm afraid of, Pastor Griggs."

"So you don't … "

"For me, it's a hard No."

"Why?"

"The visit itself? Sure. A page in the island's history. Probably a whole chapter. But it's the aftermath that grieves me."

Shelly remained quiet; *Father Tom doesn't use 'grieve' loosely. I'll listen.*

"Pastor Shelly, I see this as a kind of fall from grace. Madeline Island's well-known, yes. But it's not famous. Las Vegas, Disney World, New York—nobody has to explain those names. But Madeline Island? You have to explain this place. That's our gift of grace."

"I don't understand…"

"Look—What the island is well-known for includes the simple fact that it's just well-known. To tens of thousands of people who cherish this place, yes—but that's still a relatively small circle. It's almost our little secret. That protects it—us—from being gobbled up.

"All it would take is an invasion of political junkies, in a campaign year, and we'll become a national curiosity. Hordes of people who have no appreciation or respect for the beauty, the tranquility, the … intimacy of this place could overrun this slice of Eden. And you can't get intimacy back."

Shelly, feeling a bit ashamed for her first response, had no argument for the Father, and conceded. "We will pay a price for this."

Father Tom had more. "It's simple: more land privatized. Trees cleared, roads built, infrastructure crowding nature out, and one after another summer home covering more and more ground. The Island is already gentrifying, pricing people who have lived here for generations out of their own homes. That will be on steroids after His Majesty the President walks the land."

"And then," Shelly added, "who will do the island's work? Those who prepare our meals, who clean our rental properties, staff our businesses—some of them were born here, but are already being pushed to living on the mainland, and commuting by ferry to their jobs."

With a decade of observing the seasonal flood of visitors crowding this precious and fragile place, the priest lamented, "And a lot of the people who come will be merely curious, without any stake in protecting this … this community."

Rev. Griggs had another concern. "As word gets out, I see something else: conflict. Arguments pro and con. Neighbors taking sides. This is a question that we've not had to answer."

"Yes. Politics is divisive enough. Why infect this island with more win/lose thinking?"

The two clergy were silent, each imagining the impact ahead. Then Father Tom spoke, in words that formed a prayer: "May it never be."

"Amen."

They did not know that a very private island resident would soon mirror their concerns, and put those concerns on paper.

⁑

"This is all native wood?"

"Yes."

"You cut it yourself?"

"And aged it, and milled it."

"Your reputation is well-earned."

"I do my best." He said no more, knowing from experience that silence is golden, especially when it drives his guests to embarrassment and a hasty retreat.

"Well, ah, thanks, Michael." The buyer handed over the check, a sign of surrender in a futile attempt to converse with the bearded craftsman who preferred cash, tolerated checks, and refused credit cards.

Michael Erickson slammed the tailgate closed and waved the driver off. Another table, a drop-leaf piece in white oak, was on its way to a "summer person's" dining room. The buyer had gladly paid an above-average price for Michael's above-average masterpiece. His style was simple, straightforward, and unbending, not unlike Shaker furniture in lack of ornamentation, but distinguished by Erickson's trademark inlays in tabletops and drawer fronts, with hand-carved wooden knobs and pulls, its brass hinges recessed in the wood, hidden from view.

Michael actually preferred birch, with accents in other woods. The satin finish was always light in hue, the inlays in darker shades. And birch was plentiful. But if he couldn't talk the customer into that ... Oh, well. They just don't know what they're missing.

The new owner, failing to converse with the craftsman, was awed by the attention to detail. Michael gave his customers few additional satisfactions. Woodworking he loved; customers he needed, but solitude he craved, and the sooner these wealthy urban types left Erickson's shop, the sooner Michael could re-enter his secluded world.

The Range Rover moved down the driveway as he walked back to his shop, his tattered Reeboks the only break from a "woodsman" stereotype as they crunched on the gravel. Erickson's visage was striking: deep-set eyes, enormous eyebrows, an upper body that spoke of raw power. Had he been vain, he would have been proud of his physique. But Michael held such vanities in contempt. The rest of his appearance was classic north woods: faded jeans, plaid flannel shirt, suspenders, and gray t-shirt showing in the open collar, a coarse, reddish beard, mustache, and graying, unruly hair pulled into a ponytail.

He added a few pieces of wood to the barrel stove, and began the next order, glad for the return of solitude.

CHAPTER ELEVEN

AMERICA AT ITS BEST

Normally, the color of the fire hydrants would not have sparked a debate. Nor would a town of two hundred people have considered hiring a landscape architect to upgrade the lamppost-mounted flowerpots, or a tech consultant to upgrade La Pointe's website. But the president was coming.

Rumors had been flying about the strange run on reservations at local inns—including hundreds of guests who were told that the room they'd booked for the Fourth of July weekend was no longer available. After all, the president …

But the honor of announcing Eastland's visit had been assumed by Congresswoman Crandall, and she chose the time and place for effect.

Memorial Day on Madeline Island can be hot and sticky. It can also rain. It can snow. This time, it rained. The men of the Red Cliff VFW Color Guard came, as they had for years, on the 10:00 a.m. ferry through a nasty chop. They were met by about a hundred islanders and weekend visitors huddled in rain gear at the Town Dock. A simple but moving ceremony brought together summer visitors, life-long islanders, and proud veterans of Ojibwe descent in a moment of truce between cultures.

The weather did not stop the singing of a traditional patriotic song, nor the laying of a wreath on the water by the widow of a local veteran. Nor did it stop the three-volley salute fired by the VFW veterans or the haunting sound of Taps, reminding the gathered of what Memorial Day honors. In moving simplicity, this was America at its best—a time for people to cross racial and generational lines to honor their shared heritage.

But this year, there was one change. Pastor Griggs was politely asked to defer her traditional reflection. In her stead, Congresswoman Crandall would speak. Her talk was predictable, for the most part. But then, her big announcement: "My fellow citizens: in just a few weeks we gather again to honor our nation and its heritage when we celebrate Independence Day. And when we do, it will be for us an Independence Day we will never forget. Because it is my high honor to announce that, through the efforts of my office, the President of the United States, Robert Alan Eastland, will spend Independence Day weekend here, in the Apostle Islands."

That was the day before the monthly Town Council meeting—just enough time to generate an excitement bordering on hysteria by the time the gavel fell. Before the meeting adjourned, proposals included re-naming a street after President Eastland, painting the fire hydrants red, white, and blue, asking Eastland to be Grand Marshall in the 4th of July parade—which this year would be a day early—and a counter proposal favoring the First Lady, not the male president, for the entirely symbolic ride in the lead convertible.

There were, of course, contrarians. Not everyone welcomed presidential attention to their quiet refuge. One called for asking the president to not come at all. Others wanted the president to meet with a delegation opposing deforestation of federal lands. One individual proposed (unsuccessfully) that they petition the president to legalize marijuana.

Questions were raised. Can we park *Air Force One* on Madeline's little airstrip? (No. He would arrive by helicopter.) Would the president be required to obtain a Wisconsin fishing license? (Something would be arranged.) Isn't this finally reason enough to finish painting Town Hall and pave its parking lot? (We'll see.)

Representative democracy, it is said, thrives on reasoned deliberation by those whom the people select as their leaders.

This was democracy, but with less reasoned deliberation. The president is coming! They were ecstatic, and the next day, as the Town Clerk transcribed the minutes of the meeting, she smiled at the number of times "historic" and "unforgettable" appeared in the handwritten notes.

⁜

La Pointe, Wisconsin, has not been spoiled by success. There are no theme parks, traffic lights, or fast-food franchises. Nothing is open all night. And while it welcomes visitors, it is reluctant to compromise itself to accommodate them. You must take La Pointe as it comes: laid-back, unpretentious, and protective of its ethos. If it's not exciting enough—well, you're free to go to Las Vegas or Orlando. When you come to La Pointe, you are not entering a town built for the sole purpose of extracting your money. You are visiting someone's home. You're welcome to come, but no one will make much of a fuss over you. Unless, of course, you're the President of the United States.

There was a run on paint at Bayfield's only hardware store; American flags sold out in half an hour, and a frantic call was placed to the manufacturer's 800 number for as many replacements as they could ship.

Some who lived in this semi-wilderness had come for the same reasons others visited here: clear air, pure water, and above all, tranquility. Hearing the news, they feared that this visit would diminish what anonymity remained for the region. For them, a presidential visit was an honor they could do without.

Police Chief Albert Benson heard the news of the presidential visit with mixed feelings. Yes, a memory for the ages, for a community that richly deserved the honor—though it represented a gigantic headache for someone who was thrilled to have almost nothing to do.

Michael Erickson was perhaps the last person on the island to hear, on one of his occasional visits to a local watering hole.

"Hey, Erickson! Heard the news? President Eastland is coming to the island this summer."

"Why?"

"Fishing vacation."

"Why don't we just send him some fish and ask him to stay away?"

"Michael! How unpatriotic!" The patrons laughed. Michael didn't.

"Maybe he'll order some of your furniture for the White House." There was more laughter, but Erickson remained unamused.

"I pick my customers carefully. He's not on my list."

Driving away from the tavern, he pondered the news. *The man responsible for what I can never forget—is coming here?* So, Michael Erickson began envisioning a plan, just as he did every hunting season. *With all his so-called expert bodyguards, and all their urban ways? I wonder how they'd cope with someone who understands this place. Perhaps I should find out.*

CHAPTER TWELVE

PRIZED POSSESSION

As Michael had done dozens of times before, he pulled an ancient manual typewriter from a shelf in the closet, set it on the table, and began to gather his thoughts. It would not be his first effort at expressing his First Amendment right to free speech, but the first to receive much attention. His previous efforts, mailed to the region's newspapers, had been disposed of by newspaper men and women who found various reasons why his diatribes were inappropriate for their op-ed pages. Erickson pecked at the keys, one finger at a time, until approximately two hundred and fifty words had flowed from his mind. He then sealed them in a hand-addressed envelope with no return address.

Michael rubbed his eyes. He leaned back in the chair, stretched his arms over his head, letting out a long, slow breath, satisfied that the letter captured the anger had driven him to compose it. He opened his eyes.

At first, he saw only the rough-hewn beams that supported the roof. His eyes scanned downward, capturing the unvarnished pine boards that formed the ceiling over the table, then the field stones carefully fitted to form the chimney, then the mantle … and there, above the mantle and the fire that glowed below, was his hunting rifle, coated with a light layer of dust, a rare sign of neglect.

He stepped away from the table, walked across the wooden floor, and slowly, almost reverently, lifted the weapon from its resting place. *You are my most prized possession.* Whether a Ruger, Sako, Remington, or Savage, a good firearm can be a kind of companion to one who understands the art, science, and psychology of weaponry. *You have faithfully dispatched all manner of God's creatures. But could I ever squeeze the trigger if a human target were in the sights?* No words were said. They were instincts more than thoughts, just beyond the reach of his mind. When you love weapons as he did, they take on a life of their own.

His thoughts suddenly chilled him. *Am I really contemplating …?* He placed the rifle back on its hand-crafted cradle over the fireplace. He picked up his letter, and dropped it into the fire. He began a more reflective version for the president's consideration.

Your visit will draw hundreds—thousands—of people who have no appreciation for our history, no sense of the spirit, the feeling, of this place. This is our home, we who prefer the quietness, the solitude we have here. Worse, those who will come have no idea—nor do you, Sir—that this has been holy ground for people who have held this island as sacred for centuries, long before people like us arrived and took much of its fish, its trees, its quiet, away. Noise. Commotion. All because you and other people like you decide to "visit" a place that has never invited you. Yours is no "visit." It is an invasion.

An hour later, a new letter was sealed in a new envelope—a shorter missive, uncharacteristically mild, still objecting, but without the vitriol of the letter now reduced to ash.

Michael Erickson didn't deliver his epistle to the Post Office window during business hours. Instead, he dropped it, well before the next sunrise, in the outside mailbox.

A few hours later, the island's postmaster took note of the envelope as it spilled from the mailbox in front of the 150-year-old post office. Of course, he knew who had sent it—he had become a minor authority on handwriting, and when he saw the addressee, on that basis alone almost called the authorities. But he thought better of it. Knowing the letter's author, that would be the responsible thing to do. But it may also tip off that author, who would not be amused.

He wasn't supposed to pay attention to much more than the zip codes of outgoing mail. Honoring the public's privacy is a postal tradition as well as federal policy. But in a small island town where you know everyone's business anyway, it was asking too much to expect that he would not notice the more interesting pieces, and try to guess what may be inside.

He pondered his decision for a moment, knowing what he should do and what he would do anyway, which was, essentially, nothing. He postmarked the letter and sent it on its way.

⁘

Martha Stansfield, twenty-two-year veteran of the White House Mail Room, was on the receiving end. She quickly examined the envelope for signs of trouble. She found nothing particularly disturbing except for a rather incomplete address, and no sign of its origin except its postmark. It was addressed simply:

> The President
> The White House
> Washington, DC

As one more subtle protest against government regulation, the author had deliberately omitted the zip code.

She knew, based on experience, that it was likely to be more than another request for White House memorabilia. Ms. Stansfield decided not to inform the Protection Research Section of the Secret Service just yet. It appeared to be only a sheet or two of ordinary paper, but the contents might not be friendly to her employer. She then carefully opened it and found above the name of one M. Erickson of La Pointe, Wisconsin. She did not know that an angry, convoluted diatribe against "Big Brother," "killers" and "developers," warning of "dire consequences" if the president "disturbed the peace" of "God's island" had almost preempted the unremarkable letter in her hand. There was no explicit threat, and thus no response needed.

Had Michael's first letter reached Ms. Stansfield, the files of the Secret Service Protective Intelligence Section would soon include one bearing the name of Michael Erickson. He would join perhaps 40,000 others that the agency was charged with watching because of their potentially threatening words or actions. Given the recent decision by the White House, his letter would have received more than passing scrutiny. In the parlance of the Secret Service, Erickson would have become one of several hundred "lookouts," people who warranted special monitoring.

CHAPTER THIRTEEN

TO SERVE AND PROTECT

The hardest part of planning the president's vacation was finding a place to land a helicopter. *Air Force One* would fly to Duluth on Friday, June 30. A helicopter, *Marine One*, would whisk the family the ninety miles to their destination. But where that helicopter landed mattered. It had to be a reasonable distance from the president's living quarters. "Reasonable" meaning close, of course, and amenable to security. As always, the president's security.

As every Secret Service agent knows, security is relative. The nation had lost presidents to assassins, and nearly lost several more.

The Secret Service was established on April 14, 1865 by order of President Lincoln. Several hours later, he was killed by a bullet from John Wilkes Booth's Derringer.

But presidential protection wasn't its original mission anyway. It was and is a branch of the Treasury Department, and its first agents battled counterfeiting, not assassins. It took nearly a century to recognize the need to protect the lives of public officials—and the stability of a nation.

There had been plenty of warnings.

1835 saw the first of several miracles, when President Andrew Jackson, attending a funeral, almost precipitated his own. The unguarded president was outside the church when a gunman walked up to him, put a muzzle-loader to Jackson's chest, and pulled the trigger. Nothing happened. Before anyone could react, he pulled out a second weapon, fired—and again, nothing. The next move was Jackson's, who nailed his assailant with his cane.

Thirty years later, John Wilkes Booth pulled a trigger that worked, while the president's bodyguard was in a nearby saloon.

In 1881, President James Garfield was shot twice in the back. In 1901, President William McKinley was attacked during an exposition in New York City. Teddy Roosevelt was campaigning in Milwaukee on October 14, 1912, when a local bar owner shot him in the chest (the bullet was slowed by Teddy's eyeglass case and a 50-page speech). Roosevelt told the police not to hurt the shooter, and then gave a 90-minute speech, beginning with: "Ladies and gentlemen, I don't know whether you fully understand that I have just been shot, but it takes more than that to kill a Bull Moose."

FDR was attacked in 1932; he escaped, but five people were wounded, one—Chicago's mayor—fatally. Puerto Rican nationalists killed one agent and wounded two others in a failed attack on President Truman in 1950.

No one can forget November in Dallas, 1963. But few remember that JFK almost didn't live to occupy the White House. Shortly after the 1960 election, the Kennedys vacationed in Palm Beach. Richard Pavlick planned to drive his dynamite-laden car into the president-elect's limousine, but had a change of heart when he saw Kennedy's wife and daughter waving good-bye from the door. A few days later, he was arrested.

In more recent years, Squeaky Fromme shot at President Ford in 1975, John Hinckley, Jr., wounded President Reagan in 1981, and even the White House has been attacked, by an assault rifle blasting away at the north side, and an airplane crashing into the south face.

Perhaps the most bizarre threat happened on a battleship, when the Commander-in-Chief was fired upon by his own Navy.

In November, 1943, President Roosevelt was bound for the Tehran-Cairo Conferences during WWII, on the safest means possible for a traveling president. He was aboard the USS Iowa, surrounded by an entire fleet of escorts. During a scheduled drill, the destroyer escort William D. Porter accidentally fired a live torpedo. Swift maneuvering by the battleship's skipper averted disaster, as the torpedo missed the ship by 20 feet.

Finally, the legendary fire of San Clemente. President Nixon liked a roaring fire in the fireplace—even if he had to turn on the air conditioning to make the room bearable. On October 29, 1970, the president was in bed when the smoke alarm went off. The overheated fireplace had decided to work mischief, in the room immediately beneath the sleeping chief executive.

The agent on duty woke the president and got him clear of danger; others grabbed fire extinguishers and raced to the scene on a golf cart. One found a fire hose and with no firefighting experience began blasting away at the wall where the fire had started.

As the local fire department charged through the door to fight the most important fire of their careers, there was their president in pajamas and a bathrobe, greeting each one at the door with a handshake, thanking them for coming. He never missed an opportunity to campaign.

Such was the task of the Secret Service. But ultimately, there is no way to guarantee the president's safety—it is an exercise in minimizing danger, but not quite eliminating it.

⁂

The president's lodging was still being debated, both in Washington, and at his destination.

"Maggie, Bayfield wants the president." *Desperately*, Walter Kolquist could have added. And he built a strong case. "Look—we're perfect. We have elegant B & B's. They offer accommodations fitting for a commander-in-chief. The mainland affords greater mobility, amenities, and accessibility. It's ideal. And you know I'll break my butt to make it a flawless weekend."

"I know you would, Walter, but the island has its advantages too. I've tried to recommend Bayfield to the White House. But to them, privacy would be easier to assure there. They tell me there's just something about an island for being away from it all."

Not to mention the "pull" of a certain congresswoman. She had been elected to serve the entire district (that included her ally Walter Kolquist). She knew this project could not succeed without the soon-to-be disappointed banker's support, and reminded him that much of the lodging, dining, and eager shopping would spill over to the mainland anyway. That softened the blow. Money often does.

But her family's property ties were on the island—fifty acres of prime undeveloped land discretely titled in her cousin's name, just waiting for the right price. She well knew the value of a presidential stay as a marketing tool. Final score: La Pointe: One, Bayfield: not quite Zero, but not the grand prize.

⁜

The local minister wasn't sure a presidential visit was a good idea. She was convinced when approached by a trio of her congregation's leadership. Marvin Pound, town board member, local fisherman, and church president, spoke first.

"Pastor, we've been talking."

"And … " She twisted uncomfortably in her chair, and not only because she suspected what they've been talking about. Everything was becoming uncomfortable for Pastor Shelly Griggs. She carried a welcome but cumbersome gift in her belly, due for a grand appearance in late June.

"And, we think you should write a letter inviting the president to worship at St. John's this summer—"

When two seconds passed with the minister still desperately praying for divine guidance, Rollie Sanders, local carpenter and chair of the church's Trustee Committee, blurted out his personal reasoning—one not argued by any of his colleagues.

"What a great moment for us! It would be the highlight of our whole history!"

And the fact that God is here each week doesn't excite you? the Minister was tempted to ask.

"Pastor, it's really an elegant idea. I suspect the island would expect us to invite him," Marvin added. "Frankly, I think he's unlikely to attend. But he will certainly respond in some way, perhaps with a representative of some note." Rollie smiled his trust-me-on-this smile. The pastor, thankful that she would be on maternity leave during the summer, said, "Of course. Let's do it."

Sandy, the church's treasurer, added her own practical rationale. "I bet it's our best offering all year!"

The Reverend, knowing that she'd be off the island, had already handed Sunday responsibilities to Dr. Franklin Neale in her absence. She would, of course, miss preaching to the president, if in fact he showed up. She was in love with the people she served, in a community so refreshingly different from her Los Angeles roots, and secretly hoped he would show up, and give her congregation the gift of a memory for the ages. But she'd rather enjoy her first child—a girl, she just learned—than preach to a politician. *They'd rather talk than listen anyway*, she mused.

She grinned. *When did Marvin discover the word "elegant"?*

CHAPTER FOURTEEN

CLOSE ENCOUNTER

Franklin Neale walked to Michael's shop, just over a mile through the woods, finding the workman cleaning his tools. It was Saturday, a week before the festivities would begin in earnest.

"Checking up on your chairs, Doc?" Erickson even smiled a bit; Frank returned it.

"I hope I can get a sneak peek, Michael. You have no idea how I'm looking forward to siting on something besides folding chairs."

"Not to worry. On schedule to be finished by … Labor Day."

Erickson liked Neale. They're not close in age; Dr. Neale beat Michael by almost three decades. But of all the islanders, year-around or summer, in Michael's mind he's one of the more tolerable ones. Still, Doctor Neale was shocked to hear Michael say, "Come on inside." The Doctor followed him into the small, rustic cabin, one virtually no one else has seen.

He spied a photograph, a faded print of a group of soldiers, standing in what appears to be a field camp.

"Who are these guys?"

"My old unit."

"Keep in touch with them?"

Michael's voice changed from relaxed to stiff. "No."

"Why?"

"Because they're all dead."

Michael walked into a small screened-in room and leaned against a post supporting the roof. The professor followed, sensing that, *This may become a delicate conversation ... a thin place. Tread carefully.* He waited for Michael to speak.

"I've never told anyone this."

"You don't have to go there, Michael."

"We—my unit, the guys in the picture—were in Cambodia, when the government was pretending none of us were. We were directing traffic for the guys dropping bombs."

Michael, Neale sensed, *is about to re-live something.*

"It's about midnight, a few clouds, quarter moon; just enough light to see. We're there so if we see anything we can call down some air strikes. We're crossing this swamp, we hear noise, we drop. We see this enemy tank escorting three trucks, moving south."

Erickson took a long, deep breath. Neale didn't move. He kept his eyes on Michael's face.

"We're a hundred meters from any cover, so we try to sink into the muck and not move. We radio our position. We're concerned 'cause there's air patrols around, and we don't want some trigger-happy flyboy dropping bad stuff when we're close enough to these bad guys to smell their breath. We want distance between them and us. While we watch from the weeds, they stop. We hide, face down in the soup.

"The guy in the lead truck gets out, so do the other drivers, and a guy from the tank gets down. We're thinking: *Uh-oh. Maybe they see us. If they do, we're dead.* Instead, they stand around, talk for a few minutes; laugh; all the while, we're just laying in the weeds. They don't see us. We just lay there.

"About a minute later we hear this noise, sudden like— *Whoosh.* And everything in front of us disappears in a ball of fire. Enemy soldiers run for cover into the bushes, but we can't do a thing. Whoever is up there has no clue there are friendlies in the swamp.

"This F-4 screams past and turns for another pass. Our radio guy starts yelling to someone on the radio to call off the attack. Just as he starts his call, a 500-pounder that pilot had already released lands in the river, 50 yards in front of me. Just like that, two of my guys disappear. We never even found dog tags. Then another 500-pounder, just to the right and about 15 yards closer. This one wounds our radio operator and kills our medic. I get up and run for the radio; the Vietnamese might see me and shoot me, but I'd rather be killed by them than by our own guy up there somewhere. I start hollering our position and beg someone to call off the attack; then I tell our guys to run back toward the tree line. It's my best instinct, my order. But it's a mistake."

"The enemy begins shooting?"

"I wish. Then this would have some honor to it. But the NVA are running the other way for cover. Never see them again. Meanwhile, our guy in the sky comes back over, sees movement, and opens up with his Gatling gun. Trouble is, *we're* the movement he sees. Ten seconds later, everyone in my unit is either dead or wounded. I still have some fragments of official U. S. Air Force 20MM in my thigh. Your taxes paid for it."

The room went silent, and *even the birds*, Franklin noticed, *have stopped singing*. He had no idea what to say; Michael couldn't speak without breaking down.

Finally, Michael turned to his guest.

"I laid there bleeding all night, my guys ripped to shreds all around me. I was their leader. They looked to me for orders, and I led them to their deaths."

More silence. Michael turned away, talking to no one for an uncomfortably long time.

"When it was clear, I crawled to each one I could find. A couple lived until just before dawn, but there was nothing I could do except try to comfort them. The rest—I couldn't even recognize most of them.

"A couple hours into the morning, a chopper came and snatched me, and picked up what they could of my guys."

"God be with their families."

"Yeah. Sure. Hopefully more than He was with my unit that night."

Franklin was desperate to respect what—and who—Erickson was remembering.

"Do they investigate these things? What do they do?"

"Yeah, they investigate. Then they file a report, the kind they hope no one ever reads. Just another tragic 'friendly fire' accident.

"I wasn't supposed to see the report, but a friend of mine in Military Intel returned a favor, and I got a copy. Still have it. The pilot got credit for killing a tank and three trucks. 'Classified,' it says. We weren't supposed to be there, remember?"

"Did you ever encounter this pilot?"

"No. Never will, either."

"Is he dead?"

"Wish he were. Almost was; shot down about three weeks later, spent 6 months as a POW. But he's very much alive and well, I'm afraid."

"How do you know?"

"I see him now and then."

"Around here?"

"Not exactly, unless on TV counts as 'around here.' His name is Robert Alan Eastland."

CHAPTER FIFTEEN

A LARGELY UNNATURAL LIFE

Later that evening, Robert Alan and Mary Lee Sherman Eastland were awake in their elegant living quarters, on the third floor of the nation's executive mansion. While the front of the 132-room White House appears to have only two floors, there is a third level seen only from its southern exposure—the world's most prestigious walkout basement.

They shared a bedroom near the southwest corner of the White House. Immediately to the east of the bedchamber is the President's Study. Beyond that is the Yellow Oval Room, which is as close to a living room as the White House has, occupying the central part of the south facade and marked by the distinctive rounded protrusion that creates several floors of oval rooms, visible from the south lawn.

But no Oval Office. It isn't in the White House at all. The president must walk down two flights of stairs, and then stroll past the Rose Garden and Press Briefing Room to that famous chamber in the West Wing executive office area. This night found them in the President's Study.

The presidency. They had devoted much of their adult lives to attaining this. And like the Neales, their as-yet-unknown counterparts in the Midwest, they were sharing a room at the end of a grueling day. All their days, it seemed, were grueling. But Robert and Mary Eastland shared little else.

"How are you tonight?" She stood behind him as he sat at his desk, signing dozens of letters delivered to his room at the end of the day. She caressed his tight shoulders, in part to draw him away from his work. She was seeking at least companionship, and possibly intimacy, an increasingly rare event in the life of the First Couple.

"All right, I guess."

She kissed him on the temple, moving her arms down around his chest in a light embrace. *Perhaps a more direct approach will penetrate his shell—*

"Not tonight. I've got more where these came from. Sorry." He never looked away from the repetitive scrawling of his signature.

"It's been so long … "

"Not tonight." He kept writing.

Robert Alan Eastland was perceived as a solid family man. Three years after he laid his first wife and daughter to rest near their home in Nebraska, the congressman married Mary Lee Sherman, daughter of a giant of Wall Street. They began to build a new, and attractive, family. He would father a son, Aaron, now sixteen, and a daughter, Shannon, now thirteen. Eastland's new family went from notoriety inside the Beltway to national prominence in the first presidential campaign. They were no small part of his election; his wife was eloquent and witty on the stump, the family was absurdly photogenic and as such too tempting for the press to ignore. The tabloids made sure that no one could buy a bag of groceries without the Eastland's in living color at every checkout counter: skiing, playing tennis, riding horseback. Priceless, but free, campaign exposure.

To his opponents, Eastland was disgustingly good looking. He maintained his 6' 1" figure well, his blond hair slightly thinning on top, though still attractive.

The nation remembered Eastland's grief as the then-congressman was deprived of his family in a plane crash twenty-two years before. Ironically, they had died while being flown out of a war zone to safety. An unseen explosion. The discovery of wreckage. There were unconfirmed reports of anti-aircraft fire; even reports of rockets. But in the files of the State Department, little else was recorded, except that their bodies were returned to the congressman for burial in Nebraska, in the family plot. Nothing was said about how they met their end.

But there was one who knew.

⁜

What people who loved each other would treasure as time with each other, this president treasured as time for concentrated paperwork. Mary Eastland had paperwork of her own, and had developed the habit of saving some for the evening, sharing the private study with the husband she hoped would notice her presence and desire to exploit it. She usually hoped in vain.

Life had been good, but not what she longed for. She had known only a life of privilege and had learned that her role was to exude confidence and grace. But having achieved the goals set out for her, she was lonely, empty, disillusioned. There's an addictive quality to wealth and power, but it never occurred to her to walk away from the gilded cage.

Still, she yearned for at least one space in her tightly orchestrated, largely unnatural life, where she could find intimacy, warmth, and love. Fame and power were there in abundance. The office her husband occupied provided all the adrenalin rush any person could desire. They had their children—Aaron, who, though moody and withdrawn at times, was handsome, intelligent—a pop culture icon in his own right.

And Shannon. She was beautiful, in the early years the dream of every young girl: happy, energetic, smart. Approaching her teens, some noticed a reserve … a temper … a fragility that was harder and harder to airbrush out of her public persona.

The First Lady felt guilty for not accepting that the nation's interests must come before her longings. But still: why would a man like Robert Eastland, president or not, spurn the love of a woman who, she thought, was attractive enough to draw any healthy male away from his paperwork? She did not know that his reluctance was not governed by the paperwork in front of him as much as a demon within him.

⁜

The Pastor at St. John's Church had sent a carefully worded invitation to the president, telling him how honored her little flock would be as his host for worship on Sunday before the Fourth of July. She expected a form letter, graciously declining her invitation. *Which was fine,* she thought—*even better, really.* The logistics, the pressure, the commotion, in a church that in the wintertime is attended by maybe two dozen people? *Overwhelming,* she thought, as she quietly prayed for a thanks-but-no-thanks response. She would be on maternity leave during the busy summer months, thanks to the unexpected gift from her husband.

More likely, she thought, she'd hear nothing at all.

What she got in response was a visit. Two weeks before the president's arrival. A nicely dressed woman knocked on the parsonage door, showed her an impressive-looking badge, relayed the president's delight at being invited, and, *Well, can I take a preliminary look at your church?*

She was there for an hour, walking through every room (there aren't many), every entrance. She estimated the chapel's capacity. She walked around the property—especially the wooded, undeveloped land behind the church. She overwhelmed the very pregnant clergywoman with information that was also included in a formal-looking packet. She took pictures. Lots and lots of pictures.

CHAPTER SIXTEEN

THE FRUITS OF ONE'S CONVICTIONS

The pen is mightier than the sword, and often precedes it.

The year was 1957. Khalil Wazir, known to history as Abu Jihad, engaged in the first of many passionate discussions about the fate of Palestine in a changing world.

"Our people are asleep! They must be awakened, Ahmad, or we will be erased from the face of the earth!"

He and his friends were troubled by the injustices perpetrated on them by the Israelis, and a world blind to the displacement of an entire nation by the establishment of Israel.

"We have been betrayed, brothers! The West has given the Jews our ancestral home. And the Zionists were only too happy to push us into the desert. Where are our Arab brothers? Why did they not fight for Palestine when we needed them?"

Ahmad was equally passionate. "Fight? With what army, brother? We are a paper tiger. You cannot fight the West—or the Jews—with horses and camels. Learn this and learn it well. If we would reclaim our homeland, it will be through long and bitter struggle. And it will be *our* struggle. We have no true allies. There are those who will help us—to a point, while we serve their purposes. But there is no one we can trust, except ourselves and Allah. We must fight our own holy war."

"A holy war, brother Ahmad? Allow me to ask the very question you asked: 'With what army?'"

"We are our own army, Kahlil. If, that is, we have the courage to fight."

"And die, probably."

"Yes, brother, if Allah wills it—to die, in service to God and the people of Palestine."

And die they would, almost all of them. But not until they had engineered a clandestine war that would make its mark on the Middle East, and draw the fortunes of leaders around the world, including a future American president, into its web.

By October of 1959, they had formed a paramilitary organization to fight for the cause of Palestine. It would bear the name *Fatah*, a word from the Koran that meant "opening." Fatah grew into a network of uniquely structured cells of ten to fifteen members each—unique, in that their members did not know who the others were. Secrecy is a fragile thing in the close-knit Palestinian community, and you serve your brothers best if you do not know them.

Fatah's first endeavor was not a war but a magazine, the "pen" that birthed the swords that would bloody the Middle East. *Our Palestine* was in large part financed by a then-wealthy civil engineer named Yassir Arafat. Through the magazine's tireless recruitment, Fatah spread its message of Palestinian pride and national destiny, contributing to an evolution of anger and hope among a displaced people. And it contributed to the establishment of their dominant voice: the Palestine Liberation Organization.

But it was the Egyptian government, not the Palestinians themselves, that actually founded the PLO in 1964. This new organization was seen by Ahmad, Abu Jihad, Yassir Arafat, and Fatah as a despicable puppet, a rival. In order to regain the initiative in leading the Palestinian people to freedom, Fatah initiated their first military operation (or terrorist attack, depending on whether you were perpetrators or victims). They planted a bomb in an Israeli water treatment facility in 1965. It failed to detonate. But Fatah gradually learned how to be effective in drawing Israeli blood, and by the time they were absorbed as the paramilitary wing of the PLO, they were good at the art and science of terror.

✛

Abu Jihad and Yassir Arafat would never meet Robert Alan Eastland, and likely never heard his name. Eastland, for his part, would know Arafat's name and reputation. But the one-time civil engineer's passions would unleash a generation of inconclusive attacks, reprisals, bitterness, terror—and on one fateful night, Fatah would scar the legacy of Robert Alan Eastland.

CHAPTER SEVENTEEN

BEFORE THE STORM

The bedside phone rang six times before a hand dragged it from its cradle.

"Good morning, Mr. Bates. This is your wakeup call. Is there anything else we can do for you, sir?"

"Yeah. Turn back the clock."

Finally, the day had come. The sun would rise on Thursday, June 29th, over people frantically at work in the village of La Pointe. Balloons and flags sprouted everywhere. It seemed that every lawn mower on the island was running, many before breakfast. Paintbrushes flew in all directions, touching up any less-than-perfect surface. A rented street sweeper cleaned Main Street—again. Nautical pennants were flying from every mast in the marina. The few who tried to sleep in were awakened by generators powering a growing makeshift village of vans crammed with media gear, their satellite dishes oddly out of place in the little village.

The island grocer was desperate to replenish his shelves. He'd doubled his usual beverage orders as a matter of course for the 4th of July festivities, but this year he had tripled it, and was still running out.

The ferry line dreaded these days. Their fleet of four ferries would run incessantly, while two rented passenger boats added desperately needed capacity. The lines of waiting passengers would soon extend from the Bayfield ferry dock well into town. They had already run each boat twice, filled to capacity, and it was not yet 7:00 a.m.

On one of those earlier ferries, a weary journalist made his first visit to Madeline Island. He'd caught a late flight from Reagan International to Minneapolis-St. Paul, then the last flight to Duluth. He slept until his 3:00 a.m. wake-up call, showered, dressed, and was out of the parking lot by 4:00. With Dunkin' Donuts coffee in the cup holder, two chocolate-covered donuts on the console, and a map in his lap doubling as a napkin—he barely made his rendezvous with a 6:00 a.m. ferry.

The *Madeline* is ninety feet in length, with a capacity of two dozen or so vehicles. Its most prominent feature is its superstructure: a two-level affair offset to the port side, allowing tall loads to ride the center of the gray steel deck built for heavy trucks. But on this day the *Madeline* was crammed with an assortment of visitors, workers, local residents, SUVs with government plates, and a growing army of journalists. For many aboard on that morning, it would be a workday of finding, compiling, and reporting the news to a waiting world.

The passage to the island, refined over the generations, rarely varies. The lines are cast off, the ramp is raised and the engines are reversed. The starboard engine is given more power than its port side twin, turning the craft clockwise as it backs into Bayfield's boat basin. A few seconds later, the port engine powers forward, accelerating the pivot; the starboard engine joins in after the vessel has made its turn. The *Madeline* clears the breakwater and points toward its destination.

"Been here before?" A cheery female voice interrupted the slumber of a Washington journalist, who kept his eyes closed.

"No."

"Welcome to Wisconsin." The voice grew closer as the yet-unseen speaker leaned against the door frame, ruining the last vestiges of Gary's sleep. "I'm Samantha Wells. You a reporter too?"

"Yeah—*Washington Post*."

Her eyes widened. "Gary Bates! I recognize you! Wow. I'm with WLOW TV in Duluth."

Bates noticed through half-open eyes that she was rather attractive. But he was annoyed by the fact that at six in the morning, she was so bubbly. Must be a rookie, he surmised. "Nice to meet you. See ya later." He closed his eyes in a vain attempt to salvage some sleep on the 20-minute ride.

⁜

You can hear it before you see it. You're on a morning walk or sitting near an open window when a deep, steady rumble marks the approach of the *Madeline*, its engines hard at work. When the vessel is a quarter mile or so away, an additional sound is added—that of water being pushed around the ferry's blunt bow.

Once the vessel enters the small harbor, the work is done by the captain's deft touch on the throttles: forward, astern, forward, astern again, until the boat slides along the breakwater, barely moving until it touches the dock. Lines are secured, the ramp lowered, and the vehicles drive away.

As visitors leave the dock, the village of La Pointe spreads out before them. Most of the vehicles that morning turned left, toward the bay-side homes on Nebraska Row. Their interest was in the island's guests of honor, who would stay at a stately, elegant manor that would serve as the White House after their arrival.

Had the visitors turned right on Main Street, they would have entered La Pointe's modest downtown. Further on, a Craft Hall and St. John's Church greet them, then an inn, marina, and golf course, before the road disappears into the trees and toward many of the Island's private getaways.

⁜

It began over the Four Corners, where Utah, Arizona, New Mexico, and Colorado meet. Manuel Jesus Lopez tossed his tools in the back of the battered pickup, slamming the tailgate in disgust. Rain again. The painting would be delayed; the way this cloud was bursting, it could be tomorrow or even the day after that before the old pump house's clapboard siding would be dry enough to hold paint. Manuel drove back to the ranch that had been his family's home for four generations in southwestern Colorado. There were always indoor chores that needed attention. Anyway, Maria would have dinner on the table in a couple hours.

The combination of airborne moisture and summer heat can be explosive, triggering spectacular thunderstorms that in turn can birth larger weather systems. Those systems often drift east, drawing moisture-laden air north from the Gulf of Mexico. On Thursday, June 29th, the U. S. Weather Service office in Denver took note and began monitoring whether the upper level disturbance over the Navajo Indian Reservation would in fact organize; every sign was that it would, and be carried to the northeast by the jet stream, gathering punch along the way.

CHAPTER EIGHTEEN

FOR THE GRANDCHILDREN

Standing on the deck of the *Indiana Harbor*, First Mate Harry Slack couldn't hear the Pratt & Whitney engines of the 747 overhead. But he'd heard the news that morning, noted the estimated time of arrival, and arranged to be on deck as the 1,000-foot vessel took on 65,000 tons of Montana coal. The coal is shipped in mile-long unit trains from the west, and it will take seven of them to fill the *Indiana Harbor*.

Loading a bulk carrier of this size is both art and science. Improper loading could unbalance the ship, and even damage her. It was hard to supervise this process with one eye to the sky as well. But Harry had a mission, one he had meticulously planned for, ever since he heard that he and the president would converge on this fateful day. He would not fail. He'd seen the procession of C-131 transports coming in for the past hour. Limousines and communications gear, he guessed. It was that, and much more. And now he saw what he'd been waiting for: *Air Force One*.

On this Friday morning on the last day of June, he was berthed at the Midwest Energy Terminal in Superior, Wisconsin, across the bay from Duluth. As it happened, his ship was directly under the baby blue and gray airplane's glide path.

In a secluded corner of the main deck, he opened the nylon case he had pre-positioned behind the crane used to move the hatch covers. He couldn't leave the ship—this was his only chance.

He pulled out its contents, and lifted a black object to his shoulder. The big plane was now within range, perfectly positioned, not quite overhead, moving at a speed slow enough for easy tracking. He took careful aim, locked the target in his sight, and squeezed the trigger. This set off a sequence of electronic commands. And his camcorder captured the moment for his grandchildren.

⁜

Two thousand feet above the *Indiana Harbor*, the president looked down on a remarkable sight: 1,500 miles from any ocean, at the western end of Lake Superior, rests a world-class seaport. That international commerce happens in the Midwest surprises many a visitor. So does the geography. Duluth clings to a steep, rocky hill rising abruptly nearly 600 feet from the shore, and its resemblance to San Francisco is one of its more obvious features. But there are differences: in Duluth, temperatures can drop below zero.

⁜

"The entire process is numbing. Simply numbing."

A weary First Lady leaned back in the leather chair, eyes closed. Secret Service Agent Kim Nguyen at her side watched her intently. *They really need this break*, the agent thought. It was a rare moment when one of those assigned to protect the First Family had opportunity to engage them, but Ms. Eastland was in a reflective mood, and had initiated the conversation.

"I don't know how you do it, Ma'am."

Mary Eastland smiled. She opened her eyes, and glanced out the window. "The president actually envies the man who wants his job, I think. It's amazing how brutal this business is. While Robert—excuse me, The President—was settling into the Oval Office, Mr. Brady, rest his soul, was just one of several people lining up to challenge him this time around. Governor Marsh included."

"Your husband has the advantage of already being the president."

"But the ex-governor has one advantage over my husband: Marsh's only job is to campaign full-time. My husband still has to preside over a rather independent-minded nation, police an ever-changing list of global trouble spots, deal with terrorists—"

"And Congress, Mrs. Eastland?"

Mary Eastland laughed softly. "Yes, and Congress! And, campaign full-time to keep his job."

The plane entered a thin cloud bank, and when it re-entered clear air the horizon to the right was filled with the dark blue mass of Lake Superior.

"Ms. Eastland, I'm not supposed to be politically oriented, but I follow the news. And based on what I've seen, we—excuse me, your husband—won't face a serious convention challenge. If that's true, then the election could shape up as a clash of political giants."

The First Lady smiled. "Very astute for an 'apolitical' agent, Ms. Nguyen."

"I remember" (it was the agent's turn to reminisce) "that when I first was assigned to the White House, I sensed the crowd's energy when the president appeared."

"Robert and I felt it too." *It's rare*, the agent mused, *for the First Lady to refer to her husband by name in front of the staff.*

The First Lady looked past the agent at an opening door. "Speaking of whom … are we landing soon, Mr. President?"

Eastland was emerging from the cockpit. "Yes. About ten minutes out." He'd worked hard to earn the trust of the flight crew, who were not amused when he playfully asked if he could fly the 747, but enjoyed swapping talk of airplanes and Vietnam days with a fellow combat pilot. He dropped into a matching seat across the aisle.

"You look tired, Robert."

"Guess we need a vacation, huh?"

One of Eastland's most vivid memories was the rush of his first ride on *Air Force One*. The huge 747 gave Eastland sheer, unadulterated pleasure. But with the campaign ramping up, the big plane would become his second home. He'd give anything to not spend another night trying to sleep on an airplane while it flew him to or from Washington.

What scared Eastland (and others close to the stresses of the Oval Office) was the loss of perspective when one must deal with so many things simultaneously. *What if I miss something? What if I overreact, out of sheer fatigue? I could start a war just because some two-bit dictator pushed too hard when I was tired and crabby.*

CHAPTER NINETEEN

ARRIVAL

Air Force One touched down at the precise moment specified: 1:45 p.m. on Friday afternoon, the 30th of June. It taxied toward the Air National Guard terminal at the eastern end of the Duluth airport, where local dignitaries were eagerly waiting. So was a public that was kept a quarter mile away behind chain link fences.

A motorcade would maximize the contact with the public (make that "voters") and minimize the imperial tone of this vacation. But when a president travels on the ground, the security requirements call for guarding every street, every alley, every driveway along the route, even in the sparsely populated forests of northern Wisconsin. Consequently, *Marine One*, pre-positioned two days before, would whisk the First Family directly from the National Guard base to the airport on the island, traveling most of the route over Lake Superior, just offshore.

But the route to the island was not a straight line. Virtually unnoticed, approaching the Wisconsin shoreline, *Marine One* dipped discretely south, passing over a seemingly unremarkable tract of land. It was important that the helo's primary occupant be able to say that, yes, he had seen the magnificent primeval forest then-governor Frederick Marsh had, through inexcusable dereliction of duty, put at risk.

At last, Madeline Island welcomed its president. Landing on the tarmac, surrounded by the people of La Pointe, President Eastland would have to wait a few minutes more for his vacation. Dressed in jeans and a maroon knit shirt, he received gifts from the town chairman and the sixteen students of the local elementary school—gifts of modest monetary value, but offered with immense and genuine pride. Eastland may have been elected by and for the people, but in this place and for this moment, he could have been emperor.

The town chairman's voice cracked with emotion: "Mr. President, Ms. Eastland, Aaron and Shannon: on behalf of the people of Madeline Island, it is my high honor to welcome you. It is a moment we will never forget, and I want to assure you that we will do everything we can to make this a memorable vacation for our nation's First Family!" The small invitation-only crowd applauded enthusiastically. They had no idea how memorable this vacation would become.

It was the First Lady, not the president, who thanked the town folk for their hospitality, and expressing her eagerness to do some sightseeing—and shopping—while the president fished. Then the president, remarkably brief for a campaigning politician: "On behalf of Shannon, Aaron, Mary Lee, my entire staff and myself, thank you. I hear the fishing is great," he stopped to allow the cheers to subside. "And I intend to catch my limit!"

The people cheered again, and the First Family settled into the limousine, and made their way down the spectator-lined road to their home for the next few days, an elegant Bed and Breakfast on Nebraska Row.

CHAPTER TWENTY

A PRIVATE MATTER

Late on Friday afternoon, the president's first house guest was Mark Neale.

"Thank you for seeing me, Mr. President. I didn't think you'd have the time."

"Actually, I wanted to catch you before this 'vacation' spins out of control."

An aide served lemonade and snacks as they settled into Adirondack chairs on the patio overlooking the lawn, with the waters beyond dotted by dozens of watercraft enjoying a warm, sun-filled midsummer day.

"I know, sir, that the campaign is already dominating your time, but I'd like to look back at 1996. What did you learn in your first campaign that helps you prepare for this one?"

Eastland smiled, leaning back in the cane rocking chair. "I was struck by how a campaign can be as boring as it is exciting. Even a relatively uncontested primary season is grueling. Four states in a single day. A hundred-, a thousand- or five-thousand-dollar-a-plate dinners. Interminable introductions by people seeking to impress the person who came to impress the voters. Phone calls by the hundreds to 'close friends' of the candidate. Super Tuesday.

"We arrive at each site and wait, until we begin the same long walk down deserted hallways, and then we're rushed into a gathering that is already in progress. I give the same basic speech, again and again and again. Then another long walk, another wait. It's not exactly wash-rinse-repeat, but it's close. And each time I need be fresh and passionate."

"It's interesting," Mark observed. "You're is always entering events-in-progress, aren't you?"

"And, we learned quickly in 1996 that it's important to come in speaking their language—matching their energy, actually."

"So how do you read the crowd?"

"We learned that you can't wait until you're at the microphone. Some 'crowd reading' is done before we land. We do our homework on what this audience wants to hear: urban, rural, wealthy, middle class, labor, even who the home team is, and if they just won or lost. At the event itself, my staff reads the crowd, and I'm briefed before I make my appearance.

"We watch the monitor in the back room while warm-up speakers do their thing. We pick those 'warmup acts' carefully, by the way. They may be the crowd's congressperson or senator, but they know that they aren't the reason the room is full. Their role is to build the excitement. Then I come out to people who already support me but are hungry to see me in real time. And when I come out, I pretty much sound like a local. I need to talk their language—their emotional language."

"You're not afraid to use a celebrity once in a while?"

"No, but they're vetted carefully. Message is everything. Some celeb's are there to boost themselves, and that's okay as long as they know they're on a very short leash. Their number one job is to make *me* look good."

"Mr. President, what is your family's role in the campaign? I've seen the First Lady, sometimes with you, sometimes as your surrogate."

"Mary's my best advocate. She's a better speaker than I am, frankly. And her charity work fighting breast cancer gives her credibility with, well, half the human race."

"How about your son? I'd think he'd be a great resource.

Not old enough to vote, but old enough to influence a generation of first-time voters. Of course, I shouldn't be telling you how to run your campaign!"

"Mark, I'll take all the advice I can get. And you're right. He could be an asset. But just between you and me, Aaron's been reluctant to put himself out there. Maybe just a phase. He's finding his way through a very strange, very public world."

"By the way, Mr. President, I don't want to be presumptuous, but my son Tony is Aaron's age, and if your son gets bored hanging with the grownups, feel free to have him reach out to Tony. I think they'd like each other."

"We've already thought about that; in fact, I was going to ask. It might be good for Aaron. It also might be a good look for this president too!"

It was a rare moment in which both biographer and president saw common benefit in the simple act of bringing their sons together. They didn't know that it would be the last such moment.

"I don't want to leave out your daughter, Mr. President." Eastland's smile evaporated, his back straightened, his eyes looking toward the table. Mark sensed something has changed. But since he started this …

"Perhaps you feel she's too young for an active role in the campaign. And it must be a tender time, since she's about the same age as Monica—"

Eastland cut the writer off. "Let's not go there. That's a private matter."

Mark was embarrassed. And puzzled.

The president stood. "That's, ah, enough for today. Thanks for coming."

Eastland offered a perfunctory handshake, a grim face, and an abrupt departure, leaving his biographer alone in the room, wondering what he could have said that offended the president. He gathers his notes and walks toward the door, thinking, *Did I just step on a landmine?*

CHAPTER TWENTY-ONE

TWO REPORTERS AND A KINGMAKER

"Well, Ms. Wells, they're only allowing one camera inside. You and CNN will have to duke it out for camera rights on Sunday morning. Good luck arguing with Carrie."

"I know, Mr. Bates. I also think that she should get the nod. She has equipment and experience neither my cameraman nor I have. I'm okay with that. Besides, I at least got a press pass."

Bates assumed her to be just another minor-league local reporter, and wanted to keep his distance. But on a hunch, he asked her a question that would change his life. *Since she probably knows more about local issues than I do* ... He was right; she had done her homework. But he also had, albeit barely above the subconscious, more personal reasons to chat with the rookie.

"What do you know about this church deal tomorrow?"

"Got a few minutes?"

Half an hour later, Gary Bates and Samantha Wells snagged one of the few remaining tables at a lakeside restaurant. Over burgers and fries, a diet soda for her and a Lite beer for him, Samantha Wells painted a picture of what to expect on Sunday morning for the *Post's* most famous and least religious correspondent. Not that he was all that interested in small-town religion. His interest was in the small-city reporter.

"So, now that I've overwhelmed your defenses with the fine local cuisine—tell me what I can expect in church."

"You go to church much?"

"Not since my grandmother's funeral. I'm a card-carrying pagan."

"Too bad. You're missing out."

"Not based on what I remember from Confirmation class in the 8th grade. I didn't think God was so boring."

"You're right. God is not boring. Unfortunately, some ministers seem to work overtime to make God seem that way."

"So, you're a church-going Christian woman? No offense, Ms. Wells."

"Please call me Samantha."

Maybe the veteran journalist felt his masculinity challenged by a young female dictating how she should be addressed—or maybe Bates just bristles when someone corrects him—

"Okay, Sam. All I mean is that I remember dreadfully boring sermons preached by robots in robes who couldn't connect with the real world to save their souls. So is this what the president and the rest of us will be forced to endure on Sunday? Please tell me it ain't so, but Christianity seems to be more about everyone's bedrooms than their souls. And why are they trying to be the nation's moral police?"

"I'm not proud of everything some of us do. Persuade, yes. Coerce? Never. There are a lot of us who want no part in that. Me? I just want to love my neighbor—" She swallowed her first bite of her burger—"And by neighbor, I mean everyone."

"That's very noble. But is there any news value in my enduring church instead of sleeping in—which is what God, if God exists, made Sunday mornings for in the first place?"

"I think you'll find Sunday interesting. The regular preacher's on maternity leave, so a retired religion professor is filling in. I suspect you'll find a nervous lay minister, preaching to a president. I have no idea what the preacher will say, but I don't think there will be fire and brimstone. I'd guess he'll just try to connect person-to-person and be encouraging."

"And will I also find budding young reporter Samantha Wells nervous if she ever gets a chance to ask the president a question?"

"I will be terrified."

"Nice to meet an honest TV reporter. Moving on … Do you care who wins this election?"

"Yes, but what I care more about is: when the dust settles, what happens to the people on the margins? Seems that in politics, if you can't donate, you don't count."

"Seems like you're siding with the losing side in this election. Eastland's gonna win, and the poor won't get many favors from him or his party."

Samantha remained silent.

"Did I upset you?"

Samantha looked past Bates, who thought he did in fact upset her. Both of them were quiet. Finally, Samantha spoke.

"No. It's just that I think you may be right. And it breaks my heart."

None of this really interested Gary Bates. But it kept the conversation going between one male from Washington and one female from Duluth, and he was fine with that. "Does anything actually interesting happen on this here island?"

Samantha put her sandwich down. "No one is saying much, but my sources—"

"You, Samantha, in the infancy of your career, already have sources?"

She leaned forward, looking straight at him. "If I may continue."

He picked up his Miller Lite. "Okay … "

"My sources tell me that there's a new controversy brewing on the mainland. The state holds title to some forest land, the paper industry wants to harvest it, and the Indigenous community says it's theirs and they want it left alone."

Finally, Bates, surmised, something he could actually report. "Did you say the state?"

"Correct."

"Thank you." *State, as in ex-governor Marsh's turf? Somehow, it just might be ...* He filed that mental note, when the rookie challenged him.

"Now you tell me something, Mr. Hotshot Washington Reporter."

"Such as..."

"Such as, who really runs the Administration?"

"Why, Sam—" He handed Ms. Wells a paper napkin. "Gooey stuff on your left cheek, by the way. The president runs the Administration, of course."

She took the napkin and, without looking, removed the offending stuff while speaking. "Wrong answer, Mr. Bates. That it isn't Eastland's style."

"What do you know about Eastland?"

"Tell you what: after church I'll tell you. If you promise to answer my question."

"Deal."

She had educated herself well on the dynamics of the Eastland White House. She could be forgiven for not knowing that those dynamics were set almost twenty-five years before, on a less-than-promising day in which showing up was considered noble.

CHAPTER TWENTY-TWO

THE DAY AFTER CHRISTMAS

Lincoln, Nebraska, December 26th, 1975

"Enjoy the rest of the holidays, Mr. Scott."

"Thanks."

Christmas was over, and the New Year would mark the nation's Bicentennial. Peter Scott closed the door behind him and walked away from the Personnel Office serving the University of Nebraska's administration. His status as a ex-football star for the Cornhuskers offered little hope of a job, and he needed one. He did not know it had been the next to last job interview of his life.

"And thanks for nothing."

He headed for one final stop on his so far disheartening search for employment. It would be at the state capitol. The Nebraska state offices were virtually deserted, but Peter Scott was hungry, frustrated, and down to his last lead: an office for helping Vietnam veterans, freshly discharged after an unpopular war.

He expected more of what he'd experienced all through December: impatient interviewers with few interesting jobs to offer and no desire to take seriously one more ex-soldier looking for work. Scott was numb, mechanically filling out applications while expecting nothing. So far on this day after Christmas, no one had any gifts to give.

But a familiar name on the door ignited a sense of hope:

Robert A. Eastland
Director
Office for Veteran Services

Bob Eastland? The same guy who recruited me out of high school? Gotta be.

It was. The Director of Veteran Services was an ex-Nebraska football star himself, who had recruited promising high school seniors from the Class of 1965, Peter Scott among them. Eastland had served his country in Southeast Asia, enlisting in 1969, trained as a fighter pilot, and on his 43rd mission was shot down on Christmas Eve in 1973. He spent a grueling half-year in captivity until he was released in 1974. Scott also served his country, but on the ground.

Scott formulated a strategy: he wouldn't be a job seeker, just an old football protégé catching up on old times. He'd meet Bob Eastland as a peer. He walked in.

"No, I don't have an appointment. Just let Bob know Pete Scott is here."

The receptionist cautiously interrupted Eastland's phone call with news of Scott's presence. Eastland hadn't thought about Scott in years, and was puzzled by someone he hardly remembered paying a social call. But it was a dreadfully slow day. He ended the phone call and came out to meet his visitor.

"Long time, no see, Scotty." Eastland extended his hand.

"Yeah. Congratulations on the new job. Good to see an old Cornhusker making good."

Eastland's secretary groaned in dismay. "Not another football player?" The two men chuckled; Eastland put her mind at ease. "We're harmless."

"Unless you're from our dreaded rivals in Oklahoma," Scott added. Eastland laughed and turned toward the door. "Come on in. Sandy, hold my calls."

"There haven't been many to hold, Mr. Eastland."

"Which means …"

"… that most sensible people took the day after Christmas off, and urged their hard-working secretaries to do the same."

Eastland grinned. "What time is it, Sandy?"

"3:50"

"Take the rest of the day off. I'll lock up."

"Wow. Forty minutes early."

"Merry Christmas."

Once inside Eastland's office, two veterans caught up on the years since Scott's last performance in a football uniform. They sized each other up.

"What did you do in the war, Scotty?"

"Special Forces."

"Wow. Where?"

Scott grinned. "I could tell you, but then I'd have to shoot you." Eastland laughed; then asked a question few veterans would ask:

"You kill anyone?"

"Yeah. Lots of folk."

"Bother you?"

"Not really. What I remember is that I was really good at it. How about you?"

"Air Force. F-4's."

"So you escaped the mud and mosquitoes, huh?"

"Not exactly. Shot down North of the border, probably not too far from where you were disturbing the peace. Six months as a guest of Chairman Ho Chi Minh. Pity we couldn't get together; I could have used a Green Beret or two."

"So, you're a war hero?"

Eastland look contemptuously away. "For what that's worth." Scott was puzzled at Eastland's cynical assessment of his status as an ex-POW. To Scott, they were among the only heroes of an unpopular war; *Eastland should carry the label with a degree of pride us foot soldiers could only dream of.* But as the conversation wore on, Scott understood.

Eastland was Captain of the Nebraska football team. Kathryn Rossberg was a cheerleader—stunningly beautiful, confident, eager to tame a man. It was passion, if not love, at first sight. They married six months after their first date, and began a roller-coaster marriage that resulted in the birth of their daughter, Monica. Their marriage survived Robert's hitch in the Air Force, including his combat record—and his capture by the Viet Cong.

But when he returned, the passion was hard-edged, intolerant, grim. It was as if the deprivation of a Vietnamese prison triggered a hunger, a need to compensate for what he had, for six months, lost. And even a passionate, beautiful, seductive woman wasn't enough to quench his desires. An affair nearly ended the marriage but somehow, Kathryn refused to let him go; she shared one desire with him—a lust for success and power— and they found a common bond in his pursuit of political power.

After the war, the Eastland family of three relocated from their small, remote Nebraska hometown to Grand Island. An education in the state capital had made him hungry for a political career, and Grand Island seemed perfect: they could raise their nine-year-old daughter in a town large enough to serve as a springboard to greater things. Thinking his status as a veteran and a POW could entice the voters, he sought to become Grand Island's mayor, despite less than two years of residency there, and as he met with Peter Scott, he was just weeks removed from a humiliating defeat at the hands of his neighbors and friends, in the November off-year election. Kathryn was still unpacking after the move to Lincoln.

In this last week of December, both Scott and Eastland found in each other a belated Christmas gift. They would discover how much they had in common: the same drive to succeed, the same political philosophy, and the same craving for power.

Eastland offered his fellow veteran a job on his new staff, and would learn to use Scott's keen instincts not only to help find jobs for Vietnam veterans, but to develop a strategy for moving to Washington following the 1976 congressional races. It would prove a most successful arrangement. Scott would become Eastland's "handler," using the up-and-coming politician to achieve what he couldn't achieve directly.

It soon became clear that Kathryn's role in Eastland's career would be, bit by bit, overtaken by Peter Scott; she would be the model candidate's wife and mother, but little else. She grew to despise Peter Scott; the feeling would be mutual, and the Eastlands as husband and wife settled into a performative, image-conscious charade.

On January 2nd, 1976, Peter Scott began working in the office next to Robert Alan Eastland—an arrangement he would share into the new century. It would take him to the center of political power. It would take him around the world and embroil him in events that would shape much of that world. And, ultimately, it would take him to Northern Wisconsin.

This alliance, seemingly advantageous at the time, would lead to another proof of the Law of Unintended Consequences. It would, in time, lead to the fall of people in high places.

THE PROBLEM WITH KIDS

In planning the weekend's activities, one concern stood out: What about a thirteen-year-old girl and two mid-teen boys? There was reason for concern. Aaron Eastland was not known for a gregarious social style. Aaron was handsome, having inherited his father's blond hair. He was slightly taller than average. A very public figure, he was eagerly sought by his peers, and their socially ambitious families. There had been a date or two, well covered by the tabloids. But no relationship, no girlfriend. He could be proper in public, and even had given an address or two to groups of young people. *Groups.* The White House staff knew that one-on-one settings were a roll of the dice. He could be sullen, withdrawn, and had occasionally refused to give his peers the time of day. Especially in recent years.

But Aaron knew that as the First Son, snubbing either his parents or his peers in public was just short of a capital crime—which made him resent his role even more.

The role of the First Daughter was even more complicated.

She was maturing, and fast. She too knew that her role was predetermined in this campaign year. But she had developed a strong will and a sometimes-disturbing capacity for anger, often directed at her parents. Assuming the boys found some common ground, would she be welcome in their company? In any case: *What do we do with Shannon?*

Scott suggested the two sons be introduced, to see how things went. If these two young men didn't hit it off, things could be awkward for their parents, and that had political overtones. But Aaron's mother seized the opportunity, in a rare moment of agreement with the chief of staff.

So on Saturday morning, Press Secretary Ellen McCay placed a call to Mark Neale. Who she really wanted to talk to was Tony. Mark, delighted that his offer had borne fruit, held the phone toward his son. "Tony: the president's press secretary wants to talk to you."

"Me?"

"You." Tony took the phone, handling it as if it were a grenade.

"Hello?"

"Good morning, Tony. I'm Ellen McCay, and I work for the president. Could I ask you a question?"

"I guess …"

"Tony, the president's children are here, and frankly they have nothing to do. I'm told that you're the perfect person to help Aaron Eastland enjoy his stay here. Would you be willing to at least meet Aaron, and see if he could join you for something this afternoon?"

Tony's mind was racing. *He wants to meet me?* "Okay. I—I—Maybe we could go to the beach or something?"

"That sounds great, Tony. Can you be ready in, say, fifteen minutes? I'll send a car."

"Yeah. I can be ready."

"Wonderful! See you soon!"

For a moment, Tony was terrified. But then it hit him: *They're on my turf. I know the island, and I can take this kid to the best beach on the lake. And it's big enough that we won't be surrounded by people. Big Bay, here we come.*

The press secretary found the Eastland children in their rooms in the Manor, sitting with headphones attached to their Walkman players, reading. *They look bored out of their minds,* she thought. *At least one of them has an option now.* She walked past Shannon and got Aaron's attention.

"Aaron? I hope this is okay, but I have a kid on his way who's your age and lives here. He's your father's biographer's son. Name's Tony. He can show you around."

"Do I have to?"

"Aaron, you really kind of do. It's a positive look for your father. But please?"

Aaron shrugged. "I'll be ready."

After Ellen McCay left, Shannon looked toward her brother. "So I'm stuck here and you get to do something?"

"Yeah. But if this kid's okay, maybe you can tag along tomorrow."

On his way, chauffeured in a government Suburban, Tony wondered what proper protocol was. *How do I greet the president's son? I'd better think of something ...*

He need not have worried. Aaron was standing by the driveway, and when the SUV stopped, he opened the door for his guest.

"Hi, Tony. I'm Aaron."

"Hi." Which at that moment was Tony's entire vocabulary.

The First Son's typical modus operandi was to make just enough small talk to not be considered rude, then retire to solitude. But he welcomed Tony Neale into the Manor, and after about fifteen seconds they dispensed with formalities. Aaron wanted to go some place "fun" and Tony suggested the beach. "It's away from town, and a lot quieter."

"Let's do it."

For the next four hours, two sixteen-year-old men from Washington, D.C. found common ground at the water's edge on the mile-long beach at Big Bay, escorted by agents who kept casual sunbathers away from them. Aaron's judgment? *Tony's cool, and I think I can trust him.*

Tony risked inviting the First Son to join him hiking the next day. Aaron agreed. Tony was pumped.

⁂

Late on Saturday evening Shannon Eastland was alone, the music playing in her ears barely above silent. Her diary had laid open for half an hour as she fought with herself, fought for the courage to write what she had held inside far too long.

Her only audience had been her brother, an hour ago. What she had just told him made him more than angry. She now sought the courage to tell her diary. She would not, yet, write all that Aaron had heard. But she would start: *I told Aaron. He promised to keep it quiet for now. He gets it. Finally, someone listens to me ... but how do we tell anyone else? And who?*

CHAPTER TWENTY-FOUR

A WOMAN WEEPS

Christmas Day, 1977

A military transport bearing the Star of David approached the Egyptian airfield at Ismailia. The Egyptians knew that a plane from their enemy to the east was inbound, but they made no attempt to stop it. On the contrary—they gave it priority clearance and rolled out the literal red carpet for its occupants.

The feet on that carpet were on Egyptian ground for the very first time. They belonged to Prime Minister Menachim Begin, arriving for a groundbreaking visit with President Anwar Sadat. It was Sadat's 59th birthday, and Begin offered him a traditional Jewish birthday greeting: "May you live 120 years." His wish would not be granted.

In an act unheard of among western heads of state, Sadat got behind the wheel of the Cadillac and drove Begin to the presidential retreat on the Island of Knights, which had been re-named just days before as Gezirat el Salaam: the Island of Peace.

The two pivotal world leaders drove through the Egyptian countryside like ordinary friends. The route was well guarded, but their journey was perilous. Begin's peace overtures to Egypt were opposed vehemently by many in the Knesset; Sadat was opposed not only by many Egyptians, but by most of the Arab world.

Israel was suggesting limited Palestinian self-rule and giving up the Sinai Peninsula as part of a peace settlement with her Arab neighbor. Egypt was suspected by other Arab states of seeking an independent peace with Israel; Sadat was accused by Syria's President Assad of "treason" and "capitulation."

The West Bank, Israel's vulnerable enclave on her border with Jordan, was the stickiest point. Begin's proposal of limited Palestinian autonomy was unsatisfactory to Egypt. Israel feared that more concessions would lead to a separate state led by their archenemies the PLO, who feared being left out of any agreement. They stepped up their terrorism in an attempt to derail a peace process that they passionately believed must not succeed.

President Jimmy Carter called that Christmas morning, Washington time, and wished them well.

On that same Christmas morning, Kathryn Rossberg Eastland wept. She had not slept on Christmas Eve; sleepless nights were becoming the norm, her mind an endless stream of feelings, most of them painful. She wondered how she had allowed the charade that was her marriage to last. She wondered if bitterness and loneliness were sufficient grounds for leaving the man she'd married with such high hopes, who was the father of her only child, and was consumed by his ambition and indifferent to his wife. Perhaps. In any case, she did not know she was just weeks away from knowing more about this ambitious man with such a promising future. And when she did, leaving him would be her only option.

CHAPTER TWENTY-FIVE

SUNDAY

Sunday finally came, announced by the pre-dawn arrival of a security team: agents in suits and sunglasses, Navy SEAL sharpshooters in flak jackets and black fatigues, a counter-sniper team, and local law enforcement, all of whom arrived at St. John's Church moments before the satellite truck from CNN started its diesel generator. There had been security on duty since early the day before. Discretely standing by were members of the Technical Security Division, who began the morning with a bomb sweep of the little church, and then stood by with explosive-ordnance disposal personnel.

For the first time in the 180-year history of Christianity on Madeline Island, parishioners weren't admitted to church without a ticket. Also, for the first time, St. John's Church was closed to visitors. Tickets had been prepared by the Secret Service, to ensure that the actual congregation could find a seat amidst people with badges, security clearances, and some role in running the country. Some were carrying guns.

There were precisely five who didn't carry guns but recorders, notepads, and one camera. They, too, had been issued special laminated photo passes similar to those worn by the White House Staff and the Secret Service. They were, some long-time worshipers said, more distracting than the sharpshooters.

The presidential motorcade arrived, precisely five minutes before the service was to begin. The regular worshipers had already arrived as instructed, half an hour prior to the service.

They had passed through a metal detector and were already seated, anxious for the guests of honor. When the limousine stopped outside the church, the agents made their customary visual sweep of the area before opening the doors for President Eastland and his family. They were escorted in and took their seats. Two minutes later, the organ sounded the beginning of worship, with the Leader of the Free World in the second pew, right hand side, smiling.

At the allotted time, Dr. Franklin Neale read his text, from the Book of Proverbs: *"The king's heart is like channels of water in the hand of the Lord; He directs it wherever He wants. Everyone's path is straight in their own eyes, but the Lord weighs the heart."**

"Mr. President, distinguished guests, among whom are your wonderful family … to all who are here: Welcome. Whoever you are, wherever your life journey has taken you, this is a welcoming, safe, and love-filled place.

"Re-directing water. It isn't as easy as it sounds. Neither is changing the direction of the human heart. But to the ancient people who first heard these words, God not only could but did change the courses of rivers, streams, even seas. It's striking, really—the idea that kings, who were perceived as above all coercion, could be somehow redirected by Someone above the king. Quite a concept, isn't it? That even monarchs—and presidents—are people, accessible to their Creator.

"They listen to and seek out counsel, just like their ancient counterparts did, at least the ones who survived, and even now, those in power lean on advisors, consultants, cabinet officials—a host of people whose purpose is to make their case for a course of action.

"I have often wondered if, and how, public leaders may be directed by God. Seriously. Lincoln's courage in liberating 19th Century slaves? Truman's agonizing over the use of The Bomb in 1945? Or Kennedy, facing down the Russians and their missiles in Cuba?

"Or, the myriad 'little' decisions that leaders make every day, that cumulatively shape human history? The appointment of judges. Negotiations with Congress. It is a fact of life at every level of every institution: leaders often lead by being themselves led.

"It is presumptuous for me to speak to this gathering about leadership. The scope of my influence does not compare with the scope of those who carry the weight of a nation on their shoulders. I could not, Mr. President, do what you must and so ably do.

"But the fact remains: many of the principles that guide leaders are the same, regardless of scale. Among those principles is this: there are things more important than power. Mr. President: it is your character, your example, that we need from you. We long to trust you—and that matters more than the platform of your party or the promises you make in seeking our votes. It means more to us that you lead with your life than with political skill. In spite of the stature of your office, it means more to us that you be humble … than regal. Demonstrating that you too can feel what we feel. Being honest about your mistakes rather than trying to hide them. In other words: it's how you love, as well as lead, that compels us.

"I don't know you, except through what other people say about you. I am not privy to whether you pray, or read sacred texts, or even if you have a clergy person to whom you can go. Mr. President, they say you are the most powerful person in the most powerful nation the world has ever seen. They say you have an opportunity to re-direct history. With that comes immense pressure, and countless seemingly impossible dilemmas that require a Solomon-like capacity to choose wisely. For that very reason—I have good news, Mr. President. I believe that a God who loves you and those you lead seeks in ways often invisible to move the needle toward justice, peace, and compassion. May you seek that wisdom.

"You, sir, a mortal like the rest of us, can be a leader who is led by, with all due respect, the real 'most powerful Person in the world,' the One who made the world in the first place. And that's all you have to be. God asks of you only what is asked of any of us. Humility. Integrity. Trust.

"I pray for you, Sir. May we all do the same. We wish the very best to you, too, Mr. President. And to your wonderful wife, and your precious children. We want you to know that you have our prayers, our support, and our love. God bless you, Mr. President.

"Let us pray."

The service ended after the congregation sang "America the Beautiful" and a benediction from Dr. Neale, who walked down the center aisle to the back, where he stood as people walked by, shaking his hand and thanking him for the service. The scholar-turned-substitute-preacher awaited a handshake from his president, which he received. He also heard the president—loud enough so his staff would catch the hint—invite Dr. Neale and his family to the evening's festivities. The Neales were flattered. The White House staff were suddenly frantic, adding four unexpected guests to the barbecue.

Scripture from Proverbs 21:1-2 (Common English Bible)

CHAPTER TWENTY-SIX

POLITICS, AND THE MEASURE OF A MAN

That afternoon, Robert Alan Eastland finally got his wish. The borrowed Grand Banks motor yacht was a perfect choice, a classic trawler design which did not flaunt its elegance. It presented a moderate image for a president, classy but not blatantly opulent. It was made available courtesy of a family acquaintance (and donor) from Nebraska, and was under escort by a fleet of Coast Guard and Sheriff's craft, a helicopter, and (at a strictly monitored distance) several speedboats chartered by the press. While it may have lacked the solitude he knew in more private days, there was at least the water, the wide horizons, and an occasional nibble on the line.

He didn't catch his limit; only one fish had the misfortune to mistake Eastland's lure for lunch, and was released, being too small to keep. But more fishing was scheduled for later in the weekend, and this politician was determined to grab his share of trout and walleye—and a few Wisconsin votes. Peter Scott took a futile turn at fishing but was consoled in the fact that while the fish of Lake Superior were unimpressed, he'd orchestrated a masterful photo op, bait that the press was devouring with wild abandon.

⁂

All day long, Secretary Malone had been grousing. He'd envisioned a very public moment that politically, he'd insisted, it should have been. The whole point of this trip was to draw attention to Marsh's inconsistencies, and the dispute between the Ojibwe and the State of Wisconsin should have been Exhibit "A." This meeting should be carefully staged for maximum exposure: invite the press, cameras and mics in the "On" position. Let the secretary, who considered himself a master at playing the kind and understanding listener one moment, the outraged advocate of justice the next, work his magic.

That's what should have happened.

But the Red Cliff tribal leaders had objected, calling instead for a private "Summit" between senior leaders of the United States government and leaders of the Ojibwa nation. Someone at the White House inexplicably caved in to the tribe's demands, blowing this opportunity for Secretary Malone to be the face in the news.

Unknown to Malone, it was not a cave-in. It was Peter Scott, whose vision for the trip had shifted the Red Cliff issue from main event to spare tire, to be used only if Eastland himself could not remain the focus of attention. The president, and Scott, found a need to feed a hungry press corps. Once again, Tom Malone was pushed to the perimeter. Within the hour, he would thank his lucky stars.

When white people meet Chief Wade Sanders, they are disappointed. He doesn't match their stereotype, which is more a comment on the ignorance of whites than on any shortcoming of the chief's.

Chief Sanders had earned the trust and respect of his people over his fifty-two years. He was intelligent and visionary, having turned down offers of college scholarships and a chance to "make it" in the dominant culture, preferring to remain close to his people. His community was his calling.

He drove a well-worn three-quarter-ton Ford F-250 4 x 4, which may have been rusty but was kept in a state of mechanical perfection. So was his fishing boat, named after his daughter, the *Jamie Anne*. It was not pretty. A pale gray hull and boxy home-built superstructure with exhaust stack, stove chimney, radar dome and various antennae protruding from its top. In that, it matched the majority of small-business entrepreneurs who fish the Great Lakes' cold, clear, and abundant waters.

Today, the chief's objective was as far from Malone's as night is from day. He was dressed in a suit, an awkward concession to the representatives of the United States then en route to his village. His white shirt was new and purchased just for the event, since he'd not worn one in seven years. Around his neck was a western style bolo tie with a silver and turquoise neck piece, a gift of a fellow chief from the Navajo nation.

Wade Sanders had been born and raised in Red Cliff. As chief, he had not always found joy in some of the proposed solutions to his people's challenges. He found casino gambling profoundly distasteful. He refused to call it "gaming"; it was "gambling" to him, and always would be. In his mind it was wrong, but he supported it because it was the will of his people. They were eager to seize an opportunity to generate cash and a measure of self-determination. The result had been far less lucrative than its boosters had promised, but less awful than he'd feared.

This was simply another difficult encounter with the white community. He'd battled prejudice and the jumble of contradictory government policies all his life, and often stood in the crossfire. He now would represent his people in another controversy, with those who rarely understood what mattered to Indigenous people.

He stood outside the tribal offices, with the elders of the Red Cliff band and representatives of other Ojibwe communities, awaiting the arrival of Secretary Malone. To his mild surprise they arrived on time, a caravan of seven vehicles: a lead Blazer from the County Sheriff's department; a sedan of Secret Service; an Expedition carrying the secretary and his aide, and several sedans carrying various media and Interior Department staff.

The secretary got out, recognized the chief from briefing photos, shook his hand warmly and complimented the chief on his leadership. Chief Sanders, with a barely perceptible smile, welcomed the secretary, introduced his fellow leaders, and offered the secretary a tour of the forested land at the heart of their dispute with the State of Wisconsin. It was a ten-minute ride: the government vehicles were led by a Red Cliff police escort through the land and a ten minute ride back to where they started. The chief then invited the secretary inside the Red Cliff governmental offices, to a conference room only large enough for about fifteen people: Ojibwa elders, the chief, the secretary, and two of Secretary Malone's aides.

Once seated, things began in earnest.

⁜

Meanwhile, Tony was Aaron's guide for the afternoon, along a forested trail in the middle of the island. As expected, they were surrounded by security personnel, but given distance enough for private conversation. Even so, Tony noticed that Aaron was less talkative than he was the day before. Something was on his mind; Tony remembers, " … worried about Shannon …" more than once from Aaron. Undeterred, Tony had decided: he will invite Aaron to sail with him tomorrow. He was unaware that Aaron was far less interested in either the forest or in sailing than in taking the measure of his new friend: *Can I trust Tony? Can he handle some really bad news? My sister's life may depend on it.*

CHAPTER TWENTY-SEVEN

THE TREATY IS NOT THE ISSUE

Mr. Secretary, the sovereign Ojibwe nation, acting in good faith, entered into a treaty with the United States that guaranteed in perpetuity our access to the land in question."

Malone smiled. "'Perpetual access' is our understanding as well, Chief Sanders. Is that access being denied by any action of the government?"

"No. Our access is not being denied." Malone stared blankly.

"Then—ah, what is at issue here?"

"What is at issue is not the treaty."

"Not the treaty?" Malone's voice was rising. This was not going where he'd expected.

"Not the treaty. Technically, it is being honored. Our problem, Mr. Secretary, is ethical, not legal."

"How do you mean?"

"We will still have access to ancient hunting and fishing lands. But when the loggers are finished, there will be nothing to hunt or fish. It is our contention that stripping the land of its forest cover effectively abrogates a solemn treaty, even though it is technically still in force. It will take at least two generations to restore the forest. And even then, it will not be the same. It will be a different forest, an artificially created, sterile, managed forest, designed by short-sighted mortals, not the Creator."

"I understand."

"No, sir, you do not. Secretary Malone, it may surprise you to learn that I read the newspapers. I watch FOX and CNN. I understand politics, and I understand that your boss is seeking re-election. And I understand that your visit here is politically motivated. Sir, with all due respect, if you had your way, there would be cameras lining the walls around us."

Malone knew that, with every word, he was being stripped naked before everyone in the room. What the Chief was saying was true. Having it told directly, not in a diplomatic dance around the truth, was something Malone was unprepared to endure. He nearly lost his composure.

"Chief Sanders, I assure you that we are deeply interested in the plight of this community."

"Perhaps you are, Secretary Malone. I can't read your heart. Frankly, I have no desire to make the president's re-election either harder or easier. Your purpose for this meeting may have been noble and sincere, or not. Our purpose for this meeting was to call the United States, through its State of Wisconsin, to account for the audacity to consider trading away, not trees and land, but a community's—a nation's—heritage."

Malone was conciliatory. "I understand, gentlemen, that the State of Wisconsin is on the verge of leasing logging rights on some very unique land."

"Of course you do, Secretary Malone. And you know that it could make your opponent look bad, and that's why you're here. But if we're honest—and I intend to be—while we have different agendas in this matter, we also have an opportunity to do some good. It may be Wisconsin's call legally, but on behalf of the community which elected me, I am formally calling on the United States to restrain the State of Wisconsin from forever destroying the natural and cultural and, to us, spiritual value of this land."

⁜

The secretary, in the back seat of the Expedition, leaned back and breathed a sigh of relief as the procession returned to

Bayfield and the ferry. He had dodged a bullet; this could still be politically advantageous. And he was thankful that no cameras had captured the agony of the previous hour.

CHAPTER TWENTY-EIGHT

A BOXER AND HIS TRAINER

Gary Bates sat across from Duluth's newest journalist on plastic folding chairs, at a plastic patio table in a makeshift picnic area outside a food truck, all part of the island's attempt to handle the flood of tourists, government officials, and press. The food was good, the flies annoying, and Bates was finding the young lady spreading mustard on her hamburger more attractive by the minute.

He began the conversation, strictly professional of course, with an innocent enough question about the Vacationer-in-Chief. "So … what do you know, or think you know, about Eastland?"

"Ex-football player. Ex-Vietnam POW. Came from a prosperous family. His father owned an insurance practice that could have been his. But I think he wanted more than what small-town America could offer. He married … Kathryn Rossberg, I recall. But after the birth of their only child—"

"Her name was Monica."

"You've done your homework, Mr. Bates. So why do you need my wisdom?"

"Your wisdom is more fun to listen to than mine. Keep talking."

"After Monica's birth, he avoided the draft by enlisting in the Air Force. Shot down in '73. You know about that, I presume."

Bates chased a bite of his cheeseburger with a drink of Lite beer, directly from the bottle. "Tell me, young reporter, what you know about his political life."

She was cutting her burger in half—no onion, no cheese; lettuce, mustard, and a pickle. "He moved from his birthplace to Grand Island, tried and failed to win the mayor's seat. Locals said he lost because it was obvious that he'd sought bigger prizes. Impatient ambition doesn't play well in Grand Island, I guess."

She's done her homework too, Bates concluded. "Go on …"

"So, he got a job assisting veteran job seekers and began networking for a run at Congress, won a seat in the late-'70's, built an up-and-coming reputation in foreign affairs. Lost his first wife and daughter in a plane crash in Lebanon."

"I'm impressed by your knowledge, fellow journalist."

"You say that to all the girl reporters."

Bates laughed. "Actually, Samantha, I only compliment people who deserve it. What else do you know about him?"

"First of all, thank you, and secondly, what else I know about Eastland is what I know about Peter Scott. Eastland's number one guy … they're real tight. Scott hails from Omaha, I think. Eastland was one of Nebraska's football legends and recruited Scott, who loved pummeling the opponent's running backs, and yes, I know football. My dad is a coach.

"Anyway, Vietnam found both of them. Scott was drafted after graduation, while Eastland was already flying combat missions. Scott fought the Viet Cong on the ground; Eastland from the air until he was shot down. After release from prison camp at the end of the war, Eastland returned home as a war hero. Scott returned to Omaha as just another veteran.

"But they both returned as different people. Hard-edged, I guess. A grim focus on making up for lost time."

She stopped to take a bite out of her lunch. Bates waited until she continued. "Eastland likes to delegate. He's not a hands-on type like Carter. He prefers to paint with a broad brush but has lots of little painters filling in the details. Trades on his reputation of integrity; all things considered, he's apparently earned it. But Scott's shrewd and gets things done. That's what I know."

She's not only done her homework, Bates mused, *but she knows how to sift the data for what matters. I like this kid.*

"Now, Mr. Bates, you tell me: who really runs the Administration?"

"Why, Samantha, the President of the United States. Just like the Constitution says."

"Okay, you have a sense of humor. Now who really runs the world?"

He grinned, turning the nearly empty bottle in his hand. "Simple: your friend Peter Scott."

"He's not my 'friend,' sir."

"I would hope not! Anyway," Bates continued, "nothing happens without his knowledge and approval. In fact, not much happens without his thinking it up first. He's driven, focused on his work and not interested in much else. He is definitely not the life of the party."

"He doesn't get a lot of press coverage for such a major player."

Bates looked intently at his food, thinking for a moment about the subject of the conversation more than his attractive counterpart. "Sam, I suspect his years in Vietnam had a lot to do with his intensity."

Samantha leaned back in her chair. "I'll bet you're not too far off the mark."

They were not. As a Green Beret, Scott achieved recognition for excelling in the art and science of clandestine warfare. American voters would gladly elect a war hero, provided his service was not too messy. But they would be reluctant to elect what amounted to an assassin to public office.

Power politics was almost an exercise in restraint for Peter Scott. A culture of death had burned something out of him, and he did not care to rediscover his inner life. Politics was his passion, his mistress, his current battlefield. And for this, he had no regrets. Nor much of a conscience, for that matter.

Bates thought for a moment, and then added his assessment. "Scott calculates Eastland's every move. Eastland trusts his chief of staff to be his strategist, and an effective keeper of the gate. Scott's responsibility is clear: to get the job done one way or another. They work closely together—"

"—like a boxer and his trainer."

"Yeah," Gary said, "but they are not really friends. That's the intriguing part. My guess is that they share too many secrets to be friends. This strange … symbiosis seems like a combination of mutual benefit and mutual fear."

Samantha nodded thoughtfully. "This president has no intimate friends, does he?"

Bates nodded. "Pretty lonely life. Kind of like mine."

CHAPTER TWENTY-NINE

OUR DARK HORSE'S LEGIONS

Ms. Wells swallowed another bite and explored new territory. "Did Scott ever have a personal life?"

Bates shook his head. "Not really. Married and was abruptly divorced in '77. He remained single thereafter. There were high profile but brief flings, potential courtships, I guess. But he had neither the time nor the interest—nor the charm—to keep love's flame alive."

"Unlike you, Gary—can I call you 'Gary'? I'm guessing you still have a heart. Does the battle-hardened *Post* journalist still have a heart?"

Bates didn't respond. Perhaps because he didn't know.

Samantha wiped the mustard from her lips, looked off to the horizon, and after a moment's reflection, spoke.

"Here's how I see it. I think that political leaders have to appear noble and principled, but are frequently aided by almost predatory operatives who aren't distracted by scruples. I think our president sensed, correctly as it turned out, that as Scott proved himself in an Asian jungle, he could be effective in a political one."

It was time for the veteran reporter to share an insight of his own. "Sam, who's your favorite president?"

"Lincoln."

"Great! Got time for a story? It might flesh Mr. Scott out."

"I'm listening."

"Part of my thesis at Yale. I think Peter Scott is cut from the same bolt of cloth as one of America's most obscure political kingmakers. June, 1860. The brand-new Republican Party had gathered to nominate their candidate for president in Chicago. They met in a hastily built wooden monstrosity that seated 6,000 people. For the first time in history, the press gallery was equipped with electronic communications gear—"

Samantha lit up. "Telegraph terminals!"

"Bingo! 900 reporters applied for its 60 seats. Pretty smart, actually. Remember what their Democratic rivals were doing?"

"I'm sure the ace reporter will enlighten me."

"They never got around to nominating a candidate. They were deadlocked over the platform."

"Slavery?"

"Right again, Rookie. The status of slavery in the territories." Bates was reveling in one of his favorite stories. "There was no suitable compromise between the antislavery North, and the South."

"I'm still trying to figure out if this story has a point."

Gary chuckled, and sipped his beer. Putting his bottle down, he said, "Just be patient. It does.

"The Republicans expected to nominate Senator William H. Seward of Illinois, who had an apparent lock on the nomination. But a lesser-known candidate, also from Illinois, waited just outside the limelight. I'll bet you can guess who."

"I'll bet I can. Interesting. Sometimes it is best to be just offstage, ready to step in when the star tumbles."

Bates nodded, enjoying this chance to impress an attractive female—and show off his political smarts. "Seward tumbled. Had they voted the evening he was nominated, he would have walked to victory, and near-certain victory in November.

"But there was a minor inconvenience: the proper forms hadn't been printed. No problem. Just adjourn for the night, crank up the presses, and clinch the victory in the morning.

Meanwhile, our dark horse's legions lobbied through that night, convincing delegation after delegation that Seward's views on slavery were just too strong for the nation. They weren't told how intolerable their own candidate's views would be."

"So a wild guess—I bet some relatively unknown skinny guy named Abraham won?"

"And on the third ballot, and Seward—whose election may have prevented the Civil War!—walked away with nothing."

The TV journalist held up her hands in mock bewilderment. "That's a wonderful history lesson, the point of which still eludes me."

"Allow me to enlighten you. This was orchestrated by Judge David Davis, a shrewd Nineteenth Century political operative with a sophistication worthy of the Twentieth. Scott is like Davis: too rough, too intense, to win the trust of many voters, directly. He gains power by getting someone else elected, doing what the candidate cannot do before a watching public. And Judge Davis? Campaign manager for Honest Abe."

"Fascinating. Now I have one more question for the esteemed correspondent from the *Post*."

"Which is..."

"Beer. It's a turn-off to this innocent Midwestern girl."

"You're not really from the Midwest, and that's not a question."

"Deal with it." She patted him on the shoulder as she got up and left. In spite of, and in part perhaps because of, her jab, he smiled. He really liked this kid, and not only for professional reasons.

⁜

While the president fished and made conversation with local dignitaries, Scott was below decks, talking by satellite phone to Secretary Malone, who had just survived his "fact-finding" trip.

"Scott, I'd like to pull a press conference together later this afternoon. It's as we suspected. The Native Americans are furious, and it won't take much encouragement from us for them to become a serious problem for Marsh."

"Good. But not tonight. Plenty of good press today; let's milk what we've got, then throw this at the press tomorrow when nothing much else is happening."

Malone was anxious to have his moment in the sun but knew the value of patience. He was a team player after all.

⁘

Two days after the low-pressure system was first noticed, it had moved out of the Rocky Mountains and headed across eastern Colorado and western Kansas, with building winds and thunderstorms. Before it left the mountains, it had dropped several inches of rain in some areas, swelling rivers and streams beyond their banks in southern Colorado. Lightning had ignited several modest fires to the south in New Mexico. Its track through the Midwest was becoming clearer, the Weather Service noticed. And they didn't like what they saw.

CHAPTER THIRTY

PLAYING IN A MINEFIELD

Sunday evening was calm, hot, and muggy. The mosquitoes were as persistent as the press at the barbeque on the lawn of the manor. Several tents provided shade from the retreating sun, while the main course sizzled on the dozen or so charcoal grills scattered across the lawn.

For the Neale family, the afternoon had been occupied by two major tasks. One: return about a dozen phone calls promised to family and close friends. And two: reconsidering—after having already decided the previous week—what they would wear. As many guests of the president have learned, the least casual task is selecting the appropriate casual attire.

They arrived with the other invited guests. Security personnel greeted them and checked their names. The process was a pleasant surprise. Guests expected airtight security, which there was. They also expected a gauntlet of questions, searches, and scrutiny, which there wasn't. The security staff politely thanked them for coming and wished them a wonderful evening as guests of the president who, they emphasized, "is eager to visit with each of you before the evening is over. Your president is deeply grateful that you have welcomed the First Family to your island home." They were urged to visit the refreshment tables, courtesy of the White House.

Then they were asked to walk single file through a metal detector.

Members of the president's party circulated among the guests, although the most popular attendee was Kirby, the president's Dalmatian, running from guest to guest, soaking up the attention.

Peter Scott chose to work the crowd alone. Few recognized him, apart from those active in Republican politics. But he still enjoyed the thinly veiled awe from those who knew who he was. Tom Malone was more recognizable, walking side-by-side with Congresswoman Crandall, who introduced him to the mesmerized locals excited at being surrounded by VIP's, the national press, and soon, "your president." Only a few caught the scripted nature of things.

Among those locals was Walter Kolquist. He'd been stung by not bringing the First Family to his community. Eastland would not set foot in Bayfield. But Kolquist could still claim victory, as many of Eastland's entourage, hordes of press and a crush of spectators, would—and generously fill the town's coffers in the process.

After all the guests had arrived, their official host walked out of the manor, in the company of the ever-present protective detail. Guests were formed into a receiving line, warmly greeted but given no real chance for presidential conversation. The Neales: Franklin, Mark, Debra, and Tony, expected nothing more. But the president, while working the crowd, caught up with that morning's lay preacher, and decided to play with the distinguished Dr. Neale.

"I'm delighted you came after such a busy morning, Doctor. By the way—I was intrigued by your sermon. Tell me: do you really think God is involved in what I do? Influence I understand. I deal with it for a living. Whether the Divine influences me—I don't recall ever feeling that."

Scott hated when Eastland did that. Too risky. You could offend a guest and lose a vote; maybe more. Even an unknown private citizen can become uncomfortably famous if they feel offended, and don't mind telling some hungry journalist. *Why, Robert, would you risk embarrassing this guy?*

Dr. Neale was aware that he'd better have something resembling an answer. But he had nothing to lose. "I don't think God manipulates you, but—"

"Precisely," the President interrupted. "I do feel pressure from, shall we say, more visible sources. Like the people who attend functions like this one!"

There was laughter—then the president pressed his case. "Don't get me wrong; I believe in God, I really do. But I think God leaves politics to the politicians."

Dr. Neale welcomed Eastland's challenge. "I will say this: Politics matters to me. I care deeply about what you do. But my loyalties are not partisan. My faith holds my loyalty. There are others who feel the same about theirs, and we often share the same concerns."

"Fine," Eastland said. "It's good when religions get along."

"Yes it is. But to be honest, our faiths, and certainly mine, may not always get along with your politics. And when that happens, we will challenge you."

"Perhaps," Eastland replied. He was pleased with himself, enjoying the verbal joust. He was doing no real harm to the professor, while trying to steer the conversation away from religion and toward his own turf. But the professor wasn't finished.

"I respect the political world you lead. But I doubt that it alone will bring a just and equal sharing of life's blessings. Competing parties, lobbyists, donors, and pragmatic values need those of us on the outside to hold you to your promises. Not only your promises, but God's. To be honest: I believe that God's vision isn't simply improving what we have, but contradicting most of what we see and do. You and I aren't enemies, Mr. President, but we're differently rooted. Power is the politician's currency. My currency is love."

"This morning, Dr. Neale, you mentioned love. Were you thinking of 'love your neighbor' or something else?"

"Yes, 'love your neighbor.' But love sees all others, including our enemies, as beloved."

"Dr. Neale, I have serious issues with that."

Franklin knew that pursuing that line of thinking would lead the conversation to an abrupt and perhaps ugly ending. But he had something to say that, in his mind, was more important—provided he seized the conversation before it spun out of control.

"Mr. President: When I used that word this morning, I wasn't thinking of our political differences. Not at all. I was thinking more personally, of the regard and affection for you from the people in that room—including my own regard, respect, and affection for you as my president. But there's something more. If there is an ultimate political power, it's not socialism or democracy or free markets, and certainly not tyranny. It's the love we see through ordinary people loving their neighbors, feeding and clothing and sheltering those in need—and, with all due respect, even protesting, when their cause is dismissed."

The president saw a chance to pull the conversation back to his home turf: politics. "Sounds like you lean left! Tell me, Dr. Neale. Do you consider yourself a liberal or a conservative?"

"You should think of me, Sir, as a subversive. I don't want mere progress. My faith drives me to seek a world radically re-shaped by a God who is not a passive spectator, Mr. President. A new, abundant world for all God's children. And nothing less. I've been in front of the White House myself, Mr President, carrying signs and chanting, and I suspect I'll be there again before long."

Some people may be hard-pressed to step out of their role. But Dr. Franklin Neale was more than a professor on this particular Sunday. Even conversing with the president, in his mind he was not only a minister, but a witness for a distinctive, transcendent way in the world.

He also sensed that either the president or his coterie of handlers would recognize the growing risk of this conversation, and gracefully move the verbal jousters into separate corners. He had, he figured, one more chance, and he jumped at it.

"Maybe God isn't overly engaged in politics and certainly not interested in left or right. I think God goes past political ideologies to justice, leadership—and leaders themselves. With all due respect—and I do respect you and your office—I think God is very interested in you, as both president, and as a person. God loves you, Mr. President."

Franklin wondered what had prompted him to make that last remark. It sounded dreadfully out of place. To tell the president that he was loved, by God or anyone else, seemed either trite or impertinent. It was as if everyone listening to the conversation had been flash-frozen in place, waiting for the president's response.

Eastland was stunned. Contrary to what others within earshot surmised, the words had touched him in ways no one there could imagine. For the president did wonder, when he allowed himself to face his demons, if it were possible for anyone to love him. Had he crossed some line beyond which love was no longer possible? In a quiet voice more vulnerable than presidential, Eastland simply said, "I hope so."

Scott saw no political upside and plenty of potential for a theological debate to become a minefield. A diversion was in order: a re-connection between Aaron and the Neale boy, and this time, Shannon would meet Tony. Scott took charge of the actual introduction. "Ms. Eastland: meet Mr. Tony Neale."

It was an innocent enough suggestion, and it would lead to the demise of his political career.

CHAPTER THIRTY-TWO

READING TONY NEALE

To everyone's surprise, Shannon didn't hesitate. Surrounded by people who were not part of her all-too-pretentious Washington world, she walked right up to Tony, took his hand and shook it. "Hi, Tony. It's about time we met! Thanks for taking care of my brother—Aaron has told me about the fun the two of you've shared. I think it's time all three of us had some non-adult conversation. Let's begin at the punch bowl. Mom, Dad: may we be excused?" By the time the parents assured her they were free to go, they were speaking to the backs of three teen-aged heads walking toward the punch bowl.

This may have seemed like an innocent opportunity for the First Children to enter a different world, one more honest than the continual posturing, pushing and shoving in social Washington. But to Aaron and his sister, this was an opportunity. They were on a mission, and Tony would be drawn into it. Within minutes they were walking around the grounds, shadowed by the agents assigned to Aaron and Shannon, and engaged in animated conversation. The president, the Neales, the press, and Peter Scott noted with relief that their conversations seemed lighthearted. Along the north perimeter of the manor grounds, an area lined by stately oaks and tall shrubbery, Shannon took the lead in asking her new acquaintance about life on the island. The discussion turned to school, what one did in the winter, and Tony's love, sailing.

And: parents. What, Aaron asked, was Tony's mother like? Shannon asked about his father. Were they close? Did Tony trust them? When he had problems with his parents, whom did he talk to? Tony was puzzled by their oddly focused questioning—and the urgency in their voices, especially Shannon's, as they probed the relationships within a family they had just met. Tony could not know that the First Children were wondering: Is this the time, and could this new acquaintance be the place to start?

After they had walked nearly around the grounds, Shannon was suddenly quiet, deep in thought, while Aaron was testing his courage.

Tony knew that his place in this gathering with these children was well defined. But these new acquaintances were surprisingly approachable. Feeling that he had nothing to lose, Tony invited his new friends to sail with him the next day. Aaron's eyes lit up. "I'd love to! Can Shannon join us?" Tony nodded. "Great! We'll ask our parents, and we'll call you if they're okay with it." Tony was delighted. His tentative suggestion was embraced by the president's children. The writer's son felt honored to be chosen for a friendship that would become much, much more.

Samantha Wells noticed too. She had been assigned to local coverage, and prior to that moment, she'd mixed her thrill at being this close to the First Family with frustration at not being assigned to the "hard news" events. The more senior reporters, heavily favoring the national press, followed the president's fishing expedition, plus the handful of local journalists who followed Secretary Malone.

Samantha chafed at another human interest story, but being the only journalist to overhear this plan in the making, she knew that "soft" or not, it was her story at the moment.

Her colleagues, in any case, would be somewhat disappointed. The fishing trip provided only a photo op, and not much of one at that. Malone was up to something, but was playing it close to the vest. The timing of any public comment would be determined, not by the badgering of the press, but the judgment of the White House. Had they known the White House's agenda, the press would also have followed Gary Bates, who was legendary for being in the right place at the right time.

CHAPTER TWENTY-THREE

EACH OTHER'S WORLDS

Driving home, Mark Neale and his father engaged in a spirited review of the evening. They'd enjoyed it, and Tony was thrilled—A chance to get to know America's most protected teenagers? What's not to like?

Debra tried to match their enthusiasm, but something bothered her. She had learned to listen to her instincts. They were telling her that something was wrong.

Her discomfort began while observing the First Family at the barbecue. Perhaps it was just the pressure of their public lives that made them respond in a way that troubled her. No, it was the chemistry between the elder Eastlands and their children. This is not a happy family.

⁜

An exhausted Gary Bates emailed Washington on Sunday Night, submitting his report for the morning edition. He was surprised when his editor called him back after midnight.

"Anything to justify your trip to the north woods? Or are you just working on your tan?"

"Too many mosquitoes. Actually, Malone visited the Reservation this afternoon."

"And—"

"And, he took a drive with them through the woods. Got out and walked around at one point. Then a mysterious closed-door session with tribal leaders."

"And—"

"Be patient. The national press covered the president's fishing trip. I think the big fish are on the mainland, and no one else seems to suspect anything. Malone had just me and a few local reporters who had no idea something could come out of his little excursion. But I've developed a good local contact who tells me there's political quicksand up here for Marsh, which I'll know after a few more pieces come together. My contact promised me first crack at this one, and he's calling me back in a few minutes. He owes me an explanation."

"You might recall that newspapers have what are known as deadlines."

"I'll have something within the hour." *I hope*, he thought.

"Met any interesting single women, Bates?"

"Yeah. She's a blonde."

His editor stared blankly at the receiver in his hand, now emitting only a dial tone.

⁜

In the early hours of Monday morning, the National Weather Service was convinced that the growing storm system, having swept out of the Rocky Mountains on Sunday, would impact how a lot of the Midwest celebrated the Fourth of July.

The storm system, now in Nebraska, was organizing into a typical summer phenomenon. There was plenty of rain, some hail, and enough thunder and lightning to ruin more than one round of golf near Lincoln and Omaha. A few severe thunderstorm watches were issued; there was even an unconfirmed report of a funnel cloud.

In fact, they noted, there was a chance that northwestern Wisconsin would be affected. They faxed their data, including their projections for the next 48 hours, to Washington.

CHAPTER THIRTY-FOUR

PRESIDENTS FOR BREAKFAST

Monday, July 3rd, dawned clear and calm. The lake was a mirror, rippled only by the fishing boats heading out at sunrise. One carried the president for a two-hour trip, to be followed by another in the afternoon, sandwiched between the parade and the evening festivities. For presidents, even holidays are strictly scheduled.

The press gathered by 9:00 a.m. in the village, as directed by the authorities. Among them were Gary Bates, Samantha Wells and Strobe. After instructions telling them where they could and (especially) could not position their cameras and mics along the morning's parade route, they would be allowed to set up and test their equipment under the watchful eye of federal employees. Following the parade, they would have a quiet afternoon to re-position their gear for the Independence Day celebration that would include another outdoor meal for the administration's guests, then fireworks to cap the evening. Apart from those following the president's fishing adventures, the press would wait all day for what would, with luck, be a 30-second piece of footage from the festivities to be uplinked to Duluth or New York or Atlanta—and may or may not be deemed newsworthy by the unseen editors.

While Strobe and his peers jostled for the best camera spots, the journalists attended to their stomachs. At 9:30 a.m., the Madeline Island Chamber of Commerce hosted the press at an outdoor breakfast. This would be their big day, and they wanted the journalists telling the world about the president's holiday to tell that same world what a wonderful place their island was.

Gary Bates almost didn't attend; a little sleep would have been nice. But there was someone he wanted to see.

"Good morning, Samantha of TV-land." He'd seen her arrive and got into the breakfast line about a dozen reporters behind her. That gave him enough time to see where she'd sit—he hoped, of course, that she wasn't sitting with a colleague. *Sit by yourself, Samantha, and you won't be alone for long.*

What he didn't know was that the TV reporter had seen him out of the corner of her eye and made sure to sit conspicuously alone. By the time he'd grabbed his coffee (black), a large plate of scrambled eggs with salsa, five links of sausage, and a cinnamon roll, she'd found a small table for two, and began spreading the cream cheese on her bagel.

"Good morning, Gary. How was the secretary's trip to the mainland?"

"Boring. How is our budding teen-aged friendship?"

"They're sailing together this afternoon on the Neales' boat."

Bates was mildly surprised. *Aaron Eastland must really like this kid,* he mused. *Bet the Eastland handlers were thrilled with that.* But another budding friendship was more interesting to Gary Bates.

"On the record for a moment. I'm doing tomorrow's piece on reactions of midwesterners to President Eastland. What might yours be?"

She looked at him quizzically. "Why would you interview a fellow journalist who's only been a midwesterner for about three months?"

Bates shrugged, forked a portion of scrambled egg, and dipped it in the salsa. "Because you're here. I'm putting my questions together in my head, and a little conversation sometimes helps me focus. I think you've got a better grasp of things than the average person."

"What do you mean?"

"Well, for starters, you understand that the presidency is a great office."

"Occasionally occupied by great presidents."

"Speak on, Citizen Wells."

"Do you really want my opinions on things political, Mr. Bates?"

"Humor me."

She put down her as-yet-uneaten bagel and opened the carton of skim milk. "The occupant of the Oval Office is the closest we have to a monarch, and the White House is not unlike a palace. But there are huge differences. The Constitution provides very little definition of presidential power; so powerful presidents create their own. But Americans have a strong antipathy toward too much political authority."

"So, what, in other words, do presidents have to be?"

"Entrepreneurs. They build coalitions, define agendas, orchestrate public opinion. As far as the person at the top is concerned, America's a mosaic of sorts: East Coast, Midwest, West Coast, retirees, blue-collars, intellectual elites, all of whom must be courted, tamed, and handled with care. Successful presidencies happen because at or near the top someone is gifted in recruiting and managing powerful people. The occupant of the Oval Office, if he—or she—is to retain it—"

"Do you really think 'she' will apply in our lifetime, Sam?"

"Yes. It will happen. And he, or she, must fulfill certain roles. The office is rich in symbolism and drama."

"Presidents among other things have to be good role players."

"Right. And great presidents not only play the role—they create it. That's true, by the way, not only of the president, but of the president's spouse and family. Frankly, I think it's an impossible burden."

"There's not much room for error, is there, TV Person? And by the way—you didn't learn all this in 'TV Makeup And Hairdo' Class—"

"Political Science minor at San Diego State, okay? I are educated, Mr. Bates. I can even read your columns."

"You obviously have excellent taste."

She grinned, paused, and decided to press her case. "Presidents simply can't have an 'off' performance. They may have just come out of a briefing on the threat of nuclear terrorism, but when the president walks into a room full of school kids, the only permissible role is to smile, relax, and appear totally captivated."

"It's absurd, isn't it?"

"But it's also real, and it's inescapable."

Bates decided to change the subject to the real purpose for this "interview" with Ms. Wells. "Would you like to get together tonight after the fireworks?"

"Um, what would we discuss then?"

"I'm asking you for a date."

Samantha grinned, and finished pouring herself a glass of orange juice.

"But I hardly know you, Mr. Gary Bates. I'm not that kind of girl."

"Then call it a professional courtesy. Even reporters have needs, Ms. Wells."

"Needs? Or wants?" She got up to walk away, then looked back over her shoulder. "See you tonight."

Suddenly, Gary Bates was looking forward to the fireworks.

CHAPTER THIRTY-FIVE

THE LAST LOVE FEST

There was a call to return when Gary Bates stopped by his motel room after lunch. He recognized the number and postponed a much-needed nap long enough to call his boss.

"Perkins."

"Bates. What's up?"

"She's a blonde, eh?"

"Very blonde."

"But then, it's Wisconsin. They're all blonde Scandinavians up there, right? Descendants of the Vikings?"

"Sure, Perky. And white guys can't play running back. Why, sir, are you such a sucker for stereotypes?"

"Is she cute?"

"Answer my question first."

"I use stereotypes because our readers think in stereotypes, and I don't want to forget how to read their minds. Simple, sweeping, and quick—that's what the public wants. It's a kind of mental shorthand. Now you answer my question: Is she cute?"

"Yes, she's cute. But as far as your north woods Scandinavian comment—she's from San Diego."

"Wow," Perkins said with mock thoughtfulness. "I guess the Vikings landed in southern California. By the way, Ace Reporter Bates, I'm dying to hear about your love life, but have you been gathering any news? Or just charming the local females? You're spending my very generous expense account money, and I'd love to have something to show for it."

"Tomorrow, before the president returns to Washington. Probably a hastily arranged press conference; they'll give it a sense of urgency. Malone—and this is not for publication until I release it—will accuse Marsh of bungling relationships with Wisconsin's Native Americans. He'll charge Marsh with sacrificing ancient and solemn national commitments and selling out to the profiteers. See? I told you I was working."

Hanging up, Gary Bates mused, *Archibald, your cultural blinders are light years behind your readers. Lucky for you, your readers don't see your biases because when we write, we don't heed them.*

⁜

For the first time since Calvin Coolidge, a sitting president rode down La Pointe's Main Street. The rest of the Independence Day parade was as it had always been: whimsical floats, small bands, banners, police and fire vehicles with lights flashing and sirens screaming. There were differences: this was July 3rd, and the president was there.

And this year, there were more spectators than participants, as everyone who could fit on the morning ferries, and others who anchored off the beach and rowed their dinghies ashore, lined—packed—the streets. This had not pleased the security teams, but they'd expected it, and had brought nearly a hundred additional federal resources.

At the end of the parade, Patrick Henry's speech was recited as it had been by the same individual for years, complete with three-pointed hat and a resounding "Give me liberty—or give me death!" Except this year, Patrick Henry was terrified, conscious of speaking to more than his usual audience of neighbors. There was a speech by the president—brief; he was on vacation after all—but the fact remained: he was there. And several hundred cameras captured the moment for posterity.

Presidents must be a different person in different settings, speaking the language of each constituency. Some have been exceptional in meeting this challenge: Ronald Reagan, John Kennedy—and Robert Alan Eastland. Speaking to the crowd on this midwestern island, Eastland's relaxed manner made him appear approachable, likable, sincere; a good neighbor. He spoke simply but warmly, capturing the essence of Independence Day: a true community of Americans, celebrating with their neighbors the joy of hard-won freedom. It was refreshing, he said, to see people in T-shirts and sandals, not suits.

His opening line, "This feels like home," was met with cheers and enthusiastic applause; he patiently waited for it to fade before continuing.

"It really does. I come from a small town, with the same warmth and genuineness I find among you today. One difference: the scenery here is pretty tough to beat!" More cheering from the decidedly partisan crowd. "—And the fishing's better!" The people cheered again.

"If I may put on my official hat for just a moment—" He spoke of our rich heritage, of being part of a community where each citizen can make a difference. The Fourth of July, he said, calls us to cherish freedom's gifts.

"A couple weeks ago, I visited our troops in Europe. They are proud, they are committed, and they are confident. But it's so easy for us to forget they are there, twenty-four hours a day, in places where they may be the first line of defense for their country and their country's allies. I was honored to serve with another generation of Americans, who held their heads high and kept the faith despite being part of an unpopular war.

"Friends, we owe them our deepest gratitude. There is no greater way to honor their legacy than to seize moments like this, when people from all across this nation have gathered on this island, in the nation's heartland, to celebrate what binds us together. I am proud to serve you. Thank you."

He walked away from the podium to the cheers and the heartfelt love of his public. It was a love fest, a rare and touching moment for all those gathered. It was also a triumph—he'd held them spellbound. He reveled in knowing how well he could work a crowd. Yes—a true love fest.

It would last less than twenty-four hours more.

CHAPTER THIRTY-SIX

WATER, DEEP AND CLEAR

That afternoon, another presidential preference—in this case, a First Children's preference—was giving the Secret Service fits. Aaron and Shannon Eastland had been invited by Tony Neale for an afternoon's sail, on the 19-foot Rhodes sailboat that was the joy of the Neale family. Aaron and Shannon accepted the invitation.

On a 50-footer, there's little chance of a capsize, plenty of protection, and lots of room for a crew, including those responsible for protecting their thirteen- and sixteen-year-old charges. But a 19-footer is best suited for two people, and there would be three this day, out in the open for all to see and at the mercy of Lake Superior's fickle weather—which was becoming a growing concern.

Once again, the agents in charge were confronted with the fact of their limited authority and almost unlimited responsibility. They could respectfully request that the First Family reconsider such a risky activity. But with few exceptions, they had no right to forbid it. They still had to Serve and Protect.

The innocent afternoon sail would cost the taxpayers thousands in planning, consulting, and protective measures. Hasty research into the characteristics of a 19-foot Rhodes. Weather updates from NOAA, with special focus on wind and wave predictions. A thorough inspection of said vessel for structural flaws and potential for sabotage. A Coast Guard report on recommended Personal Flotation Devices.

The Coast Guard, already on alert, would have fully-crewed launches cruising nearby; the helicopter crew would be at the ready. No—on second thought, the helo would be circling overhead, a rescue specialist in a wetsuit ready to drop into the water within seconds. Navy SEAL sharpshooters and Secret Service agents would occupy a couple of speedboats, in part to protect Aaron and Shannon from hypothetical waterborne assassins, and in part to keep the press at a respectable distance. All this so that the President's children could have a "private" moment with their new friend.

Peter Scott showed particular interest in their safety, it seemed. He insisted on personally arranging for their personal flotation devices and promised to make sure they wore them.

⁑

"Are you nervous?"

"Very," Shannon admitted. "To tell you the truth, I've never been on a sailboat before."

Tony was surprised. "You're kidding. I would have thought you'd have had lessons from some official Navy guys or something."

"My sports were tennis and horseback riding. I've never spent much time on the water. So you'll need to tell me what to do. I promise I'm a fast learner."

Two Secret Service agents untied the boat's lines and pushed it away from the dock as the sails filled with a gentle offshore puff. The boat moved silently into the bay.

Shannon received her first sailing lesson. "See that line around that winch? That's called a 'sheet'. When the sail at the front of the boat—it's called the jib—begins to flap, just pull that line, until the sail stops flapping."

Aaron was surprisingly nervous. Tony would have to coach him as well. Once again the First Children were on unfamiliar turf, if a lake can be called anyone's "turf."

"The water's so clear! How deep is it here?" Shannon asked.

"Probably about fifteen feet or so."

"And you can still see the bottom? That is amazing … Tony!" Shannon grabbed her friend's arm as the boat suddenly leaned over in a puff of wind. Her more experienced new friend laughed, reassuring the president's children that "heeling" was part of a sailboat's mystique. After a few minutes, Tony gave Aaron the tiller; it helped him to relax. And for the first time in a long time, Aaron and Shannon felt that they had power over their lives.

They engaged in a half hour of light conversation, as if this really were nothing more than three teenagers enjoying the water in July. But Aaron's mood began to change as they begin talking first about their parents, then specifically about their fathers. Tony boasted about his dad; Shannon became quiet, distant, and, Tony noticed, teary. There was a long silence. Tony wisely waited rather than giving in to his urge to probe. Then Aaron pointed to the nearest boat, and said, "Do you think they can hear us?"

⁜

This was the time. Shannon would tell Tony, Aaron would confirm her story, and three teenagers would share a truth that would unleash a firestorm.

⁜

By the time this part of the conversation ended, they had drifted nearly a mile and a half from home. That morning's gentle, northeasterly breeze was building, as it swung to the south. They sailed home in silence; the building wind shortening the trip.

⁜

Peter Scott slammed the headphones down. *That idiot will never learn,* he thought to himself.

Scott's second thought sent a chill down his back. *I helped him build a political dynasty, and its future promises even more. But only if he stops making these kinds of stupid mistakes. Without some quick damage control, there will be no future.*

His final thought, almost lost in the frantic mental search for his next move, brought a sense of satisfaction. Once again, his instincts had been right. Planting bugs on Shannon's and Aaron's life jackets hadn't been paranoid after all.

CHAPTER THIRTY-SEVEN

THE LAST WORD

Samantha Wells called Gary Bates, waking from a sound afternoon nap. She got right to the point.

"Something's wrong, Gary."

"What do you mean?"

"All three kids come in after a delightful afternoon's sailing with each other, right?"

"Right …"

"They're brand-new friends, right? Enjoying one of the best afternoons of their lives, in front of the entire world, thanks to people like you and me."

"Don't lump me in with the rest of you TV types."

Samantha was in no mood for jokes. "So why did they come in looking like they'd seen the Devil himself, make a beeline for home, say not a word to any of us—"

"Sam, maybe they had an argument. Kids do fight."

"Gary, they just met. They're still on their best behavior. They haven't had time to find things to argue about. And no way is that writer's kid going to tick off the First Son and Daughter. They're not having a little teen-aged spat. Something serious happened out on that sailboat. The Neale kid is really shaken."

Good instincts, Gary thought. *It might be nothing; it's the president's somewhat mysterious kids, not the president, so there may be no news in this at all. But apparently, something very strange happened, and you never know. Maybe there's some news there—not much else going on.*

"Samantha, I'll snoop around the president's residence. We'll compare notes at the fireworks."

Nap time was over; Gary Bates was back on the clock.

⌗

Abu Jihad, the 42-year-old military commander of the PLO's Al Fatah faction, had personally trained thirteen volunteers for this mission. Eleven men, two women. All under 21 years of age; all ready to die for their people. Today, March 10, 1978, was their day to die.

They would die gloriously. Israel would be denied its arrogant ambition of dictating the future of the sovereign Palestinian people. They would add another chapter to a seemingly endless cycle of attack and retaliation, Palestinian against Israeli against Palestinian against Israeli again, over and over. This war would continue unabated, as if both sides were determined to impose a peaceful solution through violence and terror. It would call into question the notion that retaliation can bring ever peace. Instead, it speaks to how powerless are they who simply must have the last word.

On the other side of the world, rookie Congressman Robert Alan Eastland and his strategist saw an opportunity. "Couldn't I score some points on a 'fact-finding' trip to the Middle East?" Peter Scott agreed. "It's dicey, but a huge upside if we can get you some visibility, in Israel at least, maybe Lebanon—well, that's too hot right now—but Israel and Egypt, definitely. That would work."

"Okay. Also: Kathryn's always wanted to visit—"

"No way. Too dangerous."

"All the better. She's up for an adventure—and if we leave her and Monica in Jerusalem, they'll be safe."

"Monica too? You're rolling the dice, Robert."

"Worth it."

And so it was: a rookie congressman, eager to make a name for himself, flew to Jerusalem in the early days of a war, with his wife and daughter.

He would return a widower.

CHAPTER THIRTY-EIGHT

A HOT AFTERNOON

The president's children had cultivated one other special relationship: Agent Kim Nguyen, a Vietnamese-American and child among the "boat people" of the 1970's who fled their homeland. She was now in her mid-forties, having risen to the top of her profession in part because of the discipline and tenacity she had learned from her parents, for whom every decision had life-or-death significance.

In her assignment at the White House, she had developed a liking for the Eastland children, especially Shannon, and often perceived her as the younger sister she had once had, before dehydration and disease claimed her on an overcrowded sampan in the South China Sea. Agent Nguyen was determined to get to know this reclusive kid.

As a part of that strategy of winning Shannon's trust, she occasionally bent the rules to help her when she wanted something unusual—usually, snacks. She was puzzled, and troubled, by recent changes in Shannon's moods. Nguyen saw signs of depression and withdrawal, more pronounced at certain times, less so at others. She sensed a pattern here; Shannon was most out of sorts when her parents were nearby. The agent wasn't trained as a therapist; still, she wanted to discern what was happening.

Samantha Wells was determined to make the most of her assignment. During a lull in the day's activities, she found Agent Nguyen relaxing in one of the town's restaurants. She walked over. "Hi. I'm Sam Wells of WLOW in Duluth. You're with the Secret Service, right?"

"Yes. Kim Nguyen."

"Must be fascinating work."

"It often is."

"Seems you spend a lot of time with Shannon Eastland."

"I'm sorry, but I really can't discuss my work."

"Oops. No, I'm sorry. Should have guessed. Anyway, I've noticed she and her brother have hit it off with Mark Neale's son. I find that amazing. Bet she's a lonely kid."

Agent Nguyen actually would have enjoyed a conversation about her charge. But she simply smiled. "Very observant, Ms. Wells."

"I'm sorry. I'm sure there isn't much you can say publicly. I'm new at this."

"Really?" Kim found it refreshing to speak to someone that hadn't become jaded.

"Really. I've only been on the job since March. The more experienced reporters are following the big shots today. My orders were to stay behind and cover the afternoon on the island, which so far hasn't been terribly dramatic. Everyone appears to be taking a nap."

Nguyen laughed. "Some are. But not the president's daughter."

"What can you tell me about her?"

"I really can't say much." Agent Kim looked away, and for a moment spoke thoughtfully and a bit more transparently than she intended. "She's a really nice kid. I hope this is off the record. I shouldn't be discussing her at all."

"Not to worry. Thanks for your time."

⁜

For a community hosting the leader of the free world, it had
been a surprisingly quiet day. At least it was for Mark Neale.
He spent Monday making sure that all the interested relatives
got a courtesy phone call to say that, yes, it's been a wonderful
experience and yes, the president really is engaging and yes,
there were sharpshooters surrounding the church on Sunday
morning.

⁜

March 11, 1978

Their Zodiacs came ashore about 18 miles South of Haifa,
near the kibbutz of Ma'agan Mikha'el. Armed with Kalashnikovs
and rocket-propelled grenades, their plan was grim and simple:
to travel as far as possible, and kill as many Jews as possible,
hopefully ending the carnage with a glorious martyrdom in Tel
Aviv.

Their first casualty was Gail Rubin, who five years before
had emigrated from New York City to Israel. Her fatal mistake:
being on the beach when the terrorists landed on that Sabbath
day. She was killed on the spot. They would simply keep killing
until they themselves were killed for their cause.

They stopped a northbound bus with a hail of gunfire that
wounded the driver and some of the passengers. They ordered
everyone off—then herded them back aboard, turned the bus
around, and moved down the highway with shouts of "To Tel
Aviv! To Tel Aviv!"

For 30 miles they drove, shooting and lobbing grenades
randomly at oncoming traffic. Seven miles north of Tel Aviv the
bus met a roadblock. Its tires were shot out and it ground to a
halt in the ditch alongside the road. Then the carnage began in
earnest.

Israeli police stormed the bus, smashed the windows,
and hollered for those inside to jump. Not everyone made it.
Whether it was a bullet finding the fuel tank, or a grenade from
a terrorist, the packed bus exploded in flames. When the fire

was extinguished, there were twenty-five bodies huddled in the rear of the charred bus. One was that of a five-year-old girl, still clutching a toothbrush.

Prime Minister Menachem Begin vowed that Israel would "cut off the evil arm" of the terrorists. "The architects of this bloodbath," he continued, "cannot enjoy impunity."

He also, in light of Israel's worst domestic terrorism attack to that point, postponed his planned trip to Washington to consult with President Carter. It was perhaps just as well. He would have met a frustrated president, angry at Begin's refusal to give up land Israeli soldiers had bought with their own blood in 1967. Construction of the settlements on the West Bank continued, much to the consternation of the Arabs, the Americans, and even some in Israel.

An up-and-coming United States congressman from Nebraska, Robert Alan Eastland, was already on the eastern side of the Atlantic, and saw a need for first-hand data for his congressional committee, as well as the opportunity for some political capital. The Cannon House Office Building, for all its stature, did not house the office he ultimately sought. With his family and trusted aide Peter Scott, he had come to the Middle East to better serve his country, and to seek his political fortune.

CHAPTER THIRTY-NINE

DISCLOSURE

Tony walked quickly to his room. He said nothing. He made no eye contact with his parents as he brushed past, ignoring a question from his mother and leaving his parents staring at each other in disbelief. He had given the same treatment to the reporters who had waited on the beach when the young trio returned and, without smiles, stepped from the boat and said good-bye. Two walked to the government Suburban that was their ride. One walked, silently and abruptly, to the one tasked with driving him home.

He closed his door more firmly than usual—enough to startle his father, who had witnessed Tony's rush through the living room. Mark looked toward Debra. "What was that about?"

He figured it was time to debrief Tony on what should have been a memorable afternoon. But his mother, who read Tony's body language more perceptively, intervened. "Let me do this." She waited a few minutes—then walked to Tony's room.

The author knew from experience that sometimes, when a crisis developed in the life of their son, the most effective therapeutic act an educated parent like himself could perform was to butt out. And butt out he did, despite hearing an occasional cry loud enough to penetrate the cottage walls.

When Ms. Neale came out, Mark was too engrossed in the final draft of his book about the incumbent, to see the rage in Debra's eyes.

"We need to talk."

"In a minute, Hon; I'm almost—"

She slammed the laptop's screen down, almost on his fingers.

"Now!"

They went into their bedroom; Debra closed the door and paced back and forth along the wall. Her face was red; her fists at first clenched at her side, and then pressed against her temples. She was in a kind of pain that physical trauma could not produce.

"Deb—what on earth is going on with Tony?"

"It's not Tony."

"Wait a minute—" He took her hands. "What happened out there?"

"I cannot believe it."

"Deb—"

She glared at her husband. "Mark, I just cannot believe it."

He tried to make her sit down on the bed. She pulled away and looked him in the eye.

"Mark—Tony and the Eastland kids had a long talk out there."

"And …"

"And …" She turned away, slamming her hands down on the dresser. *She's never acted like this before*, Mark thought.

She turned back, momentarily regaining composure.

"Mark—I don't know what we are supposed to do with this. But according to our son, our beloved president is a child molester."

CHAPTER FORTY

THAT SICKENING EXCUSE FOR A HOME

Mark—what are we going to do?"

A good question. What *do* they do? It was his turn to pace.

"First of all, we need to be with our son. Second, we need to find out exactly what this is about."

"I told you what it's about."

"I need to know exactly what they told Tony. There's no room for error on this." In the back of his mind, Mark wondered if everything he had written and everything he had believed about the subject of his book, almost ready for publication, was being undone.

"And then what?"

Indeed.

He shook his head. "We can't just walk away."

"This could destroy Tony. It could destroy us."

"Deb, if it's true, it's already destroying those kids. I'm scared, too. But just forget it, pretend it's not our business? It *is* our business now."

They walked to their son's room. Tony lay on his bed, looking blankly at the wall. He spoke first.

"Did Mom tell you?"

"Yes."

"So can we talk about it?"

Tony's mother sat on the edge of the bed next to him, gently rubbing his shoulder. "Yes. We can."

Tony rolled onto his back, avoiding eye contact.

"Dad, Shannon was raped by her father. More than once."

"How do you know?"

"She told Aaron. Today, they both told me."

"How often has this happened?"

"It's been happening for at least three years. She can't remember exactly when it started."

Tony's parents stared at each other in disbelief.

There was bitterness and rage in Tony's words. "He convinced her that it was their special secret. Oh—He made her promise to not tell her mother. Shannon says it doesn't happen as often now—only when they're not in Washington. But it could still happen, Dad."

Tony's mother needed to know where her counterpart stood. "Has she told her mother?"

"She hasn't. Shannon's mom's a mystery to her. She seems loving … but her mom's very status-conscious. Shannon thinks telling her would be too risky."

"That breaks my heart for Shannon all over again," Debra said. The room fell silent.

Finally, Mark wondered aloud: "Does anyone else know? A teacher? Anyone?" In each instance, Tony shook his head. Debra wondered: *If no one else—why our son?* "Tony, why did she tell you? What does she want you to do with this?"

"She didn't want me to go to the police or anything. They said I'm the only person they trust, because I'm not tangled up in their crazy world." Then this young man, growing up at a lightning pace, sat up and looked directly at his parents.

"Mom, Dad, Shannon was amazing. She told about her father coming into her room in the middle of the night. He'd cover her mouth, and begin undressing, touching…I still can't believe she could say those things. She didn't yell or anything, but I could tell she was angry. She looked straight at me and said, 'This is my body now, and no one will ever do that to me again.' Aaron was—it was like he was ready to explode."

In one sense, it was simple: in violating his daughter, a father had violated an unambiguous body of law. But for the Neales, it was impossibly complex. Very ordinary people now knew a horrible truth—*was* it true?—about a frighteningly powerful person. At the moment, neither Mark nor Debra nor Tony knew what to do with the rape of the First Daughter.

"I can't believe he can get away with that in the White House," Mark said to no one in particular. "It's got to be crawling with Secret Service at all hours."

"Shannon said that the White House is always busy. The family is left kind of alone, at least at night. But during the day she said she was surrounded by all these high-powered, self-important, type-A people who work for her father—she said it feels like she's always swimming in a shark tank."

Debra turned her attention to the First Daughter herself. "Okay—What is she going to do?"

Tony shook his head. "They don't agree on that. Aaron wants to tell the world. Shannon doesn't. Not yet, she said. She wants to embarrass her father and ruin his career, actually. But first: she wants out—away from her parents. She said that when she gets home, she's going to find a chance to … her words: 'run as far as I can from that sickening excuse for a home.' Then she'll feel safe to speak out."

Mark was skeptical. "'Run away?' From the White House?"

"I told her it sounds crazy, but she's sure she'd be okay. She hates being famous—but she thinks that if she runs, being famous means she'll have all the support she would need. I guess she's right; I mean, nobody would want her living on the street."

Deb reacted strongly to that rationale. "Sadly, she is right. People walk right past homeless kids, but if they're rich and famous and privileged ..."

"I know, Mom. So does Shannon. She gets it, okay?"

"I'm sorry, Tony. This needs to be about your friends, and you."

"I know," Tony said. "But still: I think breaking away looks like almost no risk for her."

"Any idea about when she'd run?" It was Mark.

"No. Like here? No way. She'd be too easy to find. She said she's waiting for a distraction big enough that no one would notice at first."

Tony's parents stepped out into the hallway, within sight of their shattered son, giving him some privacy.

Mark Neale was in over his head, and he knew it. Were this an ordinary case of abuse—if there can be anything "ordinary" about ravaging one's own child—his response was easily dictated by the law and his conscience.

"Tony's right," Mark mused. "Shannon's plan seems crazy to me—but this is one remarkable young woman, and nothing would surprise me. Is it wise? Hard to tell. Is it dangerous? Very. Can she succeed? Maybe. She is amazing." He stopped, and looked at Deb. "Wow. All the more reason to do what we can to make her plan unnecessary."

Deb remembered something: "Mark, does 'mandated reporting' apply here?" At first, it made sense: By statute, they are legally obligated to report this to the authorities.

Mark saw a perhaps fatal flaw. "Probably does. But who has jurisdiction over the president? If the allegation is true, and I don't doubt it now, what might the president do? Politics is about power, Deb, and Eastland is *President* Eastland because he knows how to use it. An allegation of something this hideous, brought by a writer who could be seen as trying to undermine him? They'd rip us apart."

He imagined a public statement unleashing a win/lose battle with a foregone outcome for his family. Raise unheard-of charges about someone whose reputation had, as far as his own biographer knew, no real blemishes, and a White House full of spin doctors and whoever else exists to preserve the president's power and reputation would orchestrate the public destruction of Mark Neale and family.

"Sure, I could just hold a press conference, make this out-of-the-blue, off the wall accusation, and then watch the world laugh us into oblivion."

Debra was beginning to understand. "We would be crucified—"

"There's an interesting analogy."

Mark took his wife's hand, and walked back into Tony's room. Together, they sat silently on their son's bed, waiting for the friend of the First Children to acknowledge them. After a while, he spoke.

"Dad, do we just sit here and do nothing?"

Mark was thinking out loud. "If we just made the accusation, Shannon and Aaron would probably never get the chance to confirm it. They'd be suddenly inaccessible, in seclusion, 'devastated,' Eastland would say, 'by these horrible, unfounded charges.' Tony, you're the only evidence we've got."

Debra's thoughts returned to her son, and how terrifying this may be for him. He could not be overlooked. "Tony: I want you to know—*we* want you to know, that in all this, we are proud of you. You are facing this with courage, compassion, and … You are amazing, Tony."

"You really are, son," Mark added. But their son wasn't finished.

"I'll do whatever it takes to help Aaron and especially Shannon. I don't care what happens to the president—or to me. I think it's time for full disclosure."

Mark was worried. *Phrases like "full disclosure" have never been part of Tony's vocabulary before. He might take matters into his own hands if we don't act. But he has no idea ... How do I let my son go through that?*

And my wife? This is already tearing her apart. She'd be seen as married to a fool. And she, not my professional duties, not even Aaron or Shannon, is my primary loyalty—isn't she?

I need to talk to someone.

He grabbed his phone and dialed his father's number, guessing he'd find him at the marina cleaning fish. *Dad, I hope you're there. If I've ever needed you, I need you now.*

"Frank Neale here …"

"Dad, stay put. I'm coming to you. I'll explain then, but we have to talk." Mark hung up, hugged his son, kissed his wife on the forehead. "Will you two be all right for awhile?" Reassured, he headed for the car, wondering who else might know what Tony had learned.

CHAPTER FORTY-ONE

FOR SUCH A TIME AS THIS

Conversations between father and son were a common occurrence: walking on the beach, sitting on a fallen maple trunk, cups of coffee at the ready. The elder Neale had earned his son's respect. Throughout Mark's life, he had modeled wisdom, dignity, and irrepressible hope. In the mind of his son, Franklin Neale was a rock. In this crisis, Mark presented his father both the facts, and his fears.

"I've decided to seek a meeting with the president, as outlandish as it sounds to even attempt it. But I wish we hadn't learned this. Here's what scares me: What happens to Aaron and Shannon if this comes out? And, to Tony?"

"It's already out, Mark. If Shannon doesn't tell someone else, Aaron certainly will in time. And you know Tony will. This now has a life of its own."

"But I'm out of my league, Dad. This is the President of the United States. Eastland is a driven man. His chief of staff is, I think, even more driven. I can't imagine a scenario in which these kids aren't at some risk here. Nothing is off the table when it comes to protecting the president's image."

"In spite of all that, I'm actually glad you found out, Son. A girl's life is being stolen, and a young man is carrying a burden no one should face alone."

The writer thought for a moment. "I thought my calling was just to write." This triggered a train of thought in the writer's father.

"Mark, remind me why you are a presidential biographer."

For the first time, his son smiled. "You know why: I fell in love. I love—or at least, loved—these fascinating, deeply gifted and deeply flawed people. I love exploring the inspiring, and now, I guess, the disappointing people who lead us."

Franklin grasped his son's hand. "Yes. That's important. But not most important. Our first task is always to care. To be present when—especially when—another human is at risk. Aaron and Shannon need you. Tony needs you too. Even the president needs you, whether he knows it or not. He is best served by bringing this into the light of day.

"Mark, how many people understand as you do what this really means in the light of history? You know that this must be addressed before it destroys them, and so many others."

Mark's father sighed. "Since this is a father we're talking about—I always wondered how I did as a father for you. Tough job, being a dad."

"Dad—you were there for me." Mark smiled, looked down, then up again at his father.

"You gave me more than Saturday afternoons playing basketball in the driveway. You introduced me to the expansiveness of life, to a faith grounded in grace that's true precisely because it's too good to be true. You modeled integrity, you honored the dignity of people—especially women—and you invited me into the joy of the written word. That was an offer I couldn't refuse."

"Thank you."

There was a long pause. In the distance, a muted droning from the engine on a fishing boat could be heard, barely audible and muffled by the trees. It slowly faded, replaced by the soothing music of a light wind passing through the forest. Then Franklin looked directly at his son.

"Remember what Mordecai said to Esther?"

Mark recalled the Old Testament story of a simple Jewish girl thrust onto center stage before an unpredictable king. He answered his father's question with a quote from the text:

"'Who knows but that you were put here for such a time as this.'"

His father smiled. He placed his hands firmly on the younger Neale's shoulders. "I think this applies to you, Son."

Mark was not persuaded. "Before today, Dad, that might have moved me. But I'm not sure now. I want to challenge Mordecai's words: are we supposed to believe that I was divinely put here for this? Are we just pawns on some heavenly chess board? I don't see a good outcome, and I don't feel like God's appointed hero."

Franklin looked into his Mark's eyes, and accepted his son's challenge. "Perhaps I believe it more than you might, and honestly, it's mysterious to me too. But the fact is: you are here. You may hate it, but you are. More than that—nobody is better positioned to take this on than you. Your relationship with Eastland, your standing as an authority on all things presidential—you're a formidable obstacle to anyone trying to discredit you. Kids are easy to discredit, and easier to intimidate. But you have standing, and you might as well use your voice as loudly as necessary. No one else can do this like you can."

Mark hugged his father. "Now it's my turn to say 'Thank you.'"

CHAPTER FORTY-TWO

LION TAMING

Mark Neale's letter to the president, having been penned by an author, underwent three agonizing drafts. It did not articulate what they knew about Eastland's sins against his daughter, since there was no way to control who saw it. His best chance for reaching Shannon's father was to plead urgency without detailing why.

It was delivered by Mark Neale to the security staff guarding the president's lodging. They passed it to Peter Scott.

> Dear President Eastland:
>
> I understand how inappropriate this may seem, but I am requesting a brief, private conversation with you. It is urgent, and it's about the welfare of your daughter. This is no casual request.
>
> Should this pass through an intermediary on the president's staff, as I assume it will—I ask that you please make sure that he has an opportunity to read this note.
>
> Sincerely,
>
> Mark Neale

Scott decided that he would raise the issue with Eastland, and no one else. He was relieved that the Neales, by not telling someone else, had reacted cautiously. Mark had no way to know that someone else—Peter Scott—knew even more than the Neales.

Scott counted, correctly, on Neale's grasp of how this could impact his life—and not just his almost-finished biography. He also knew that Mark Neale was, ethically and professionally, invested in telling the truth. That gave Scott distinct advantages: information, resources, experience, and the will to play hardball.

He called the president and insisted that they meet immediately and privately. Then he checked the itinerary for Aaron's and Shannon's whereabouts. They were at the manor. Good. They would be kept on a very short leash. For Scott, this was not a moral but a political crisis. The end game was damage control: this cannot be allowed to surface. He had kept things quiet before.

Just before confronting Eastland, he conferred with Agent "D.C." Barker, who began making arrangements for a discrete assignment, to be executed on Scott's order. Unfortunately for Scott, circumstances would render his plans irrelevant.

The president was enjoying the afternoon. Briefing papers sat unattended on a table in the lounge, while Robert Eastland occupied the screen porch, a glass of wine in his hand. Looking out, he saw a growing fleet—sailing yachts, power cruisers, fishing boats, gathering in the channel separating Madeline Island from the mainland with its picturesque homes and shops in Bayfield, and the wooded hillside beyond. It was a rare time of simple pleasure, and his last for a long time to come. Scott walked in and stood before him, not waiting to be acknowledged.

"Mr. President, we have a problem."

Scott's condescending tone put Eastland on the defensive. "Go on, Peter."

Scott's tone changed to a barely controlled rage that he had never, in a quarter century, directed toward the president. "Did you really think you could get away with it again?"

"Get away with what?"

Scott went right to the point. "Your son apparently found out from your precious daughter what you've been up to when no one was looking, and they spilled their guts to the Neale boy this afternoon. I must confess it was shocking even to me. I thought you'd learned your lesson, Mr. Model Father and Husband."

Eastland looked away and said nothing. He had the authority to put Scott in his place. But he did not have the power to challenge the truth.

He walked to the desk and sat down. This was dangerous indeed. He said quietly, "So, what should we do?"

"Lion taming." Eastland needed no explanation. It was a political power tool, and a game that Scott and Eastland usually enjoyed. When Eastland needed to rein in a freshman congressperson or a leader from the private sector, especially if they've publicly challenged his policies, they would be invited to meet privately with the president. Every effort would be made to impress the lion-hearted critic with the aura surrounding the most powerful person on the planet. Massive and intimidating security would be visible everywhere; the person in question would find themselves subject to the urgencies and interruptions of an administration confidently going about the business of preserving democracy worldwide. In a well-choreographed dance, they would face alternating encounters with demanding and aloof officials checking and double-checking the meager credentials of the intruder into the nation's most sacred place, shaming them for real or imagined "irregularities" that delayed the hoped-for meeting—only to be followed by a gracious escort to the next level of access, where the torture began again.

They would be taught, indirectly but quite intentionally, that if they attempted to go nose-to-nose with the President of the United States, they were minor league rookies, and this was the World Series. The "lions" outside the Oval Office became "lambs" by the time they entered it, putty in the president's hands. Scott expected to find this episode as gratifying as any, and easier than some. Eastland, however, saw no pleasure in this one. There was no room for error. The Neales must be finessed, and not driven to panic.

Scott wished he could simply put a tail on them; he would rest more easily if he knew what they were up to. But that risked raising eyebrows among the always-suspicious Secret Service. He kept his eyes open, waiting for their move. And when they made it, he was relieved that it had been, at least for now, discrete.

Scott noted the time the request for a face-to-face meeting had arrived. He decided to wait for a while, and let the Neales sweat a bit. Time is on the side of a silent protagonist. "The one who speaks first," it is said, "loses." Mark Neale had spoken first. He would be agonizing over what his note would trigger. With luck and timing, Scott hoped, he might yet be spooked into compliance.

With just an hour to go before the festivities, now was Scott's moment to respond. He placed a call, feigning ignorance of what had motivated the letter.

"Mark, I understand you wish to speak to the president. I need to know, sir, what is so important."

Neale had expected a challenge from the White House staff, and was relieved that someone as well placed as Scott was responding. He had rehearsed his opening statement and fired it off in one breath. "It is of the utmost importance, but I'm afraid I can only speak to the president about it. I understand how irregular this seems, but could I have just five minutes tonight before the fireworks?"

"Let me suggest that we meet; then perhaps we can catch the president for a moment."

"Mr. Scott, I understand how naïve this request must seem. But I have information about Shannon's welfare that he needs to address personally. If it would help, I would share my concern in writing, by phone, or whatever form is appropriate. My only concern is to be assured that President Eastland, and he alone, has an opportunity to consider what I know. Mr. Scott, I need your assistance. And the president needs your help."

Scott surmised that he wasn't going to give up. *He may be out of his league, but he's no fool, and a simple rebuff could be dangerous.* Rather than trying to deflect, Scott decided on a frontal assault.

"Let's be frank, Mr. Neale. I know what your concern is. It's what Aaron and Shannon told your son. I know everything about that."

Neale was stunned. *How could he—?*

Scott continued. "It's impossible for you to meet privately with the president. Let me suggest that we meet, you and I, tonight before the reception begins. Perhaps I can help. I'll meet you at the gate. And, sir, I assume you know well enough not to discuss this matter with anyone, agreed? Thank you."

He hung up.

CHAPTER FORTY-THREE

BREAKING THE UNWRITTEN RULE

Scott had one more task. He walked down the second-floor hallway of the manor, toward the rooms occupied by Aaron and Shannon. Aaron sat cross-legged on his bed, listening to music through headphones. Perfect. Aaron began to smile when someone appeared in the doorway, but his smile turned to apprehension when he saw who it was. Scott had broken the unwritten rule of not entering First Family rooms without being invited. Aaron slowly, nervously slipped off the headphones.

"Hello, Aaron," Scott said, deliberately withholding any trace of a smile.

"Uh—Hi, Mr. Scott." Aaron wasn't smiling either. Scott always made him uncomfortable.

"Aaron, I'd like you to listen to this, and tell me what you think."

The First Son was puzzled, and a bit annoyed. He listened cautiously as Scott played an audio file on his government-issue phone. At first he heard the scratchy sounds of wind, water, and voices seemed to blend together. Eventually he recognized the voices, then about thirty seconds of conversation between three adolescents on a sailboat. And when he did, his disinterested stare became a look of terror. They were his and Shannon's own words, which they thought had been shared in secret with someone they could trust.

He dropped the headphones, trying to control his reaction. *Did Tony record us?* He glared at Scott. "How did you get this?"

"That is none of your concern, Aaron. What matters is that I know, and I am not amused. Understand this, Mr. Eastland: this was a terrible mistake on your part. You and your sister—and your young friend—will regret any attempt to share this information with anyone else. Is that understood?"

Tears welled up in Aaron's eyes and he began to shake. "Yes, Mr. Scott."

"Good. Have a nice afternoon." He closed the door, firmly.

Scott walked stone-faced back to his temporary office in an adjacent cottage, acknowledging no one along the way. He stunned Gary Bates by summarily brushing the journalist off as he walked across the lawn. Gary wanted now more than ever to compare notes with Sam.

Scott's mind was racing through a host of possible scenarios. The evening festivities needed to be carefully orchestrated. The two families would be in the same very public place, and must appear as normal as possible. Neither the Eastland children nor Tony Neale can have access to each other. Scott would have to risk the remote possibility that one of the Neales would blurt something out publicly. They were too smart for that—or were they?

He called Agent in Charge Andrew Boyd. "Where's Barker assigned tonight …? Okay, make this change: put Barker on coverage for Aaron and Shannon … I know, but I need Nguyen to float tonight; she's become popular with some of the guests."

He hadn't lied exactly; she was a popular agent. But this evening, that was both true and irrelevant. It wasn't her contact with the crowds but Barker's contact with the First Children that concerned Scott most.

In all the agony of that late afternoon, he failed to notice the sun disappearing behind a bank of clouds moving in from the southwest. The strong southerly wind was dying, producing a deceptive calm.

CHAPTER FORTY-FOUR

CONFRONTATION

When working with amateurs, the best defense is a good offense. All guests had to pass through a metal detector, then walk around the side of the manor house to the lawn overlooking the lake. Scott made himself conspicuous just inside the security barrier, so that the Neales would see him as they arrived. As soon as they approached the metal detector, Scott walked directly toward them.

They walked stone-faced past agents and SEALs in black fatigues and flack jackets, weapons hanging over their shoulders. Samantha Wells asked for an on-camera comment while she had a live feed running to Duluth, but was ignored, leaving her to attempt a smooth search for someone else willing to speak in front of a camera. She was embarrassed, but also sensed the dissonance in their demeanor at what should have been an exuberant moment.

Tony was angry, frightened, and drained. He betrayed his anxieties by instinctively hanging close to his father. Peter Scott frightened him, and made his father nervous as well—a fact not lost on Peter Scott, who found it quite satisfying.

Scott waited impassively as they went through the metal detector. The alarm sounded as Debra entered; all three Neales jumped. She was pulled to the side, scanned by a hand-held wand, while her handbag was searched. The metal trim on the bag had conspired to excite the sensors. It was humiliating to be scrutinized by federal officials in front of one's neighbors, and terrifying when you're carrying the information they held. Mark's heart ached as the person he loved endured this indignity. He raged, that because of Eastland's actions, he and his family were being violated as well.

The offending handbag was cleared, and they were released onto the manor grounds. Scott moved, unsmiling, toward the three nervous guests. "Good evening, Mark, Debra … and Tony." His smile and the rehearsed warmth of his voice were betrayed by cold, penetrating eyes that drilled right through the sixteen-year-old. "Right this way." He ushered them away from the crowd.

Mark tried to speak first. "Mr. Scott, this is a difficult—"

"Like I said, I know what you're here for. Aaron told me everything," he lied.

"What exactly did he tell you?"

Scott stopped abruptly. The Neales followed suit. The chief of staff turned, facing the famous author and presidential expert. Scott's cold visage conveyed what words alone could not, and the author shuddered. "Sir, you don't understand what you're dealing with. First of all, you're getting your information from a, shall we say, disturbed young woman who isn't coping with the pressures of her position. She's under a lot of stress, and has never handled stress very well. Consequently, she has on several occasions won the confidence of innocent people like your fine son, and made outlandish allegations against her mother, against the Secret Service, against a foreign diplomat. And, against her father. She has proven able to persuade her impressionable brother to go along with her stories." All that was Scott's fabrication, but it was just believable enough, he thought.

"But—" Debra tried to interject.

"But, Ms. Neale, she's never made a charge like this one. Don't you understand? It could ruin the president. It's not just a prank by a troubled teen-ager anymore. The presidency is at stake. It's my job to resolve this before innocent people get hurt. This has to stop, and it has to stop now!" Scott paused, and smiled.

"I apologize for being so blunt." The smile disappeared. "But I must insist that your involvement in the Eastland's personal lives stop right here. It is not your concern. I give you every assurance that I will personally look into this further, if it would make you rest more easily. I also assure you that it's just another attention-getting episode by a bright but emotionally distraught young woman and her fragile brother. Nothing more."

"Mr. Scott, I don't want to create unnecessary difficulty. But Tony's a pretty good judge of character, and he believes them."

Scott sighed. "Sir—"

"Please let me finish. I have an obligation here. You are familiar with 'mandatory reporting'?" Neale was desperate, grabbing for any straw.

"I am, and you've just reported it. So have I. Frankly, I'm stepping over the line a bit and revealing a confidential conversation with the Eastlands, but I discussed it directly with the president earlier this evening. He's fully aware, and we've discussed it with the First Lady, Shannon, and Aaron. They know that they're not to bring it up again. They're embarrassed and are sorry for any unnecessary anguish they may have caused you fine folks."

Scott was a world-class liar, and for a moment, Mark Neale genuinely wanted to believe him. Or, perhaps, the author of an almost-finished work about the President of the United States desperately wanted to.

"Mr. Neale, you no doubt also understand the significance of another principle I'm sure you respect: confidentiality. A great deal is at stake. What you say could not only hurt the president and his family but could hurt the entire nation. Further, you do not have the option of sharing information you have learned in confidence. Have you thought of that?" Scott was now on a roll. Debra Neale was on the verge of tears.

"You also need to consider what this could do to you. I do not want to sound threatening but I think you should know the implications of this. When such charges are ultimately refuted—and they will be refuted—you could be personally and professionally devastated. Think of that. You would be at the center of one of the ugliest public scandals in our nation's recent history. With all due respect, I don't think you're prepared for that kind of thing. But that is the scenario. All because you could irresponsibly and without direct evidence spread a tragic rumor. Again—what would that do to you, your wife, your son, your career?"

Debra turned away, eyes tightly closed, lips trembling. It was finally more than this strong woman could bear. *Bull's eye*, Scott thought to himself.

There was an awkward silence, as Scott deliberately stood motionless, staring at Ms. Neale, waiting for them to break the silence. To blink. Again, Mark Neale blinked. "What do you suggest?"

Scott had one more trump card. Instead of looking at the parents, he turned toward the shaking teenager. He took one carefully measured step toward him, standing barely eighteen inches from his ashen face.

"You and your parents" (glancing at them briefly, then looking again at Tony) "must go out there, smile, and enjoy your evening. You will, of course, have opportunity to socialize with the First Family. It wouldn't look normal otherwise. But you must not attempt to be alone with them. You must not attempt, in any way, to discuss this with them, or you will be asked to leave. If they say anything, simply do not respond. We will be watching the three of you very closely."

He looked up at Tony's parents. "We will be watching all of you very closely. At the end of the evening, you may go home, and never say a word of this to any living soul. If you do, you will regret it for the rest of your lives. I'm sorry to be so blunt, but those are the facts. Mark, do you understand?" He nodded.

"Ms. Neale?"

She whispered a weak, "Okay."

"Tony!" Scott raised his voice. "Do I have your word?"

"I understand," he said quietly, looking at the floor. Scott took that for compliance. He should not have.

"Good. Now let's enjoy the fireworks." He ushered them out into the crowd.

CHAPTER FORTY-FIVE

THE GATHERING STORM

An enthusiastic and appreciative public, eager to smother the Eastlands with love, surrounded the First Family, but Aaron had never felt so lonely. He stood with his parents and Shannon as they socialized with northern Wisconsin's political class. The Neales, on the other hand, were kept discretely away, left to endure small talk with those who were not at the moment part of the president's conversations.

There, across the lawn, was the person the First Children had trusted. How the president's children behaved in public, they were told, impacted their father's political future. They must not betray their emotions. They must play the part. Especially on this day. Shannon's wellbeing—and Aaron's— depended on playing the closely scripted role.

In any case, the agent suddenly assigned to them was grim and forceful in steering them away from the guest they most longed to see.

Tony was in no mood to play any kind of role. He seethed at the enforced distance between him and his new friends. At every opportunity, he looked toward the First Family, seeking eye contact with them. Shannon was doing the same toward him. Aaron was avoiding eye contact. Tony understood. Somehow, they would talk.

⁜

There would be two fireworks displays that evening. One had been carefully planned by the people of La Pointe and executed by a two-man team. Islander Terry Allen and Chief Wade Sanders, friends since childhood, were trained in handling large-scale pyrotechnics; they alone would staff the explosive-laden barge that served as a launch pad. Madeline Island had observed this tradition for as long as anyone could remember—but not with a president as the guest of honor. It would be bigger than ever—half an hour of non-stop fire, light, and sound.

The other display was provided courtesy of the Creator, in the skies west of the island. Before the fireworks were unleashed, an occasional flash of lightning caught the attention of worried officials who had worked hard to make this evening unforgettable, the high point of the president's visit.

It was also a concern to the dozens of pleasure craft anchored offshore in a broad semi-circle around the fireworks barge, itself moored a predetermined, safe distance from the shore. The Coast Guard enforced a strict buffer between the barge and the waterborne guests, forcing some of them to anchor in uncomfortably deep water.

Had this been any other night, the more cautious skippers would have retreated to their marina. They could watch from shore, out of danger from the approaching storm. But with the chance to see the president, even if through binoculars, eagerness overruled prudence. In any case, the forecast was for just occasional thunderstorms, not likely to develop until they had all safely retreated to their moorings. Thunderstorm or not, they stayed put.

For all the planning that went into the festivities, scheduled to conclude long before the predicted weather became a factor, there was some confusion as to who had the authority to decide what to do. Was it the local authorities? The White House? Would the Washington people overrule any decision not to their satisfaction? No one wanted responsibility for a judgment that, if wrong, would have embarrassing consequences. If they pulled the plug too soon and the storm didn't materialize, those who had worked so hard on the celebration would be furious. What was worse, the national media would be merciless toward those who ruined the president's celebration of America's most important holiday, all because of a few raindrops. If they waited too long, people could get miserably wet, and the same media would still be merciless, showing quite unflattering footage of the American president running for cover. Result: No one wanted to decide. *The rain isn't supposed to hit until after eleven. Why is it showing up at nine?*

But when the original starting time for the fireworks was in jeopardy, a hastily-called and contentious conference between the local fire chief, the police chief, the Coast Guard, the Secret Service, and Peter Scott ended in a consensus to hurry things along. Scott had, of course, his own reasons for wanting to shorten the evening. It was decided that the show would begin at 9:00 p.m. instead of 9:30. Ironically, the storm clouds obscured the dusk's fading glow, bringing premature darkness anyway.

⁜

Gary Bates found Samantha with her camera operator, shooting some long-distance video of the festivities. She was obviously distracted, almost ignoring the questions from Strobe. His queries about position and lighting would have concerned a reporter who didn't have a very unsettling mystery running through her mind.

Samantha saw Bates coming. "Learn anything, Gary?"

"Drew a blank. If something's up, no one's letting on. Only unusual thing was that my staff contact stonewalled me—unusual, and possibly significant. Apart from that, nothing. I hate it when people act strangely and I don't know why. How about you?"

"Just some buzz among a few of the reporters," Samantha replied. "Most of them didn't seem to give it much thought. But there's something very strange going on. The Neale boy—the entire family—shut us out. Phone's off the hook, no response at the entrance. What do you think?"

"Samantha, I don't want to appear sexist, but you're a woman, and you have intuition. What might make three kids act like that?"

Samantha thought for a moment. *You do appear sexist, Mr. Bates.* Without looking at him, she said, "Secrets."

"Secrets?"

"Okay, maybe not secrets, but someone told something that someone else wasn't expecting. My guess it's either the First Daughter or the First Son that did the telling. My bet's on Aaron."

"And he said what exactly?"

"I have no idea, except it's serious." She looked at the *Post* reporter. "Gary, I have two concerns."

"And they are …"

"One: there might be some news here, and if I'm right, I also suspect it could be politically awkward, even embarrassing."

"Go on—"

"Two: I can't put my finger on it, but I'm worried about those kids. And who on earth is that Neanderthal?"

"Who?"

"The new agent assigned to the President's kids."

"Hadn't noticed."

"I did. They've always had that female agent; suddenly, it's Attila the Hun."

Gary glanced toward the President's son. Sure enough …

"This is scary."

"What, Gary—the agent?"

"No; that a rookie is noticing things I'm missing. Sam, watch for any signs of trouble tonight. If you're right, it's going to be hard for those kids to function smoothly. They're expected to blend into the schmoozing despite whatever may be going through their minds. Adults can do that, and politicians do it rather well. But three kids? One of them never exposed to this kind of public scrutiny before? That's another matter. Stay in touch."

CHAPTER FORTY-SIX

FIREWORKS

Scott was walking a tightrope and knew it. He could not allow the kids much time together. If they were not seen with each other, people would question what happened to the friendship that had, until a few hours ago, been a PR bonus for the election-bound president.

Scott's solution was the fireworks display. He instructed Barker to keep Aaron and Shannon close to their parents throughout most of the evening. When it came time to watch the fireworks, the Neales would be seated near the president, and the three youths would sit near each other—but not together. Shannon would be seated in the same row, but between adults she didn't know, freezing her out of any compromising conversation. Aaron would be two rows ahead, but separated from Tony by other guests. There'd be no time for un-monitored chatter.

He did not count on the tenacity of teenagers whose enforced separation was pushing them beyond worries about being compliant.

The parents took their places without conversation, thanks to Peter Scott, who placed the congresswoman and a wealthy donor between them. The First Lady was disappointed. She would have preferred a casual woman-to-woman conversation with Ms. Neale rather than another forced but necessary conversation with "important" people.

Aaron and Shannon defied Scott's instructions. Approaching their assigned seats—by Scott's orders distanced from Tony—they boldly asked the unsuspecting guests if they could take the seats next to him. "Of course—You kids should sit together!" And a horrified Scott watched as his plan was compromised. Still, conversation between Aaron, Shannon, and Tony would be difficult. Those who sat nearby tried to engage them with comments about how much fun their afternoon on the water must have been.

Scott did not realize that a TV camera was also focused on them, a local TV journalist watching them intently. *Come on, kids. I can't hear you, but I'll soon learn if I can read lips.*

As the first fireworks burst overhead, Tony, without turning his head, asked "Are you guys okay?" The president's son responded barely above a whisper while looking towards the sky. His words sent a chill down Tony's back: "We can't take it anymore. Will you help us?"

"How?"

"How did you enjoy your hike?" It was Walter Kolquist, Bayfield's bank president, enjoying the proximity to the president that he'd been promised.

"Oh, it was fine," Aaron answered.

"Where did you do your hiking?" This time, Maggie Crandall joined in, hoping the president noticed her sincere— and politically advantageous—interest in the First Family. Eastland noticed, as did Scott, and they both wished they could hear what was being said.

The blend of fireworks and the animated crowd drowned the hushed conversation for anyone too far away to hear. But with the banker and congressperson involved, Scott relaxed for the moment; such conversation would, in the company of strangers, likely be safe enough.

"It's called the Capser Trail," Tony responded. Shannon saw an opportunity. "I really enjoy hiking," she offered. "In fact, I'd like to hike it too." Without looking directly at Tony, she asked, "Where is that trail again?"

"About a quarter mile over there." Tony nodded to the right. "Just through those bushes, to the right across the road, then through the trees."

"I've heard of it," Crandall observed. "You're fortunate, Tony, to spend time in such a beautiful place."

"I know," Tony said, looking toward the trees, unsmiling. "You could disappear in those woods."

Peter Scott's instincts told him that things were unraveling. At the moment, there was nothing he could do, standing at the back of a group numbering over a hundred. He looked toward Agent Barker, who stood alongside the cluster of guests about ten seats removed from three people who should not be sitting together. Scott motioned toward them with his eyes, then pointed at his ear as if to ask: *Can you hear anything?* The agent shrugged and shook his head.

No one else caught the subtle exchange except for the TV camera of WLOW-TV.

In the van, Samantha replayed the clip, and replayed it again. Each time, she was more convinced that she'd interpreted it correctly: "can't take it any more … help us … disappear"

"Strobe," she whispered to her camera operator, "rewind to that spot again, and don't let anyone else see it." She slipped away to find Gary Bates.

⌗

It is called a "microburst." As such, it would have been almost impossible to predict. The forecast was for some unsettled weather, but much later and much milder. Barely three miles away, Bayfield got little more than a typical midsummer thundershower. But all the ingredients were there for producing one relatively small, violent storm that would concentrate its fury on Madeline Island, sweeping from one end to the other.

It first visited a deputy sheriff on the highway south of Bayfield, who called in a warning that his Blazer was nearly blown off the road by sudden winds the likes of which he'd never experienced. He also reported that since trees had blown down around him, he was trapped on a hundred-yard stretch of State Route 13.

This gave at most a three-minute warning to those on the island, time largely spent debating who should warn who. Should the local authorities be told to inform the Washington people? No; tell the Coast Guard. Wait—you can't tell the Coast Guard until the Federal liaison is told—and by the time this was resolved, the people on the island needed no further notice.

CHAPTER FORTY-SEVEN

YOU'D BETTER THINK FAST

Sally and Mike Crane sat on the cushions that normally provided comfort in the cockpit of their 26-foot Catalina. They'd moved them to the forward deck, where they had an almost unobstructed view of the fireworks. They saw an occasional flash of lightning reflected on the clouds overhead, but were mesmerized by the reds, greens, oranges and blues of the pyrotechnics, the perfect conclusion to a remarkable day.

They'd motored across the bay that morning for the island's parade, then sailed the North Channel into mid-afternoon, before dropping anchor as one of the first to arrive for the evening's climax. A delicious dinner was grilled on the barbecue bolted to the aft rail. Conversation with other sailors was liberally lubricated with wine, hard ciders, and hors d'oeuvres.

At first, the stillness of the evening had an annoying effect on the fireworks. The smoke from the explosions hung in the dead air, creating a thickening haze that obscured subsequent rounds. "A little breeze would help," Mike commented about fifteen minutes into the show. As if on cue, a gentle breeze aloft began moving the haze to the east. In fact, Sally soon noticed a surface breeze from behind, taking the edge off the warm, humid air. *Maybe it'll blow the mosquitoes away,* she thought. The breeze gave her a chill; she pulled a beach towel around her shoulders.

The breeze kept building. The puffs of smoke moved more quickly, and the luminous trails from the rockets themselves, designed to arc outward and then descend vertically before fading, were now moving at a noticeable angle to the east.

Mike sensed that the boat had started to move. The breeze coming over the stern was blowing the boat around counterclockwise, as the boat to his south was swinging clockwise. He reassured himself that there was adequate swing room for both boats—and noticed that the rotation was picking up speed, enough so the water was audibly rippling its protest as the hull slewed around. It was only then that he and Sally, and about three hundred other boaters and passengers, looked away from the show emanating from the barge and saw, too late for most of them to do much about it, the much more impressive show bearing down on them from the southwest.

The mainland had disappeared. Instead, lightning illuminated an ominous moving wall of cloud aloft, roiling and writhing, a green-gray wall of rain hanging below. The surface of the lake was still relatively flat, but the wind was beginning to tear at the water, turning what moments before had been a mirror into a white froth that soon built into waves: one foot, then two, then more.

The conversation that followed between Mike and Sally was repeated in some form on the entire fleet of pleasure boats at virtually the same moment.

"Uh-oh."

"Mike, what do we do?"

"I'm thinking."

"You'd better think fast."

The gentle breeze that had become a brisk wind became in seconds something else entirely. They were struck by a force that no one in that group of weekend sailors had ever experienced, the kind of gale that the most seasoned boaters dread.

The Catalina, caught with its port side now fully exposed to the wind, was blown over at a forty-degree heel as the water resisted the keel's sideways passage, while the blow clawed at the mast like a giant fist, trying to slam it into the water. Sally was unable to catch herself, and was thrown against the lifelines, then fell between them into the angry water. The boat continued over her, and Sally slid underneath the bow of the vessel. Just as quickly, she emerged on the other side. She was bruised, soaked and choking, looking frantically for her boat, which continued to drift downwind as it swung on the anchor. She was in trouble, and she knew it. Her husband frantically looked about in the stinging rain and wind for any sign of his wife, panicking at the awareness that with every passing second, he was being blown farther away from her. He mentally calculated how much scope he'd let out earlier that day, and realized that when the line finally went taut, he could be more than thirty yards from where she'd gone in.

Having dealt the mainland a glancing blow, the storm had used the nearly three miles of open water to build considerable momentum. It took full advantage of the unobstructed water and hit the western tip of the island and the town of La Pointe with everything it had. It caught most of the fleet with their stern exposed to the wind; they were now swinging violently around in the squall, which simply kept building to a steady eighty knots, with gusts past one hundred. Some boats were in water too deep for their anchors to hold in that kind of a blow, and each wave would lift the boat, pulling the anchor off the bottom and moving the boat a few feet closer to shore.

The fireworks barge, its rams driven deep into the sand, was virtually impossible to move while its small tug, moored alongside with its stern to the storm, took a beating from the building waves, which soon topped four feet. The tug shipped enough water to sink on the spot. That left the fireworks crew on the exposed barge, itself a threat to the fragile craft drifting uncontrollably closer.

The powerboats had the best chance; they had the muscle to push against the wind and at least ease the strain on their mooring, while the underpowered sailboats were nearly helpless. Many of them had dropped lightweight "lunch hooks," and found their lines parting with a sharp snap, or simply watched their anchors drag helplessly across the lake bed as the storm pushed them toward the rocks along the shore. Seven boats smashed against each other, the barge, and the rocks within four minutes of the first gust. Some, broadside to the waves and keels dragging across the shallow bottom, were knocked on their sides, their masts oddly slamming on the shore with each wave.

CHAPTER FORTY-EIGHT

BREAKING AWAY

It was almost hypnotic. There were a dozen dramas happening at once, and it was impossible not to be horrified by the personal disasters unfolding everywhere one looked. Everyone, if only for a few seconds, watched and listened as the tug went down with howls of steel against steel and snapping hawsers, followed by the sickening crunch of fiberglass hulls finding each other, and some of them finding the barge.

One of those disasters was engulfing Sally Crane. She was a strong swimmer, but had never needed to swim in virtual darkness, with wind screaming, spray nearly blinding her, and building seas carrying her downwind. She was in a fight for her life; she drew on everything she'd ever learned about keeping a human body on top of the water. She was desperate to find something solid to hang on to.

Within the first two minutes, she would be carried toward something solid. Under the circumstances, it could also be lethal. The waves were slamming broadside into the fireworks barge; she was terrified to see the black mass, illuminated by occasional bursts of lightning, looming larger as she drifted closer.

Mike was safe, for now. But he watched in horror as Sally tried to swim toward him, but was being driven farther away, and ominously toward the fireworks barge. And all Mike could do was watch.

It was a four-foot wave that did the damage. The confused seas, exploding against the flat-sided barge, rebounded until they hit the next incoming wave, rising almost vertically until the wind tore the tops of the waves and sent clouds of spray over the steel vessel. The mass of incoherently moving water was already claiming a 27-foot Bayliner cruiser. Its anchor was holding the craft barely forty feet from the barge, but the rebounding waves washed easily over its stern and through its wide-open companionway into the cabin below. Its occupants were desperately donning life jackets as the boat settled beneath them.

One of those waves lifted Sally at just the wrong moment, blinding her and filling her mouth with water, then slamming her into the steel plates of the barge directly in front of a stunned Terry Allen. The impact shattered her left shoulder, fractured three ribs, opened a five-inch gash on the left side of her face, and knocked her unconscious. Before Allen could react, the same wave washed over the deck, driving him against the winch that controlled the anchoring rams. Sally slid limply along the side as the first wave receded, only to be lifted again by the next.

Terry struggled to his feet and moved back to the edge, frantic to find the person he'd glimpsed—and heard, as her body slammed his barge. The lightning illuminated her white tank top; she was face down and floating on a mass of very angry water. In a moment, he realized, she'd be washed around the end of the barge and would drift quickly out of reach. He had to act.

"Chief! Over here! Bring a line!"

"Coming!"

Hearing his partner's response, Terry jumped in.

Within seconds, he wondered why. The waves rose and fell too fast for any hope of staying above them; he had to catch his breath in the troughs, while allowing the peaks to submerge him. He groped toward the form he'd seen moments before, and found her not by sight but by accident, as a wave threw her into him. Unaware of her injuries, and unable in any case to concern himself with such matters, he grabbed her arm—mercifully her right arm—and pulled her toward the side of the barge.

By now they'd drifted slightly to the north, and were being carried down the side of the vessel. Rather than fight the chaos on the windward side, Allen allowed the waves to carry him around the barge, hoping for relief to leeward. It provided scant protection, but enough for him to drag Sally close to safety. He grabbed the line thrown by Chief Sanders and pulled Sally with him to the barge. The Chief managed to drag her topside; then assist Terry out of the water. They then tried to discern what to do next with an unconscious, soaked, and injured female who in the dark may or may not be already a drowning victim.

⁜

The first few moments were caught on video by several news cameras, but even those soon succumbed to the growing fury, and journalists joined the throng of people rushing for cover. Strobe's camera, stationed on the north side of the manor's property, missed the carnage on the water, and caught instead the rush of humanity scrambling for shelter as the storm shredded what moments before had been the most prestigious gathering of dignitaries in the island's history.

The party tents blew down instantly, often on top of those seeking shelter from the storm. The power went out. Several people cried out in pain as tent poles, tree branches, even tables that were moments before laden with refreshments, whipped through the air and into the hapless crowd.

The first priority is always the president, even before his wife and children. Agent in Charge Andrew Boyd did what he was supposed to do: at the first sign this was not a gentle breeze, he took the president's arm. "Sir, it's time to get inside." With that, he began pulling Eastland toward the manor without waiting for response. By design, the president had been seated in the last row, facilitating a quick exit toward the manor should it be required, as it was now.

The First Lady followed. The agent re-assigned to Aaron and Shannon was fighting his way to the place where they had been, but he was thwarted by the rush of people headed chaotically for cover. It was about twenty seconds before he arrived at the spot where they had been; like everyone else, they were no longer there. The family was separated at a critical moment.

Aaron was the first to reach the aisle toward the Manor. Tony followed, with Shannon behind him. This was Shannon's opportunity. With the rest of the guests she, Aaron and Tony had begun moving toward the manor in virtually total darkness. They had draped a blanket around their shoulders as protection from the elements, and Tony felt the girl behind him suddenly stop. "You'll know where to look for me," Shannon said, barely audible above the howl of the storm. Tony knew what she meant. "Take this—" she released her end of the blanket, turned left, and headed away from the manor, toward the brush at the edge of the property.

CHAPTER FORTY-NINE

FIRST CRY OF FREEDOM

Mr. Scott!" The agent in charge caught up with the president's aide just before he stepped into the manor. Scott turned, shielding his face from the blast of rain and wind, and stepped back from the doorway so others had clear passage. "Make it quick, Boyd."

The agent pointed toward the beach. "I'm re-assigning some of my people, sir." Scott glanced west, knowing what he'd see.

Concern for one's fellow human beings was not Peter Scott's strong suit, and it was as uncharacteristic as it was humane that he consented. "Good," he yelled above the shriek of the storm. "Anyone you can find." He ducked inside; Agent Boyd followed, who, once out of the wind, pressed the call button on his hand-held radio and directed all available agents to the beach.

The Navy SEALs were especially useful; their assault-style clothing was more suited for rough duty, their water-oriented skills and their conditioning put them at the forefront of the crisis. But this thinned Scott's resources, and created holes in the security net.

Some agents watched toward the lake, distracted by the frantic rescue efforts along the beach. Boaters tried to help each other, aided by Sheriff's deputies and SEALs. Other agents were looking in the opposite direction, toward the people rushing to get to their cars and home. Still others had led the president, the First Lady, Aaron, and Secretary Malone into the manor, and away from the large windows, which threatened to explode inward at any moment.

With most of the action to the southwest, no one looked to the north. The huge oaks and shrubbery, of little use as a hiding place on a normal day, were unlikely to attract much attention in the middle of a small hurricane. They had Shannon's complete attention. She blended into the brush and crawled through to the other side, then half-crawled, half-ran, along the shrubbery. Within a minute, she was running between cabins and parked cars, through an unfamiliar neighborhood, guessing where she would find the forest trail that Tony and Aaron had walked just a day before. She would find the forest but not the trail, missing it by two hundred yards. Yet once across Rice Street, at least it was a forest, and as she ran through undergrowth in search of the trail, she became aware of the gravity of what she was doing.

When the Secret Service first realized that she was not in the building, she had put 500 yards between herself and those who called her father the commander-in-chief. Wet and disoriented, she nevertheless felt free for the first time in three years. She began to cry; freedom felt new, as disorienting as the forest, as exhilarating as it was terrifying, and for no reason other than sheer joy, she wrapped her arms around herself and shouted "Yes!"

⁑

Just before Aaron reached the manor, Tony bent close to his ear and said, "Don't act surprised. Don't look back. Shannon's gone. She's running." Tony slipped into the crowd running for shelter, leaving a stunned First Son being ushered inside, terrified for a sister he could no longer protect.

Tony found his parents, and they ran toward their Jeep in a confusion of wind, rain, thunder, and people. Several patio chairs and tables had blown against the windward side of the vehicle; once Debra and Mark were safely inside, Tony tossed the debris over the roof of the Jeep. The wind carried it thirty yards or more before it hit the ground and tumbled into the darkness. Mark started the engine and told them to stay low in case more debris slammed the Jeep. The howling wind tried to lift the car; its wipers were all but useless. Nothing was said as they headed for home, driving around branches and entire trees that were gradually filling the streets. Halfway to their driveway, they reached the town's fire department, where downed trees allowed no further progress. They parked the Jeep and raced into the building where a lone volunteer EMT was monitoring the radio. The EMT reported their presence on the emergency band. The Secret Service heard the report, and forwarded the message to Peter Scott.

⁜

Within twenty minutes the worst of the storm passed. The winds dropped, though still in excess of thirty knots. Waves still crested near four feet before crashing on the shore. A hard, driving rain, punctuated by thunder and lightning, repeatedly shook the now darkened island, and a storm of a different kind was about to unleash an even greater fury.

The drenched, cold, and worried Neales, blocked by trees across Big Bay Road, had no choice but to stay at the town's fire hall. Before long, a government Suburban, blinkers flashing, turned into the drive.

"We've got company, Mark," Debra said.

"Then we've got trouble," Mark mused. He remained in the doorway, expecting that the Seals were looking for them.

The SEALs exited each side of the back seat, ignoring the still-driving rain, and raced to the door. One of them spoke. "Mr. Neale? We've been ordered to speak to you and your family."

"Of course." Both SEALs stepped inside; Mark closed the door. He was about to ask what he could do, but the SEAL spoke first.

"Shannon Eastland has disappeared. Do you have any idea, any at all, about what may have happened to her?"

Mark looked at his wife; she looked back. They both glanced at Tony, but instinctively looked away; they knew that every movement was being observed, and that Tony too would be under scrutiny.

"I honestly have no idea. Is there anything we can do?"

The SEALs sensed a less-than-complete answer. As instructed by Peter Scott, they quickly scoured the room, then repeated the procedure in the garage—empty, because all the equipment was on standby around the village.

The Neales stood in silence, their silhouettes illuminated only by a flashlight. They were soaked to the skin and longed for dry clothing. And that, they knew, would have to wait until the SEALs left, and probably longer. While the hall was searched, the parents stared at their son, sensing that he knew something they didn't. Tony stood, staring into space, absorbed in his thoughts.

She's not here, Tony thought. *But I know where she is.*

⁜

She was soaked, shivering, and fright was setting in. The darkness was almost total. Her arms and legs were bleeding. Still, every step widened the distance between Shannon and the nightmare that was her home. It was a strange mix of emotions: terror, freedom, and panic.

What do I do now?

CHAPTER FIFTY

FIND HER

With the storm still wreaking havoc—the shaking in the manor was not unlike an earthquake—Mary Lee Eastland asked the agent with her, "Where are my children?"

"Aaron's downstairs. I'm sure Shannon's with another agent, Ma'am. Once we're settled in, I'll check."

A frantic three minutes later, the agent returned, and whispered something to Peter Scott, who whispered harshly back. The agent abruptly disappeared again.

"Mr. President, Mrs. Eastland—we're still looking for Shannon—"

"What do you mean, Peter?"

Scott tried to mask his unease: *Not only is she missing; she's out of my control—which makes her dangerous.* "Well— she didn't come into the manor, and I suspect she was caught in the crowds heading for shelter. My best guess is that she's simply in somebody's car sitting out the storm. The Service is checking every vehicle and structure in the immediate vicinity, so I wouldn't worry."

"Mr. Scott, I'm her mother. I will worry until I see her. So find her."

Scott knew that she had no authority to issue orders, and also knew that obeying them was his wisest response. But twenty minutes later, it was his unpleasant task to report to the Eastland's that there was no trace of Shannon, and that a full-scale search was underway, using—at the moment—only federal assets.

Telling the First Family that Shannon was missing proved to be a distraction for Peter Scott. They knew that she was more than lost. She was exposed to a violent, vicious storm. An injured First Daughter—or worse—could not be discounted. Her immediate world was capable of killing her. Her parents had their concerns: she may not survive. But Scott had his: she might—and tell her story.

"We are leaving nothing to chance," Scott reported. "We're searching every building in town, beginning here. We're inspecting every vehicle trying to leave the area. The Coast Guard is inspecting every boat—at least the ones still afloat. We're search the wooded areas around the village. At the moment, we're under a total press blackout. We've issued a statement that the First Family is safely inside the manor— nothing more. The storm will keep the media busy for now."

"Robert—would someone take her? Why her?"

The president turned his head. *She wasn't kidnapped*, he thought. *She left on her own. I know it.*

Established policy now took over: When in doubt, get the president out. Orders were dispatched to *Marine One* to remove the president, though at the moment, he was separated from the helicopter by about a mile of debris-covered road. *Marine One* would have to come to the president, and at Scott's orders, the storm-shattered grounds of the manor were cleared for the chopper.

He then began to formulate a plan for containment of the other crisis.

⁑

With only flashlights to illuminate their patient and the storm just beginning to abate, Terry and Chief Sanders could determine little beyond the fact that she was still alive. She tried feebly to move, but every attempt was met with searing pain. They knew that the shoulder had been severely injured; the gash on her left cheek was gruesome, but not the primary concern for the two trained EMTs. They knew that internal trauma was likely, and needed attention they couldn't provide on the barge. With the tug gone, they'd lost not only their transportation to solid ground, but their radio as well, and this unconscious woman may not live long enough for help to come to them. The Chief knew what had to be attempted.

"Put her in the Zodiac."

"Are you crazy?" Terry knew he wasn't and feared that his best friend was about to become a dead hero.

Chief Sanders looked at his friend. "No choice."

They gently lifted her into the inflatable lashed to the deck of the barge; the chief got in, and Allen worked the utility crane, hoisting the craft and its passengers, swinging them over the lee side and into the water. The chief used the oars to steer as the storm drove them toward the beach; once clear of the barge and in the face of the wind, the seas were still topping four feet and more.

They almost made it. But with waves breaking in shallower water, the wind flipped the Zodiac, throwing the chief and his barely conscious companion into the water and onto the rocks along the shore. Horrified rescuers along the beach, led by the SEALs, struggled against the waves to bring them to what little safety existed while the wind still howled around them.

CHAPTER FIFTY-ONE

TELL HIM EVERYTHING

The First Couple was briefed a second time on the search before President Eastland's departure. They approved a hastily-worded statement for release to the now-suspicious media. The First Lady made it clear that the policy of evacuating her husband under no circumstances applied to her. She was staying until her daughter was found. So was Aaron.

Eastland and Scott seemed eager to talk, but privately. Sensing that she wasn't welcome, the First Lady, desperate for anything to connect her with her lost child, excused herself and went to Shannon's room. In the seclusion of the bedroom, sitting on Shannon's bed, she began to shake. *Why didn't I come here before?* Her well-practiced poise was no match for the fear of not knowing where her daughter was.

Scanning the room with her flashlight, her eyes caught a journal, half-buried under Shannon's backpack. Frantic for any insight into Shannon's behavior, she picked up the diary and violated one of her promises—she began to read. The entry for June 15th troubled her— "… Dad … touching me … I was younger … maybe 8, maybe 10. When I try to talk about it, I clam up … such a father … like to kill him."

There was an entry from the night before: "I don't think I can keep this secret any more. I don't want to, in fact. I'll tell Aaron. But he'll have to promise not to tell anyone."

Mrs. Eastland walked to Aaron's room, and found him writing in a notepad by flashlight. He seemed unhappy to see his mother, who sat next to him on the bed.

"Where's Shannon, Mom?"

"We're looking for her. She'll be okay."

"I'm scared."

"Tell me why, Aaron. The storm?"

"No."

"Aaron—do you trust me?"

"Yes."

Mary took a breath and risked a question she was asking herself. "Do you trust your father?"

Aaron said nothing. The next question was the one she feared most asking: "Shannon told you about what your father did to her, didn't she?"

Aaron's response was a look of terror. "Am I in trouble for not telling you?" He also wondered, *Mom, can I trust you?*

"You are in absolutely no trouble. That was a brave and smart thing for her to do, and you should be proud that she trusts you, Aaron."

"I'm scared, Mom. But mostly, I'm angry! Dad stole something from her, and she'll never really get it back."

"I know."

"Mom … you know, Tony knows too—

Mary Lee was stunned. "The Neale boy knows?"

"Shannon and I told him when we were sailing."

The First Lady sat, stunned, and knew that the reality in which she began the day was being undone. She, her children, and yes, her husband, were entering an unknown world, with no good outcomes.

Aaron broke the silence. "Mom, sooner or later, everyone will know. I've been afraid of it coming out, but now I want it to. I want to tell the world that my father is a monster."

From the power, prestige, and elegance of the highest of privileged life, her family had been savaged as violently as the storm still shaking the manor. Mary Lee Eastland's daughter has been violated, her son has been traumatized, and she is married, in Aaron's word, to a "monster." The cover-photo innocence of two people raising two offspring in trust, love, and hope for a wide-open future will be consumed in an uncontrollable storm of accusation and judgment. She and her children have been used, reduced to the veneer over a sordid and sick reality.

But she would not allow herself to be merely a victim. *This is not about me.*

"Aaron, the story needs to be told. It will be very hard for your sister, and for you, but you're strong enough to do what needs to be done. Don't be afraid. You won't be dealing with this alone." She squeezed his hand. "I'm going to tell your father what we know. Then I'll be back, okay?"

"Tell him everything, Mom. Everything."

CHAPTER FIFTY-TWO

THE RESCUER

Michael Erickson found opportunity in the retreating storm. At the first easing of the wind, he'd taken a flashlight, surveyed his property and finding nothing amiss apart from downed branches, went back inside to await the morning. *I'll have some manageable cleanup,* he figured. *With luck, maybe some free lumber.* He took pride in how he'd built this cabin. Set well back from the road, deep into wooded land, it withstood the storm, a testament to his craftsmanship—and the fact that no trees had decided to fall on his home.

He sat quietly in the darkened cabin, as the clock approached 10:30. The receding thunder punctuating the wind and rain that still battered the island. The sounds of nature's violence were slowly giving way to peace.

He could identify most of what he heard: the first crickets, their sounds tentative at first, as if testing the air. The creaking of trees in the dying wind, the occasional crash of a wind-damaged limb succumbing to gravity, a family of raccoons moving across the driveway.

But he could not place one sound. As it approached, Michael heard the rustling of ground cover and the cracking of branches being crushed underfoot. *Something big. A deer? Bear? Could be. But <u>this</u>? Sounds more like a human. And in a hurry.*

Any euphoria Shannon felt at being free was giving way to a chilling realization: there was no going back, no do-overs, no way to avoid whatever consequences she had set in motion … and, she was lost in an unknown wilderness, illuminated only by lightning. She shivered, and she began to question her decision. *What will I do if I'm found? What if I'm not?*

The lightning revealed a fallen tree, cradled by the branches of another that survived, a small but welcome shelter from the rain. Shannon crawled underneath, wrapping her arms around her knees. In the distance, she heard the muffled sound of a helicopter lifting off, and the rasp of chain saws. Someone somewhere was working to clear the roads. They were looking for her.

A sudden crack of breaking wood brought a startled gasp, as she looked up in time to see a deer, itself spooked by her presence, turn and run to the south.

Motionless after half an hour of stumbling through the forest, she leaned back against the moss and breathed deeply. *I needed to do this … right? Shannon, get a grip. Your story deserves to be told, and it <u>will</u> be. You're not a victim any more. It will be hard, but this is your story now. <u>Yours</u>.* Years of anger, shame and fear had been framed by the role imposed on her; for far too long, her real self had been hiding in plain sight. But tonight, first crawling then stumbling and then running through wind and rain and darkness, she dared to reclaim her life. Her body. Her womanhood, defined by her and no one else.

Shannon had no idea where she was, in what direction she was moving, or what exactly she hoped to accomplish. She didn't care. For now, away was enough, as each step was a step away from her degradation.

"No more," she whispered. She found herself whispering, "No. No! NO!" over and over, each time more forcefully than before: until she let herself say aloud "Don't even touch me!"

A human voice startled her. *Did someone hear me?* A faint glimmer of light confirmed her fears: they were looking for her, and getting closer. A hundred yards behind her, a pair of deputies were working their way toward her hiding place, their voices and flashlights broadcasting their presence. She got up, turned around, and began moving again. this time more quietly, more carefully, and more determined than ever to exploit the freedom to be, for now, lost to the world.

She could not hear a lone Navy SEAL in his black fatigues, moving silently through the forest, flanking the locals. He stopped occasionally to scan his surroundings with a night scope.

⁜

Michael knew that someone was invading his private kingdom. *Who on earth would be out in this weather? Strange ... I hear a voice, like someone talking, but only one set of footsteps. No ... she—it's definitely female—is talking—to whom? I'll know soon. She's coming this way.*

Erickson sat motionless, the footsteps coming much too rapidly for him either to confront or avoid. Within moments, he heard the labored breathing of an exhausted human. The movement stopped after the intruder stepped onto the gravel of his driveway. Then, they moved toward the house, onto the front step, and silence. Slowly, the door opened, and a silhouette stood, backlit by lightning. *A kid?* Erickson was surprised. *Female. Young. Soaked, dirty ... why would any sane person hike during a near-hurricane?* On second thought: *Fancy clothes—well, they used to be fancy, but the forest has not been kind to them. This person is in trouble.*

"Is anybody here?"

Erickson said nothing; unsure of how to reveal his identity without scaring someone out of their skin. He watched the intruder step in and slowly close the door. He heard her hand feeling along the wall for a light switch. He smiled. Her hand found one, flipped it, and was reminded by the continued darkness that the switch was useless.

Then, abruptly, she turned and stepped off the porch, then back across the gravel drive. *She's heading back ... no; she came from the west; now she's headed east. Whoever she is, she has no business out here.* Slowly, feeling his way around his dark but familiar cabin, Michael gathered what he would need to track his prey: rain gear, a flashlight, and just in case, his rifle.

CHAPTER FIFTY-THREE

WALK TOWARD MY VOICE

Michael had tracked humans before, but never like this one. He would need his skills at being invisible in a forest. He smiled. He'd show these well-trained urban types how it was done. *Spooks in suits*, he smirked. He would succeed at this task, right under their noses.

Michael's first move was to not move at all. Once clear of his cabin, he stopped and listened, closely. He heard the first sounds of vehicular traffic and chain saws as roads were being cleared, a painfully slow process, especially slow for those frantically trying to find a missing kid. He could ignore those sounds. He heard *Marine One* warming its engines—strange at this hour, but again, of no particular interest. He listened for voices, or any other sign of human activity in his forest. He waited, perfectly still. When he began to move, each step was deliberate; he went deeper into the forest, parallel to the path his intruder was likely to be taking. Every fifty yards or so, he stopped, and listened.

He easily pinpointed the noises made by the two agents, following the trail Shannon had missed, and who were making no effort to disguise their presence. *That someone up ahead is being followed. A lot of effort is going into finding them. Maybe someone important? One of the city people, lost and confused? Fine. I'll find their objective before they do. Whoever they are.* He heard, and then saw, the object of his search—a young woman moving away from the flashlights and voices pursuing her.

His challenge: to make contact without frightening the unidentified but probably rattled fugitive, who by a scream could betray their location. He stepped into the woods, deftly picking his way along nearly invisible paths favored by deer, raccoon, and the occasional bear. He was moving ahead of the fleeing girl, intending to find a suitable spot to wait for her to encounter him. He knew the forest, and he would find the perfect spot to confront this shadowy figure without being spotted by others.

What even Michael Erickson's considerable tracking skills could not overcome was a well-trained Navy SEAL with a night vision scope. Lt. Charlie Mann saw Shannon; at least, it made sense to identify the moving form in his scope as the First Daughter. He assumed that he was the first to find her—until he saw another figure in a motionless crouch as Shannon stumbled toward him.

Michael wanted to make contact, but saying something, or moving abruptly, could panic her. So he did the most non-threatening thing he could think of. He deliberately, slowly and just loudly enough for someone to hear in the open air, exhaled.

"Who's there?"

"Hey, young lady. What are you doing out on a night like this?"

"Who are you? Where are you?" Her voice betrayed near panic.

"Name's Mike. Listen. You can't stay out here. I can help you. Will you let me?"

"I still can't see you."

"Relax. I'm just to your right, about thirty feet away. I'm standing up." He leaned his rifle against a tree so as to not frighten her, and slowly stood. "Can you see me yet?"

"I don't know. It's dark."

"That's okay. Walk toward my voice; Walk carefully. There are lots of things to trip on."

Lt. Mann saw the form of Michael Erickson, barely thirty feet from the girl, and leveled his weapon. He was too far away to hear Erickson's appeal. With the horrified SEAL watching, the figure that was Shannon suddenly walked into the line of fire and toward the voice. Shannon didn't see Erickson until she was almost close enough to touch him.

"Why are you out here on a night like this?"

"I need to know that you won't tell anyone I'm here."

"Okay, no problem. But who are you? At least I should know who doesn't want anyone to know her—"

"I'm Shannon Eastland."

"Eastland? As in …"

"Yes. And I am not going back to them."

"You're kidding." *Of all people—Eastland's kid? Thirty years, I've wanted to repay an old debt to this man. Now I've got his kid asking for my help?*

"Please don't tell my parents."

"Why not?"

"All I will tell you is that I just need to get away—" Her voice cracked.

"I promise you: I will tell no one where you are."

Her sudden move toward Erickson may have saved his life; it happened too quickly for even the trained marksman to safely take out the suspected assailant. *Who is this person she's so glad to see?*

"You're soaked. You'll get sick. Here—put this on."

In what little shelter the fallen tree afforded, Shannon put Erickson's ill-fitting but dry camouflage suit, one he normally wore when hunting, over her wet clothing. He'd make do with his denim work clothes.

"Who are you?"

"Name's Mike. I live out here."

"They're looking for me, aren't they?"

"There's probably a small army looking for you right now. But I know this island; they don't. We've got to get moving, and fast. Ready?"

"I think so …"

"Follow right behind me. Watch your feet."

"But I can't see anything."

"I can. Just do what I tell you, and don't talk. Someone might hear you."

The two unlikely companions set off through the tangle, guided by Erickson, and followed by Lt. Mann who, once sensing that Shannon's mysterious companion posed no immediate threat to her, called in a status report. "Subject is headed in a roughly easterly direction, in the company of an unknown individual, probably male. He seems to know where he's headed. Male is armed. Carrying a long gun."

CHAPTER FIFTY-FOUR

YOUR OWN FLESH AND BLOOD

Mary Lee gently closed her son's door and leaned against the wall. She breathed deeply, gathering her thoughts for the ugly confrontation ahead. She then went back to the manor's library where Scott and the president were, along with the agent usually tasked with Shannon's safety. The First Lady spoke first.

"Don't look for a kidnapper. Shannon doesn't want to be found."

She glared at her husband.

"Robert—she is your own flesh and blood!"

The president dismissed Scott and the agent, terrified that the First Lady would continue talking with witnesses in the room. Scott stayed outside the door. Eastland hoped he would. This would require his advice.

Agent Kim Nguyen was trying to make sense of this bizarre evening. Whatever was behind the First Lady's words, there was rage in the First Lady's face. That, plus the strange reaction of the president and his aide—something was terribly wrong.

She had developed a liking for the missing child, and decided that whatever role she played in the rest of the crisis, she would seek answers to questions these people apparently didn't want answered.

"Mr. Scott?"

"Yes." Scott's voice was flat and clipped; his mind somewhere else.

"May I suggest that I follow up with more questions of the Neales?"

Scott was impassive for a moment; Nguyen wondered if he hadn't heard her. He had, and was thinking, *Might be simpler if she's not here for a while*. Abruptly, he looked in her direction and said. "Yes—of course." Nguyen turned and headed for one of the cars on standby at the manor. When she arrived at the Fire Station, Agent Nguyen joined the Neales and got right to the point.

"I'm here under orders to question you. The White House considers you to be key in finding Shannon. You are, in other words, in deep trouble if you had anything to do with her disappearance.

"Now listen carefully—and please believe me. I think you know where she is. I care deeply about her. Not just professionally—I think she's a neat, if mixed-up, kid. I want to help her. To do that, I need you to trust me. Something's very troubling about this and for her sake, I want to know what it is. I want to talk to her before she is reunited with her parents."

She paused, breathed deeply, and continued.

"Tony: Do you know where she is?"

"No."

"Do you have any idea where she might be?"

"I won't tell you."

His father sensed, correctly, that his son just admitted to hiding something … or someone.

"They can force you to tell if you know anything, Tony."

The room became silent, all eyes on Agent Nguyen. She tried a different approach.

"Will she be safe out there?"

With this, Tony's resolve begins to crumble. "I don't know."

The agent gave him time to compose himself before she continued. "You and I both want her safe. Help me find her. Please."

"Why would I help you?"

"Tony, my one and only job is her safety. In a mess like this, no one is thinking clearly. Shannon is likely wet, scared, and alone, on an island with frantic people, some of them armed. She could get hurt.

"Listen—Shannon won't get in any trouble, and I think I can make sure you won't either, if you can tell me where we can look. Please trust me, Tony. You're the first real friend she and her brother have had since moving to the White House. I think you know why she's so upset. If you help me, I promise you I'll do everything I can to help your friend, and to protect you. Tony, you're the friend Aaron and Shannon never had. Please."

Had an attorney been present, none of this conversation would have happened. It was foolish and dangerous to incriminate oneself in what could be considered a federal crime, and then to spill one's guts to someone who worked, in effect, for the prosecution. Tony should have staked out a stronger bargaining position for the information he possessed. Or better yet, he should have said nothing at all.

His father saw Tony's face turn red and his eyes moisten. He panicked when Tony's lips began to move: *No, Tony—you can't trust these people. Don't—*

Instead, Tony took a foolish risk: naively trusting this federal agent with information that could destroy him and his parents. In his ignorance of what he "should" have done, Tony did exactly the right thing. He told the truth, and the agent questioning him knew it. Because of that, Tony may have saved his friend's life.

"She asked me for help. I told her how to get into the forest—but I really didn't think she'd try, especially in the storm. She was behind me when we went for cover. Suddenly, she wasn't. I didn't look back—didn't want to draw attention. But I kind of knew what happened."

"So Shannon's out there in the woods?"

"I think so. She might look for the trail." He paused; then he revealed why. "She's running away from her father."

Debra gasped. Mark's mind was racing. *They're packaged in the campaign as a perfect family. Up to now, that's what I've written—*

The government now knew that Tony knew; that was bad enough. But up to now, Mark and Debra didn't know that their son may have been actively involved in Shannon's disappearance. Up to now, there might have been a chance to protect Tony. That's gone now. Mark and Debra had only one thought: *What will happen to him?*

CHAPTER FIFTY-FIVE

TURNING THIS TO OUR ADVANTAGE

Back at the manor, Scott surprised the president with a hopeful, almost cheerful comment: "I think we can turn this to our advantage."

"Advantage?"

"Sure—the president who must bear the burden of a troubled child …"

"Peter, really—this is not the time—"

"Listen to me. Look at the whole picture. I understand how serious your family situation is, Mr. President. This is a critical moment for the campaign, for the country. As difficult as this is personally for you and the First Lady, we can't afford to be distracted—"

The First Lady interrupted. "This is no 'distraction!' We're talking about my daughter!"

Scott turned gentle. "I didn't mean it that way at all, ma'am. But if you love Shannon—and I'm sure you do…you both do—then we can't afford to let this get out of hand. For her sake as well as ours, we must seize control of this, and right now."

The president looked thoughtful; Scott was relieved to see him actually considering his line of thinking. "So, what do you suggest, Peter?"

This is a surreal moment, Mary Lee thought. *My children have become a threat to their own father, one of them is somewhere alone in this wilderness, and we're talking political strategy, damage control, turning this to political advantage. Advantage? In what way is this advantageous to my children? Do I want any part of this? No. If this is the price of success, it is too high.*

The First Lady stood and began to walk away. "Mrs. Eastland, you are part of this conversation. We need to be together on this."

"'Together?'" She walked out of the room, and a minute later was with her son again.

⁂

"Tell me what you're thinking, Tony." Agent Nguyen asked the question, but Tony turned instead toward his father.

"Dad—I need to help find Shannon. She's somewhere out there. She's kind of like a sister and I want to help. Will you take me to the trail?"

The Neales couldn't just go looking for Shannon, Nguyen knew—not without an escort, especially now that they were clearly implicated in the girl's disappearance. While there was legal reason to treat them as suspects, there was an overriding concern to find Shannon. That, coupled with her instincts that the Neales were not a threat to her—in fact, quite the opposite— changed the equation: They are key to finding her. This became decisive in Nguyen's thinking about her next step.

Getting to the trail was complicated by the storm-caused devastation, and in any case, the agent couldn't simply take civilians on a private search. But the thought of Tony's new friend alone in the darkness made it impossible to do nothing. At Nguyen's direction, she, the driver, and the Neales headed east, slowly weaving around the debris left by the storm.

CHAPTER FIFTY-SIX

WASN'T THAT AN ACCIDENT?

Scott was nearer panic than at any time in his life. Eastland was shaken, wavering in his once-singular focus on The Prize. The president was doing the unthinkable: he was beginning to listen to his heart. For the first time in two decades, Peter Scott and Robert Eastland had different agendas. The synergy that won them the White House was slipping away. Scott's mind was racing, looking for a way to bring Eastland back into line. He tried a conciliatory tone.

"Sir—this is a tough night for all of us. I'm not minimizing the pain you must feel. I care about your kids too. You'll need some professional help once we're back in Washington. I'll do everything I can to make that happen as discretely as possible. If we want the best for your family, let's keep this thing within the family.

"Here's how I see it: she's clearly troubled; we can't hide that now. On the contrary, it's the very piece we use. We issue a statement announcing her disappearance, as a result of her emotional problems and the trauma of the storm. Aaron? For now, we keep him close by and shelter him from outside contact."

Eastland thought for a moment, and discovered a flaw in Scott's plan: "What about the Neale kid?" Scott smiled. Eastland was climbing back aboard; he was once again a co-conspirator. Once again, Scott was a step ahead of the president.

"We can go even further with our statement. We can suggest she was enticed to leave by the son of a famous author who is politically motivated, hostile—in other words, unreliable—

and who sought some kind of satisfaction in tearing down the President of the United States. If we announce before Mark Neale goes public, then he's on the defensive, not us."

Scott prided himself for his ability to think on his feet and synthesize new data into a workable, often brilliant, plan. This one wasn't brilliant and had its risks. But it wasn't bad, under the circumstances. Its strength was Eastland's nearly impeccable reputation with a public that had never found reason to doubt his character.

Eastland, however, was still unconvinced. "And if this doesn't work?"

Scott looked Eastland in the eye, coldly. "You are President Eastland because I solve your problems. I know how to keep secrets safe. We've had to, shall we say, contain a similar matter once before."

"What do you mean, Peter?"

"Let me handle this. I'm really good at this, remember?"

Eastland felt a chill. *Wasn't that an accident? "I'm really good at this." At what? Killing?* He stopped breathing.

Scott read his mind and didn't let the president ask what he was thinking. "Sir, whatever happened back then was an accident of war, and beyond that, you need to not know anything more."

And in a moment of arrogance mixed with panic, Peter Scott revealed a brutal truth, and regretted it immediately: "Think back, Mr. Congressman. You don't think I would have allowed anything to up-end our vision, do you?"

Eastland understood now. "Don't you dare touch my children."

A Secret Service agent knocked, informing the President that *Marine One* was ready.

Scott's next words probed Eastland's commitment. "So— we will solve this problem. Isn't that true, Sir?" Eastland froze and said nothing.

"I take that as a 'yes.'" Scott walked out.

Eastland walked silently to the security detachment that would walk him to the pad cleared for the helicopter. Once inside, he sat alone as the rotors wound up, and buried his face in his hands.

CHAPTER FIFTY-SEVEN

SEARCHING

Had there been no storm, the SEAL would have had help within minutes. But progress was slow. Chainsaws were the weapon of choice and fallen trees the enemy. Travel by foot was actually faster, but faced its own limits: darkness, no marked trails, and the same danger: fallen trees. None of the Washington-based professionals knew the island like Michael Erickson did. Nor did they know who he was or where he was leading Shannon.

But Erickson knew, and for the moment, he alone. He assumed they'd find and search his cabin (agents were, at that moment, searching it). His absence made him at least a potential threat. But they had little knowledge of an unassuming cabin a mile farther north and east.

Peter Scott had neither the authority nor information to direct the search. That was the realm of the Secret Service. But lines of authority are often defined by how hard one pushes, and Scott pushed himself into this effort with an intensity that amazed even the agent in charge.

"You will provide me with a portable radio. I want a vehicle to stand by, ready to take me to the search area as soon as roads are clear. Is that understood?"

"Yes, Mr. Scott, but—"

"And I want to talk to that SEAL. Right now." He'd overheard Lt. Mann's first call and probed him for specifics on the mystery man, until an angry Agent Boyd ordered Mann to concentrate on searching. Scott conceded but kept the radio.

⁛

The president leaned back in the cabin of *Marine One*, making its way west toward Duluth. He was afraid for his daughter; genuinely afraid. He also feared that a carefully-guarded secret—including Scott's oblique, horrifying revelation—was unraveling. He wondered whether, beyond a certain island family, the truth already had. His marriage would not likely survive. His reputation would be called into question; even his manhood. The career he and Scott had built over two decades would crumble overnight.

He felt something else. Self-loathing. A thirteen-year-old girl was in that shattered wilderness. That was how badly she wanted to get away from her father.

At Duluth, the crew of *Air Force One* was ready to fire the four huge engines the moment the president was aboard. Eastland mindlessly watched the city's lights along the shore of the lake below them. The helicopter crossed the shore, and a minute later circled the tarmac and landed precisely in the center of the pad reserved for it, fifty yards from the blue-and-gray jumbo jet. A government Suburban carried the president the short distance to the ramp leading into the big plane, this time with no waiting dignitaries, no speeches, no press corps. It was a short, silent, and lonely journey.

The door was closed and the ramp pulled away from the 747. It was Midnight when the first engine began spooling up as the president dropped wearily into his seat and was apprised of the progress in the search, which was none at all.

CHAPTER FIFTY-EIGHT

A REAL FATHER THIS TIME

Press Secretary McCay finally called the press together, just after Midnight. She'd given strict orders that all live feeds would, at Scott's instruction, be cut. She then announced to a shocked media and a stunned nation via CNN that the president and his family were safe and unharmed. "There are, thankfully, no injuries to the president, his family, or his staff. President Eastland is returning to Washington, since arrangements here have obviously been compromised by the storm. He has asked me to extend to the village of La Pointe his sincere gratitude at how bravely and efficiently local authorities responded to this emergency, and extends as well his sincere concern for those who may have suffered injuries or property loss or, God forbid, loss of life in this terrible storm."

Scott then signaled to end any live feeds. Assured that the next announcement was not being broadcast, he issued a warning: "This next item is off the record and can only be released at such a time as the White House deems appropriate. We're telling you in advance only as a courtesy, since you'll need some time to prepare your reports for what I'm about to tell you. Any attempt at early release will be dealt with severely. We will confiscate your notes, your equipment—"

"There's the little matter of the First Amendment," interrupted a reporter.

"For the next few hours, the First Amendment doesn't apply. If you can't abide by this, you are free to leave now. Do we understand each other?"

All nodded in agreement.

"Very well. It is my sad duty to report that at the height of the storm, the President's daughter, Shannon Eastland, disappeared."

There was a collective gasp. No one expected this. Injured? That could have been understood. Killed? Horrible thought, but again, quite conceivable. But disappeared? What on earth could that mean? They can't find her? Or she was kidnapped? How could she … disappear?

"We have," he said, "every reason to believe that she is alive and unhurt, and her disappearance is related to the storm. We think she simply got lost in the somewhat, ah, damaged area around the manor. It would be very easy to become disoriented. The lights are out, trees and fences are down. The president has left the island and is en route to Washington because the storm has compromised security. The First Lady and Aaron Eastland are staying until we find Shannon. And we're confident we'll find her soon."

When he was interrupted by a question about kidnapping, Scott had an idea. It was time to plant seeds of doubt, should the Neales emerge as participants in the crisis. "We cannot rule that out. In fact, there are a few individuals we're eager to talk to." This opened the floodgates.

"Are you suggesting that the president's daughter might in fact be kidnapped?"

"Obviously, the storm is our primary suspect. We certainly didn't anticipate how severe it would be, nor could any hypothetical assailant have done so. We assume she's simply lost. But we are ruling nothing out. Again, there are a few people we'd like to interview."

"Who, Mr. Scott?"

"There are some people we need to talk to—I can't comment further."

"Could she have been injured?"

"Again, we have no evidence of anything other than becoming lost in the confusion that accompanied this unfortunate storm."

Samantha Wells probed further. "Mr. Scott, is the Neale family among those you wish to interview?"

Thank you, Ms. Wells, Scott reflected. He paused, letting the question soak in. Then, coldly, "No comment."

⁑

The president tried to remember when he had felt this combination of fear, rage, and uncertainty before. To him, there was nothing worse than feeling things were out of his control, and that he was at the mercy of others.

He remembered a night as black as this, a quarter century earlier, drifting under a parachute toward a jungle he could not see. He remembered the anger at himself for not evading the surface-to-air missile that shredded his right wing and killed the Weapons System Operator in the seat just behind him, throwing his plane into a roll that made ejection almost impossible.

At first he'd handled that emergency like a pro. He'd radioed a Mayday with his location. Dropping through 2,400 feet, he didn't have time to wait for a response. He executed the escape from the stricken Phantom perfectly, waiting until the F-4 had rolled roughly upright before pulling the release, minimizing the chances of ejecting toward the ground.

Once clear of the plane, the fear hit him: he was alone, heading for a landing in enemy territory, the plane's explosion on impact announcing his approximate location. Once he hit the ground, he could only, by stealth and resourcefulness, postpone his capture. It was a helpless feeling—and he was feeling it again.

Shannon, my daughter. My second daughter. She knows what I did to her. She has no idea what happened more than twenty years ago. What "happened?" What I did. I intended to be a different father to you, Shannon. And, to your brother. I meant to be a real father this time.

Within ten minutes, the Air Force crew completed their preflight checks had their one passenger of note in the air. They made the turn to the south and then east toward the capital. Fifteen minutes after leaving the ground, the pilot informed the president that the island was passing below them, discernible only by occasional lights from emergency vehicles engaged in the frantic search for his daughter. The plane then veered southeast to avoid the storm that had shattered the Third of July.

CHAPTER FIFTY-NINE

PLAY IT AGAIN, SAM

Michael and Shannon zig-zagged through the forest, seemingly turning left and right haphazardly. But Michael knew exactly where he was headed, and how best to avoid cabins, wetlands, and especially the exposed area around the airport. It would be circuitous, but away from prying eyes.

Shannon nearly panicked when they came into a clearing, and a road. "Won't we be seen?"

"No," Erickson said. "See all those branches? Nobody's gonna be on this road for awhile. Let's go." His objective, he knew, was less than a half a mile away. His task? Hide the girl.

Police Chief Benson's task was obvious: *find* the girl. He had bristled when the Secret Service ordered him to patrol the rural areas of the island, far from his village's big day and what should have been the biggest task of his career. It was obviously their way of giving the real work of protection to their own people, reducing the chief of police to a traffic cop, now surrounded by impassible roads.

But the storm had not only isolated him west of the airport; it had imprisoned those hot shots in the village. When the first radio messages crackled with news of a child's disappearance, he smiled. The real action was coming his way. He had two vehicles, three deputies, and two volunteer firefighters. He also knew who lived away from town, and sent his deputies, on foot if necessary, to recruit anyone with trucks, chains, and chain saws, to begin clearing roads. Volunteer paramedics were assigned search-and-rescue duty.

He proudly radioed his accomplishments to the Washington cops, now stranded at least a mile from where they so desperately wanted to be. It was his show now. And he would play a significant role, albeit accidentally.

Scott sensed the risks of a local cop finding Shannon first and hearing things he shouldn't hear. He called the chief, and convinced Benson with a lie: the president requested that no one who found Shannon converse with her, but simply hold her until Scott could take her into custody. It was important to keep Benson in line until Scott could get there. It was vital that Scott get there fast.

⌗

Strobe called Samantha over to the van. "There's something you need to see, Sam." She crowded into the storm-battered vehicle, and Strobe explained what she'd see.

"I was reviewing the footage of the storm, and I found something interesting."

"Good shots of the boats in trouble? The rescue?" *This could be great visual stuff, maybe even marketable to the networks*, she thought, though only as backdrop for what was now the real story.

"No," Strobe confessed, "I wasn't shooting in that direction at all. I was shooting towards the guests, trying to get facial responses to the fireworks."

"So, you got nothing of the storm itself?" She regretted the loss of the media's most prized possession: footage. But Strobe, having missed that scene, seemed quite proud of what he did have.

"I may have something more interesting. Look at this."

He hit the "Play" button, and the clip began running, showing the crowd of dignitaries gazing upward, the flashes of aerial bursts reflected in their faces.

"So?"

"Keep watching." Strobe fast-forwarded through the fireworks; soon the trees and tent flaps began showing the signs of the intensifying wind; people began looking anxiously around. The Secret Service agent approaches the president to usher him inside; others begin to move about. The wind suddenly escalates; people are standing, struggling to move to safety. Objects begin blowing through the air. The tent covering the buffet table collapses. It is a scene of pandemonium.

"That's good footage, Strobe." *Not great though; probably not marketable,* she thought.

"There's more." He scrolled back the equivalent of about thirty seconds of real-time, then played again. "Look over *there*." He pointed to the left side of the screen showing the perimeter of the property. Samantha's mouth dropped open.

"I don't believe it."

"Shall I play it again, Sam?"

CHAPTER SIXTY

THE LONELIEST HOUSE

Mr. President, we hardly know what to say. We're praying for Shannon."

"Thank you."

"I hate to bother you at such a time, but if you could review these memos—I don't need them until later in the day." Nearly all of Eastland's daytime staff, having heard of the storm, returned to the White House, ready for whatever needed doing as the search progressed. It was an aide to his secretary who'd handed him a stack of documents. He took them, hoping they'd provide a few minutes' distraction. Which was exactly why his staff had gathered these routine items: it was an effort to ease the president's distress, at 3:00 in the morning Washington time, on what had already been a long and dreadful night.

Despite dozens of staff ready to do whatever was needed, the White House had never seemed so empty. The trip back to Andrews Air Force base was uneventful, the kind that normally would have found the president sleeping as *Air Force One* flew eastward toward the Capital. Eastland didn't sleep. On the contrary, he was in steady contact with his people on the island. There was no pre-dawn ceremony upon landing; just a quick transfer to the Marine chopper and the brief ride to the White House, before the first light of morning made its appearance, on the Fourth of July.

Eastland hastily disposed of the memos. In any other crisis he would have been in the Situation Room, fully engaged, decisive, putting the considerable assets of the United States to work as necessary. But the Situation Room offered nothing that he needed, and remained dark. This was not a war or a terrorist attack. It was more of an earthquake, and he was the epicenter.

As soon as he could, he retreated to the family quarters, empty except for him and his thoughts. He yearned for sleep, but there was unfinished business, and it was in Wisconsin.

He walked past the elegant rooms he and his wife had shared for three and a half years. Up to now, they had hoped to share it for another four. Instead, he found himself entering the room of his daughter. It was clean and orderly, a tribute to the staff that made sure no one in the First Family worried about errant socks on the world's most prestigious floors. He sat on the bed, looking at pictures on the wall. One showed a smiling toddler sitting on the desk of a U.S. congressman named Eastland, in another life when she knew him only as the perfect father he would never be. Another picture of father and daughter, taken only a few months ago, when he made a much-publicized speech to her civics class. She smiled there, too. But there was a wariness in her face that spoke volumes of what had transpired since that first picture.

No one was there to see Robert Alan Eastland, President of the United States, overcome by emotions that had long been absent. Not even when Shannon's earlier counterpart and her mother had met their end.

He was haunted by words he'd heard just two days before, in a small church in a small village from an ordinary man who would never know the power of the presidency, but who seemed more at peace than Eastland did with the greatest office his nation could bestow. Words like *integrity. Humility. He was right,* Eastland mused. *I have power. Why do I feel so helpless? I have exactly what I wanted. And I thought it would be worth any price to attain it. It wasn't. My family—families—paid too much.*

There was a knock on the door. "There's a call for you, sir. It's the First Lady."

"I'll take it in my study." He walked to the private office adjacent to the President's bedroom. He picked up the phone. Mary spoke when she heard the connection.

"Is it true?"

"Mary, this isn't a secure line."

"Is it true?"

Eastland sighed. "Yes. All of it."

She said nothing; she was on the verge of crying, or screaming, or simply collapsing. She had anticipated a denial she would not have believed. But he had admitted the truth, and that was not the response for which she had been prepared.

In the silence, knowing what he had done, she asked a question she hoped he wouldn't answer.

"Have you done this to anyone else?"

The president wanted desperately to evade her probe. But he could no longer lie convincingly.

"Just Monica." He had to wait for her response, until, in unmasked hatred, she spoke:

"How kind of you, Robert, to rape only your own daughters."

"Mary, I am so sorry—" his words trailed off; his voice breaking.

There was nothing more to say. It was a relief to have it on the table; no excuses, no attempts to evade the truth. Robert had violated every law, every norm, every promise; Mary now knew. That was it.

Sometimes, when a secret is revealed, curiosity drives a host of questions seeking every detail. Mary Eastland wanted no more information. What she knew was already more than she wanted. She shifted the conversation.

"Do you think she's okay?"

Robert Eastland gathered himself enough to respond. "They'll find her. It's an island. She can't go too far."

"But will she be all right when they find her?"

That was a harder question. Would she even be alive? Uninjured? And what about the injuries that no doctor could see, inflicted by her father?

"I hope so."

"I'm staying until she's found, Robert."

He smiled. Her firmness was comforting to him.

"I'm glad you will."

She hung up.

CHAPTER SIXTY-ONE

DAMAGE CONTROL

The knock startled an exhausted Gary Bates, who was desperate for sleep. He'd gone to his room an hour earlier, missing the press conference while filing a quick report before the *Post*'s deadline.

Earlier, he had tried to find the person that would have been his date had nature not interfered. He wondered if she'd learned anything new, but figured that the aftermath of the storm had rendered their concerns at least temporarily irrelevant. Most of all, he wondered if she was okay.

After an hour of fruitless searching, he'd gone back to the motel, relieved to discover it still intact. There was nothing else he could do now that he couldn't do later; besides, he was tired, and a few hours' sleep would help. He'd set his travel alarm for 4:30, thankful he was not dependent on the island's now-nonexistent electricity. First light would make possible what was impossible on the darkened island. Or so he thought.

He had been nursing a beer, which still contained all but one swallow of its contents. *Whoever this is had better have a very good reason.* He staggered to the door.

"Who on earth is it?"

"Samantha. Open the door. We have work to do."

"Excuse me?"

She didn't wait. She walked in on a startled correspondent, her flashlight illuminating a forty-something man in his underwear, beer in hand.

"Get dressed. You need to see some footage we have."

"Sorry, kid. I'm a print journalist. I can't use video footage, you may recall—"

"I don't want you to broadcast it. You need to *see* it. Hurry."

"Why do I need to see this little piece of home movies?"

"I think I have a clue about the young Ms. Eastland. She's in some kind of trouble, and she's not with the family."

"Where is she?"

"Gary, I don't think anyone knows." This got Bates' attention.

"What do you mean?"

"She disappeared."

"Who says?"

"Scott announced it at a not-for-public-knowledge briefing about half an hour ago. The one you were apparently sleeping through."

Knowing he should have been getting this information to Washington, he winced. "I'm screwed."

"Never mind. I think I can help you recover. I have information I doubt anyone else has; possibly not even the Feds."

"I'm listening."

"I think she went missing intentionally. I think the White House knows she did. And I think I can prove it."

"This I gotta see."

"Then get dressed. By the way—" She studied him quickly, from his face down to his waist, then up again, without any attempt to hide her opinion from him.

"Yes?"

"Lose that beer. And a few pounds."

Two minutes later, Gary was dressed, and following Samantha to the van.

⁜

The president had the White House switchboard connect him to his chief of staff. "Scott, what's the status?"

"I'm on it right now, Mr. President. I'm headed out to where they're beginning a coordinated search."

"Shouldn't you stay at the manor and let the field people take care of that?"

"No, Mr. President, I think I should be out there. In fact, I think I should find your daughter before she causes us any further embarrassment."

Eastland read the tone with which Scott spoke. "Peter, if you find her, what are your intentions?"

"The key is to find Shannon and assure that she talks to no one else, agreed?"

"Peter—your intentions. I need to know."

"Mr. President, actually, it's best if you stay out of the loop. Deniability."

"What are you saying, Scott?"

"You don't need to know. As you've often said, sir, one of my gifts is damage control."

"Tell me straight out: would you hurt my daughter to keep her quiet?"

Scott paused, hoping to defuse an escalating conversation. "Mr. President, this is the worst crisis we've faced since your little escapade in the Middle East. Getting us out of that one wasn't easy; this one may be even trickier."

"Oh, my God, Scott."

"Robert—I can call you 'Robert,' can't I? Did you really think that Kathryn's and Monica's silence was unnecessary? Now if you'll excuse me, I'm rather busy right now doing the aforementioned damage control. Good night, Mr. President."

CHAPTER SIXTY-TWO

TRANQUILITY, INTERRUPTED

Franklin Neale had chosen to skip the fireworks and all the attendant commotion. He stayed home for what began as a quiet evening, reading one of several books he'd recently purchased. Their subject was the Revolutionary War, of which he considered himself a minor expert. It was almost enough to distract him from the crisis in which his family was now immersed. He'd finished reading from the Psalms, his favorite sacred text. Ironically, as a working theology professor, he had only analyzed the sacred text. In retirement it became food for the soul, and tonight, with the crisis surrounding Shannon Eastland—and now his own family—Dr. Neale's soul needed what it offered.

He could see occasional flashes from the fireworks filtering through the trees; then the distant rumbles as the sound drifted eastward toward his cottage. Then came other flashes, far too bright and too far south to be fireworks. Lightning? The distinct sound of thunder confirmed it, and the rumbling gradually moved closer. Storms were common—gifts of God, he believed, to water the earth, purify the air, and offer a symphony of sorts, light and percussion to punctuate the darkened sky. He enjoyed even the risk, in his mind slight, of violent weather, part of nature's artful drama. He breathed deeply of the night air. *At least for this night*, he mused, *the weather may offer a taste of relief from the firestorm Mark revealed. On the coming day, that storm could consume my family.*

Within fifteen minutes, his secluded cabin felt the storm's fury, tempered by the density of the forest around him. A sudden blast of wind sent him running to secure open windows and furnishings on the screened-in porch. Even before the rain arrived, the power ceased and he got busy lighting candles. If this hit the manor, he thought, it could be a serious problem for the festivities. *All those boats—they're sitting ducks.* He turned on his hand-held marine radio and heard a steady stream of frantic calls for help. He prayed for the sailors, many of whom he knew well.

The storm began to recede. His cabin survived, not that he had any doubts. Probably a few trees down; he'd check tomorrow. In the lightning-punctuated darkness and steady rain, he chose to simply wait it out. He kept his marine radio on, relieved to hear the flood of calls for help dwindle. He lit a lantern, re-opened a couple windows, enjoyed the now-cooler breezes, and resumed his reading. The elderly man stayed up later than usual, embracing the fragile peace and solitude while waiting for his family to return. *They're staying in town longer,* he thought. *It's past midnight. I hope things are alright.*

It ended with footsteps on his gravel driveway, and a familiar voice.

"Doctor Neale? Michael Erickson. I'm coming in, and I have someone with me." Without knocking, the door opened and Michael walked in before the startled older man could respond.

"Michael—" Then he saw the soaked and disheveled form with him, and stopped cold. The president's daughter?

"No time to explain. I need to hide her here. Any suggestions?"

"Michael, why is she with you, and why do you want to hide her, and why here?"

"I'll explain later. People are trying to find her, and I—"

"Ms. Eastland, are you okay? Are you here voluntarily?"

"Please help me hide. I don't want my parents to find me."

Erickson glared at Franklin impatiently. "Satisfied? Now where can she hide?"

He thought for a moment. "Up there." He pointed to a panel in the ceiling, access to a small storage area.

Michael said, "Get me a chair," and began extinguishing candles. The elder Neale set a chair below the panel; Erickson stepped up, pushed the panel aside, looked briefly around with a flashlight. "Young lady, get up there. Don't move unless I tell you. Understand?"

Shannon stepped up on the chair; Erickson cupped his hands, in which she placed one foot; he lifted her through the passage. "But can't I have a flashlight?"

"No. You might use it; someone down here could see it. Just stay absolutely still."

He paused, then looked at the professor. "She's gonna need company up there, or she'll freak out. You're getting up there with her."

"Michael, you don't think I'm climbing through that opening."

"Actually, yes, and I'm gonna push you. Get up on the chair, and step here. And I mean *right* now. We don't have time to discuss this. Now!"

"And what are you going to do?"

"Gonna guard this place. Move!" He paused. "Dr. Neale, she'll be okay. I don't know what this is about. But I promise you: I won't let anyone hurt her."

Ten seconds later, Franklin Neale was squeezing into the cramped attic. Michael replaced the access panel and pushed the chair against the wall. He then headed for the door.

CHAPTER SIXTY-THREE

BETTY'S CLUE

Agent Nguyen was neither following orders nor breaking the rules. Agents understand the importance of chain-of-command. She had been directed to question the Neales and report anything she learned. What she had learned was plenty.

She had followed the first part of her orders, and had learned more than she bargained for. While she was a professional, she was no robot. Beyond obeying orders, her training included being resourceful. She would not—yet—report what she knew. Her job was to protect the First Family. Even if that meant protecting one member of that family from another.

While Tony had talked, the agent listened not only to Shannon's young friend but to the radio that reported the search unfolding less than two miles away. Mark and Debra listened as well, and didn't like what they heard.

Those charged with finding Shannon had no idea why she fled. Did she simply panic, terrorized by the storm? Strange, but possible. Was this a stunt, a spontaneous adventure gone wrong? Unlikely. She may have an end game in mind—but certainly she's not running away from anyone. She's the president's daughter, living a charmed life, after all.

From the village of La Pointe, three main roads to the east fan out to envelope the island. One road roughly follows the island's southern shore, a densely populated area, and would be searched by local people who knew it well. But if Shannon is actually escaping something, she'd want to avoid being seen. Verdict: since her intentions are unclear, don't discount the woods.

Big Bay Road follows the north shoreline, which runs to the northeast, as does the island as a whole. On the lake side of Big Bay Road, shoreline cabins are frequent and set back in the trees. The Fire and Rescue station is there, not far from the village. The inland side of the road is more sparsely developed except for the airport, a mile from town. The land is heavily wooded, and the Capser Trail runs through there. A hasty conference between local and federal authorities determined to focus on that expansive wooded area. A "command post"—a Suburban with U.S. government plates—ventured as far as Big Bay Road allowed.

Middle Road, true to its name, goes directly east through the forested center of the island, across land dotted with occasional homes until meeting the lake after a mile or so, and swinging north. County and state law enforcement and volunteers were tasked with searching along Middle Road.

One of the cabins, set well back in the woods along the north side of Middle Road, belonged to Michael Erickson.

As the agents searching the woods reported their movements, it became clear that the Erickson cabin was drawing their attention. For nearly an hour, Mark Neale and his family hoped they'd find Shannon there, though with Michael Erickson's penchant for the dramatic that couldn't be assured.

The agents found and searched the Erickson cabin: no trace of him or the girl.

Agent Nguyen was alarmed by word that Peter Scott had arrived on the scene. Her instincts, coupled with years of observing this driven man, told her that Scott's presence was not necessarily good news. She kept that to herself until she heard that he and an agent had set out on their own from the Command Post. Something was going on.

That "something" began innocently enough. Scott arrived at the government vehicle that served as a Command Post for the eastward-moving search at 2:00 AM. He was tired, angry, and frantic. In his mind, the First Daughter must be found—

soon. His barrage of questions was met primarily by a chorus of "I don't knows." The girl was still missing; beyond that, the general consensus was that she was moving east. Erickson, by now her probable companion, was also missing.

One of the volunteer paramedics had a clue she didn't know she had. Betty Fanning, always eager to help, was within half a mile of her home on the north shore of the island. Despite some damage to her home, she joined her neighbors who were standing at the Command Post, awaiting orders on where to search next.

Chief Benson was annoyed. It was almost three in the morning; he and his volunteer search parties were eager to get to work, but first had to help give directions to the Washington people, who knew virtually nothing about the remote parts of Madeline Island. Agent in Charge Boyd described the search pattern in general terms, the locals translated that into specific landmarks, usually by who lived at or near the spot the agent described.

"Okay—we've got cabins on each side of the road. We'll focus on those between La Pointe and the airport. She's on foot in the dark with a lot of debris to deal with, so she won't get very far. You: check any cabins on the north side of the road from here east for a half mile."

"Oh, that would be just South of the Grayton place."

"Okay—Grayton. Now (pointing to the next volunteer) you: start the same search on the south side.

"Now you—that spotlight got good batteries?"

"Yeah—they're new."

"Good. Start searching the south side at the Gray ..."

"Grayton."

"Yeah—the Grayton place, going farther east along the road about another half a mile—yes, the road's still impossible for a vehicle and you'll have to walk. Report back every twenty minutes or so.

"Now you:" (speaking to Betty Fanning) "Start at this Grayton place and go east on the north side another half a mile. Hopefully by the time you get there, we can move the Command Post that far. I want to keep us moving northeast, okay? Okay. Half mile past Grayton … does anyone live there?"

"Well, yes," said Betty. "That's about at the driveway to the Neale place."

Peter Scott asked Chief Benson as calmly as he could, "Neale?"

"Yes. Franklin Neale lives back there, and his son's staying there too. It's on the lake, way back from the road."

As others received their instructions, Peter Scott stepped back from the group, and signaled for Agent Barker. He handed the radio to a nearby agent and discretely confirmed that his handgun was still with him. He and Barker held a whispered conversation noticed by no one there, and the two of them slipped away.

CHAPTER SIXTY-FOUR

I CAN LEAD YOU THERE

Over her radio fifteen minutes later, Agent Nguyen heard someone at the command post ask where Scott was. *He should be right there,* she thought. Another voice from another radio volunteered that Scott had been seen heading northeast through the woods; Barker's absence was curious, but she was more concerned about what Peter Scott was up to. Her instincts told her that it was strange for Scott to be directly involved in the search.

"Mr. Neale," she asked, "what is northeast of there?" Mark's breathing stopped. He knew exactly who now was in harm's way. "My father's cabin."

There was a pause. Then the writer continued: "If the road is clear, I can lead you there."

"Let's go."

The agent wasted no time arguing when Debra and their son insisted on accompanying her. They got into the Suburban and headed toward the Command Post, dodging debris, driving over smaller tree branches, around others.

Twenty minutes later, Mark Neale and Kim Nguyen left Tony and Debra in the Suburban with the motor running. They joined the agents and Chief Benson, who were gathered in front of another federal vehicle, illuminated by its headlights. The discussion soon focused on a cabin, the object of two very different search parties.

Gathered with Samantha and Strobe in the WLOW news van, Bates was watching the news van's monitor. He was curious, but also impatient.

"Okay," Bates said, "I see people running for cover, trees blowing down, miscellaneous tables and chairs taking flight. This I already know."

"Watch again." Strobe rewound, then hit the Play button. "Look here—" he pointed to the two boys and First Daughter watching the fireworks, then moved it frame by frame into the chaos of the storm. "Now look here—" Sam pointed to a shadowy figure in barely discernible footage, shot in near darkness but standing out only because it was moving in a direction different from the others. Instead of joining the throng headed into and behind the manor, this person, small and probably female, headed directly for the black mass on the left of the screen that marked the hedge bordering the property.

"That's Shannon, Gary."

"Right into that hedge?"

"I have one more piece to show you. Strobe?"

He pushed a couple buttons, and the earlier conversation by the children was shown.

"I think I can make out some of the words."

Ten minutes later, the TV van and its three occupants were headed down the debris-covered streets dodging debris along the way toward Big Bay Road.

CHAPTER SIXTY-FIVE

THE FINISH LINE

Before the approaching dawn, the secluded Neale cabin became the finish line of a race between one Navy SEAL, one chief of staff, and one Secret Service agent. Two county deputies, following the Capser Trail, would never find what or who they were looking for.

From the southwest, Peter Scott was closing in. He had instructed Barker to lead at a distance. Scott intended Barker to arrive first. Scott had given the radio to an agent at the Command Post, not wanting any distractions at just the wrong time. He deemed it best if he were out of reach. It was a serious mistake.

What moonlight filtered through the receding clouds barely illuminated Franklin Neale's white frame-cottage. Lanterns and candles had been extinguished; Michael Erickson had made sure of that. It was quiet. Franklin and Shannon remained, still and hushed, in a small attic over the kitchen.

Once Erickson had secured the eldest Neale and the girl, he set out to intercept any pursuers. Sooner or later "they" would come, whoever "they" happened to be. He neither knew nor cared about the agendas of the parties headed his way. To him, they all were potential threats. He headed west, into the trees around the cabin.

During the last half hour of darkness Michael heard and then saw a lone individual coming up the driveway toward the cottage. The man on the driveway stopped, then moved slowly toward the cabin. Erickson crouched behind a fallen tree, and took stock of his adversary. The person he saw was not dressed for travel in the forest; his light-colored shirt and windbreaker made him visible against the shadows. Whoever it was, Erickson noted, they were better than average at moving over rough terrain. They could be heard, but only faintly; they knew how to move with stealth. *This*, Erickson mused, *is a pro*. In this he was right. The person he saw was a veteran, a bit rusty and older, but not without residual skills being pressed into service once again. He seemed to be the only other person seeking the cabin. In this, Erickson was wrong.

Moving from the south, Lt. Mann came into view. Erickson was pleased to observe this intruder's likely path would take him west of the cabin, possibly far enough that he might miss it entirely, and wind up at the lakeshore. That suited Erickson just fine; he decided to let him pass. As yet unseen and from the southwest, Scott was shadowing Barker.

Erickson knew he'd eventually be dealing with more than one potential adversary. It was best to stay low, quiet, and immobile, until he could seize the advantage. He would only move when someone actually entered the cabin. He would confront that threat—by hand if possible; he hoped his rifle could remain silent. So far, that threat hadn't entered the cabin. Erickson would prefer to keep it that way.

⁂

The van from WLOW-TV and its three occupants were unsure about where to go next. They made their way out of the village, driving around fallen trees, rolling over downed electrical wires (no longer dangerous in the absence of power), debris from damaged structures, and past scores of stunned islanders and search parties wandering around with little direction.

⁂

Barker approached the cabin. Erickson, intent on tracking his movement, didn't see Scott, fifty yards behind. Scott was pleased that Barker (now visible to Erickson) would be the first to probe the cabin. Barker listened outside the kitchen window for signs of life inside. Hearing no sounds, the agent burst through the door, gun drawn, finding what appeared to be an empty cabin. That sudden burst of sound and light startled Erickson, and the SEAL as well; the latter would have missed the cabin entirely had it not been for the agent's commotion. Lt. Mann was still too far away to see the cabin, but recognized the sound of a door being opened and moved toward it, while Scott and Erickson did the same.

CHAPTER SIXTY-SIX

NO SURRENDER

Once the agent saw no one in the cabin, he signaled with his flashlight; this was Scott's cue. Then the agent scanned around the cabin, quiet except for the breeze ruffling the curtains near the open windows. He saw nothing amiss, until he noticed a chair along the wall, right where it should be—but soiled with muddy footprints. Another look, and he saw an access panel in the ceiling, and drew his conclusion. Picking up a broom, he quietly moved directly under the trap door, and with a sudden upward movement, jammed the broom handle against the ceiling with a loud crack. Shannon almost choked down a shriek. Almost, but not quite.

"I know you're up there Shannon, so come down now. This is Agent Barker. You're safe, but you need to get down."

It was Franklin who spoke, fearful of inviting more forceful action if they didn't comply. "There are two of us. We're coming down." Barker put the chair under the trap door, which was now being carefully slid aside by the elderly professor, who helped Shannon down to the waiting Federal agent, and with the agent's help made his own way out of the attic.

Michael Erickson had heard the sharp impact of the broom against the ceiling, then the voices. It was time to risk it. He moved quietly but quickly toward the cabin, pausing momentarily just off the porch. While Barker was distracted with moving chairs and bodies exiting the attic, he slipped unnoticed into the doorway.

"Nobody move."

Barker, lacking a clear target, suppressed his urge to turn and fire. He was also angry that he had heard no one approach the door. The noises of creaking floorboards and moving chairs had masked their approach. He did not recognize the voice.

Franklin Neale did. "Michael! Am I glad it's you."

"Who's that with you?"

"It's okay," Franklin replied. "He's a Secret Service agent. Everything's under control now."

"I'll decide that," Erickson said. He entered the cabin but stayed with his back to the door. "Agent whoever-you-are, put the gun down."

Barker was calm, but firm. "No."

"Put the gun down."

"I'm keeping it, and you'll have to trust me."

"Michael, you can trust him. I trust him."

Movement was all anyone could hope to see in the cabin, lit only by Barker's flashlight, gradually losing what was left of its power. Agent Barker sensed Erickson was within about six feet, but could not discern his intent. A member of the First Family was present, and his responsibility included protecting the young woman who at that moment was in the line of fire.

Erickson did not have time to ponder his dilemma because just then, it got worse.

"I think all of you need to drop your weapons." The voice was Peter Scott's. He was holding his gun with both hands, and pointed directly at Michael Erickson's back.

Michael responded in a steady, deliberate tone: "No."

"I repeat: drop your weapons."

It was Barker's turn. "Mr. Scott, I am not surrendering my weapon."

Scott turned on his flashlight, illuminating the four people standing in front of him, two of them holding weapons. Again, he called Erickson and Barker to relinquish their weapons.

"I am giving the orders at the moment. Now both of you put down your weapon, slowly. Any other movement, any movement at all, and I will shoot." Now it was Michael Erickson's turn. "You're Scott—Eastland's gatekeeper. I think I saw you out there. You're good. Marines? Special Forces? In any case, you're probably pretty good with that gun. You may have noticed there are three of us here holding weapons on each other. I suspect this agent here can hit a target or two. And you ought to know that in my humble opinion, I'm better than both of you."

"I suggest you shut up, and now, sir," Scott replied. "I'll consider any quick move a threat, and I will take that threat out. Am I understood?"

Michael was in no mood for compliance. "You also may have figured out that you can only shoot one of us at a time. Now—I'm not sure I care for either one of you or who you work for, but if it's all the same to you I'll side with the young lady here. Shoot me, and maybe your fellow Fed shoots you. Shoot her—I will shoot you. Whose bullet would you like, Scotty?"

CHAPTER SIXTY-SEVEN

CHANNEL 16

Shannon shook; Franklin Neale feared that the wrong word, the wrong move, the wrong tone of voice would start a small, short, deadly war. He sensed rightly that things were moving toward a conclusion, and no one in the room knew what that would be.

There are critical moments that may define a person. Some decisions allow no time for reflection on the cost. It was just such a moment for Franklin Neale. No essay he ever published, no lecture he ever presented, could prepare him for the course of action he would take, one which could extract from him the ultimate sacrifice.

It would also be overlooked by everyone present for its brevity and simplicity. With his back to the darkened kitchen counter, he discretely felt behind him, and found his handheld marine radio, still powered up from earlier in the evening. Taking advantage of the three armed men focused on each other, he slowly set it on its side, with the "talk" button on the counter. With the same hand still hidden behind him, he moved the hardbound book he'd been reading into position on top of the radio, hoping the weight would depress the switch just enough to activate the handheld's microphone, and broadcast over Channel 16, the universal hailing channel. He'd be unable to see if this actually worked. As it turned out, he succeeded.

Then, sensing that the most vulnerable person in the cabin was Shannon, the professor took her arm and pulled the girl behind him. He would, upon later reflection, wonder if he expected anyone to shoot; in the moment, his thoughts were not all that complete. He simply released himself to whatever was about to transpire.

"Please, gentlemen, there is a child here." Then, a bit more loudly for the benefit of any unseen ears on Channel 16, "This is the president's daughter, gentlemen. I don't see any benefit if someone starts shooting. Especially with Ms. Eastland here."

"I'm past calculating benefits," Michael countered. "If someone's going to die here, and if it's me, I won't die alone." Michael had decided. He would take Scott out. Scott was the most suspicious to him. He would then take his chances with the agent's handgun. He had no time to think past that first desperate attempt at resolving his crisis. Whatever happened to the child and her would-be rescuers would be sorted out in a few seconds. Scott's strange behavior was the wild card, and had to be dealt with first. Michael tensed, and began to raise his weapon.

Franklin interrupted the escalation. He spoke with passion, and rage. "There will be no violence in this place. This is a place of peace. I will not permit … "

Scott shouted at the professor. "It's time for you to leave, Mr. Neale. Now!" He pointed his weapon at the professor's chest from six feet away, screaming, "Now!"

Michael Erickson responded, this time with amazing calm. "It's okay, Doc. It's okay. Go tell someone what's going on out here. Go. Please."

"For once, I agree with the bushman." Scott lowered his weapon, if only slightly. "We just need some time to settle this. There are police and federal agents not far from us. Go ahead, Professor. Fill them in on who's here."

Franklin saw no choice. He squeezed the young woman's hand, reassured her, and walked reluctantly, slowly, out of the house.

⁜

Angelo Guerrero, the Coast Guardsman monitoring marine radio traffic, was frustrated. After all the commotion of the past few days, everyone in the Bayfield Station was on edge, and the storm had stretched their resources to the limits. Now, some idiot was holding down the "Talk" button on their VHF radio, effectively holding Channel 16, the major hailing and emergency channel, hostage.

"Just let go of the stupid button!" Angelo yelled to no one in particular. At least it was the middle of the night, with marine traffic finally quiet. Still, it was the emergency channel, and no one, accidentally or otherwise, should lock other callers out.

He picked up some voices, apparently engaged in an intense conversation. Listening more closely—there was nothing else to do anyway at nearly four in the morning—he heard bits and pieces of that conversation. Not much, but enough: " ... Eastland ... shooting ... die ... "

He switched to a police band, and broadcast to whoever in law enforcement was within radio range. "This is Bayfield Coast Guard, hailing any law enforcement or federal security on Madeline Island. Please monitor Marine Channel 16. Repeat: you really need to monitor Channel 16."

CHAPTER SIXTY EIGHT

AN AGENT NAMED SHADOW

Bates, Wells, and Strobe noticed government vehicles on the move. Guessing that they were headed to the island's airport and finding no one attempting to stop them, Strobe followed. The three intrepid journalists were stopped at a collection of half a dozen emergency, law enforcement and federal vehicles, and would learn that they were south and west of the Neale cabin. It had taken some time to get there; trees had to be cleared along the way. Strobe parked the van alongside an ambulance and switched the van's lights and engine off. People from various agencies were milling about, unsure of what to do next except to wait for Agent-in-Charge Boyd to decide. No one seemed concerned that the road beyond this point had not been cleared. Something nearby, apparently, had brought the searchers here.

Two things were clear. One: the conversation—the confrontation—on Channel 16 had multiplied the urgency of the search. Two: no one there was eager to see the media nearby. They were kept at a distance, standing behind the government vehicle that had brought Agent Nguyen and the Neales to the scene. Mark and Debra were standing arm and arm, while Tony, head down, hands folded, leaned against the Suburban. Their only light was that provided by the vehicle's headlights. Agent Boyd gave orders to the journalists: Make no attempt to film the scene or interview anyone. Observe a strict perimeter and allow authorized vehicles unimpeded access. This area was being treated as the scene of a crime. It would become a battlefield.

At first, there was not much to observe. They were within earshot of some of those milling around, although the idling vehicles muffled any spoken words.

While Agent Nguyen and the gathered federal assets confirmed what little they knew, the reporters approached Mark, Debra and Tony. Gary Bates ignored the no-interview order. "Mr. Neale, we know something's seriously wrong concerning Shannon Eastland, and that she ran away during the storm. We know your son and the Eastland children shared some troubling information. What's bothering them?"

Tony, looking toward his father, replied. "I can't tell you."

Bates was not one to take a *No Comment* answer. "We'll find out, you know."

Debra responded angrily: "He can't tell you!" Agent Nguyen, startled by the outburst, shot a stern, "back off" look toward Gary Bates; Samantha intervened. "Gary, Strobe—let me talk to them alone." The reporter and camera operator walked back to the van.

"Tony, Mr. and Ms. Neale—let's be honest. I'm a reporter. If I were you, I wouldn't talk to me. But regardless of how nosey we can be, I don't want that kid hurt, nor do you. Is there anything we can do that will help her?"

The conversation ended for the moment. They saw, in the uneven light of lanterns, flashlights, and headlights, a form emerging from the direction of the cabin. It was an older man, walking unsteadily. They guessed correctly that it was Dr. Neale.

"Dad!" Mark instinctively began walking—running, almost—toward his father, but was stopped by an agent. "Sorry, sir. Not until we've talked to him. Step back." By this time, other Federal agents had intercepted the elder Neale, ordered him to stop and asked him a few quick questions. Then, to the horror of his son, they frisked his father. Agent Nguyen, alarmed at how distressing this appeared to the older man's family, explained. "It's okay. It's our procedure any time we encounter someone we didn't expect."

The senior Neale stood, calm and dignified, unbowed by the process. After a few minutes of interrogation and receiving stern instructions about not speaking about the events of the morning, Franklin was escorted over to his son, daughter-in-law, and grandson. A tearful embrace marked their reunion. They were led to a Sheriff's SUV. The three journalists stood nearby, knowing that any attempt to engage the family would be challenged.

"Where's the kid?" Gary Bates was the first to ask about who wasn't there. "Do you think she's all right?"

Samantha was hopeful. "My guess is she's still back there in the woods, being well guarded by legions of agents. If she were in trouble, there'd be panic all over the place."

Bates was still uneasy. "I'd rest easier if I saw her."

Samantha echoed his concern, this time loudly enough for the occupants of the SUV to hear through the open windows. "I really wish you'd tell us if Shannon Eastland is all right."

Gary caught her intention, and added to the bait. "Yeah. But I'm beginning to suspect the worst. I think she's in serious trouble … "

Franklin, overwhelmed and unable to tolerate the tension, blurted out, "She's okay."

"What do you mean?"

"She's at my cabin. Michael—he's a neighbor—found her and brought her to me. She's okay. Now there are government men taking care of her. Mr. Scott, with a guy named Barker."

Strobe turned to his colleagues. "That's 'The Shadow.'"

Bates was confused. "'The Shadow'?"

Strobe responded. "The agent riding herd on the kids at the fireworks."

The journalists looked at each other; Samantha looked at Strobe. "Are you sure?"

"Yeah—absolutely. He was taking orders from Scott."

CHAPTER SIXTY-NINE

A REWARD FOR LOYALTY

D. C. Barker was a twenty-year veteran with the Secret Service, with seven years prior to that in government employ. He had served his country with distinction, wearing proudly the mantle of the Green Beret. Following his discharge, he'd found a fellow veteran in a position to be helpful. "Scottie" had connections and used them to land Barker his chance to apply to the Service. It was a favor Barker never forgot.

He was nothing if not loyal. He knew to whom he owed his career, and while his allegiance was to the Service, there was a more personal debt of honor, and in the early hours of July 4th, loyalty to Peter Scott would not be reciprocated.

Now there were four. The professor had been gone long enough that his footsteps were no longer heard in the tense, silent cabin. Scott was standing slightly behind Barker, facing the girl and Erickson. "Barker: get that rifle."

The agent complied. Suspicious of Erikson, Barker wanted both hands on the rifle, and handed his service pistol to Scott. He stepped forward, eyes locked on Erickson. He slowly reached out, never taking his eyes off the man in denim, taking Michael's weapon and then stepping backwards toward Scott. There was no way to anticipate what happened next.

Barker took his eyes off Michael Erickson and looked down at the remarkable rifle he held. For just a moment, he relaxed; an authority on guns, he admired what was clearly a carefully chosen, well cared-for piece, one that now distracted him for just a moment—

Without warning, Peter Scott brought the butt of Barker's own pistol sharply down on the back of the agent's neck; there was a sickening sound of metal hitting skin, muscle, cartilage, and the further sounds of the agent collapsing limply to the floor, the gun he had admired underneath his motionless body. Shannon gasped; Erickson froze. This, he sensed, was very bad news for this agent, for himself, and the girl.

Scott calmly reached down, placing Barker's weapon on the floor, and lifting the rifle with his left hand, still holding his own pistol with his right. He found and released the rifle's safety, holstered his handgun, and pointed the muzzle of the rifle at the fallen agent's back.

Michael spoke. "Are you going to kill him?"

Scott looked up and smiled. "No, Mr. Erickson, you are."

CHAPTER SEVENTY

THE COMPROMISE

Mark Neale needed a reality check for a very uneasy feeling. "Dad, any sign of Michael Erickson?"

The elderly man sighed. "I didn't want to worry you, but yes. He's there too."

Gary Bates didn't like what he was thinking. Feeling, actually. *Why Scott?* He stopped thinking as a journalist and began thinking about a fellow human being who may be in trouble. He turned to Samantha, away from the nearby authorities, and whispered, "We've got to get someone to see this tape."

"Why?"

"I'm not sure, but things just don't fit. Let's find a way to show someone in charge what we've got. Let them figure it out."

"Yeah, but they're not listening to civilians right now."

"Then we need to get their attention, in a hurry."

Sam turned suddenly to her camera operator. "Strobe: set up for a face shot."

"Huh?"

"Put the command vehicle in the background. Now."

"Yeah, sure, Sam. Then they'll confiscate the camera and send us all to Leavenworth."

"Don't worry about Leavenworth. We've got to cause a scene, Strobe. I hope they *do* want the video."

"Have you taken leave of your senses?"

"One more thing: don't actually start recording. I want them to see what's already there."

Gary Bates caught on. *Not bad, my little rookie.*

The camera was set up; the lights switched on, right in front of the stunned command post. Samantha grabbed the mic and began speaking. She'd make this one up on the fly, speaking loudly enough to make sure they heard every word.

"This is Samantha Wells reporting live" (she wasn't) "from a remote area of Madeline Island, where at this very moment a frantic search for Shannon Eastland, daughter of the president, is winding down. It is believed that she ran away from her family during the storm, and has been until now running from the president through the forest on Madeline … "

By this time, an agent was determined to stop what he assumed was an actual broadcast. It felt awkward, thinking that he may wind up on live television, but he stepped in front of the camera anyway. "You'll have to end this right now, Ma'am. Your orders were clear: there would be no media coverage until we say so."

Sam, playing her part, had pushed the microphone toward the agent; now she brought it back toward herself. Her impromptu scam was working, but not well enough. He was being too polite; the whole point was to make him angry enough to confiscate something.

"The First Amendment gives me a right to broadcast whatever I please. Step aside, sir. I'm busy."

"Ma'am, I'm ordering you to turn off the camera. Now."

It was Gary's turn to pour gasoline on the fire. "Agent, you're right. I wish to formally report that she has in fact been filming against your direct orders. I'm afraid it'll be all over the networks by 7:00 a.m., and who knows what she's already got? Sorry, Miss Wells, but rules are rules, and we reporters have an obligation to obey them."

Sam smiled to herself; *Gary, you're a great actor.* "I don't care what he says! I'm within my rights to film whatever I want!"

Gary pressed his case, raising his voice to match Sam's, and attracted more attention from the knot of agents at the end of the driveway. "She's got some pretty devastating video in that camera—some stuff you definitely don't want on CNN this morning!"

Agent Kim Nguyen walked over and joined the fray. "I want your camera, Ms. Wells."

"Good morning, Agent Nguyen. Actually, I'm quite eager to show you what I've got. It's in the truck."

Inside the crowded van, Strobe narrated the action, and Samantha provided the interpretation of what lip movements could be discerned. Agent Nguyen watched the most frightening video of her career; not unlike the grainy footage of Dallas, 1963. In this case it portrayed what may be about to happen to the child she was sworn to defend. There was Peter Scott, Chief of Staff to the President, apparently telling Barker: *Find her. And when you do, silence her, by whatever means necessary. No questions. That's an order.*

Moments later a shaken Agent Nguyen emerged from the van and met Agent Boyd walking toward her.

"Agent Nguyen: what's going on here?"

Instead of answering her fellow agent, she turned to the three journalists.

"Thank you for your assistance. You need to leave, immediately. I don't have time to explain why." She turned to Chief Benson. "I need you to escort these people and their vehicle back toward the village."

Benson saw no reason for this; he also resented being ordered around by a federal agent. Specifically, a female agent. "Why, and why me? Why not one of your ag—"

"Like I said: No time to explain. Move them back to the village, immediately." The Chief looked at Agent Cooper, whose icy glare moved Benson from defiant to defeated. "Let's go, people. And I don't know why either."

Nguyen was not quite finished. "Immediately!" Thirty seconds later, all the agents could see were retreating taillights, dodging branches littering the road to La Pointe.

Cooper backed up his colleague—it was what a disciplined agent does. But when the journalists were on their way, he turned to Nguyen. "What are you thinking, Kim?"

"Our subject is in trouble. I believe her safety has been compromised."

"But this Erickson guy couldn't hurt her if he wanted to. The girl's with Barker, and Mr. Scott is there—"

"It's not Erickson! I have reason to believe Scott and Barker *are* the compromise."

CHAPTER SEVENTY-ONE

BY ANY MEANS NECESSARY

The president had made his decision. It would end. Now.

Not knowing all that had transpired in the last hour, he picked up the phone on his desk, and was linked to the agent in charge. "This is the president. I need to talk to Peter Scott."

There was a pause, as Cooper, having just heard Nguyen's strange accusation about the second most powerful person in the country, pondered what to say to his commander-in-chief. He chose to say as little as necessary. "Sir, Mr. Scott isn't here."

"Where is he? This is urgent."

"He's with your daughter, Sir." Cooper immediately regretted his words.

The president gripped the phone and leaned forward; all color drained from his face. Scott, his ally, mentor, and confidant, was now his enemy, a clear and present danger, a threat to things that were becoming dearer to the president with every passing minute. The agent assumed he had just provided good news, and was shocked at Eastland's response.

"Agent Cooper—listen and listen carefully. You must get to Mr. Scott, now. You must disengage him from any contact with my daughter. You must restrain him, if necessary. By any means necessary. Do you understand?"

"No, Sir, I don't understand, but—"

"This is a direct order. I don't have time to explain. Mr. Scott must not, repeat, not, be allowed to be alone with my daughter. Again—stop him, at all costs!"

Agent Cooper went pale. After a moment of silence, he responded. "Mr. President, I suggest we switch to a secure radio link."

Eastland almost agreed, embarrassed at not doing so. Then he realized that a non-secure link was a gift. The more ears hearing his order, the greater the number of people motivated to stop the president's aide. Even Scott might hear and back off, realizing the trouble he was in.

"Request denied. Do you copy my order?"

"I copy: we are to detain Peter Scott by any means necessary, until further clarification."

"Thank you." The president hit the "End" button, cutting himself off from the stunned island.

The agent in charge looked to Kim Nguyen. "Let's go." Flashlights in hand, weapons ready, their mission was now clear: find and protect Shannon Eastland, and secure Peter Scott. Nothing else matters. Every second counts.

The Navy SEAL had his instructions now. After the president's order, he began moving, double time, toward the cabin.

At the command post, the Neales are being watched by Chief Benson and the agents. Nobody spoke. Everyone sensed that something was going to happen.

A minute later, a sound. Muffled … Was that a gunshot? The agents reacted immediately, looking toward each other when another sound—this time the crisp, loud, unmistakable *crack* of a high-powered rifle. The agents drew their guns and shined their flashlights around the perimeter. Inside the perimeter, nobody moved.

For two veteran agents closer to the cabin, the muffled sound clearly came from inside the building. Then, a muffled scream—and then the distinctive report of a sniper's rifle, barely a hundred yards ahead, followed immediately by the sound of shattering glass. They began running, guns drawn, jumping fallen logs, pushing brush out of the way, fully expecting the worst.

The SEAL had the best view. Forty yards from the cabin, he heard Scott's voice, shrill and angry. Then a figure in silhouette, framed by a window and back lit by early dawn radiating through the window on the far wall. Suddenly, the figure's hand comes up … a shot, a scream, the hand coming up again—Lt. Mann took his shot, the window exploded, and there was no longer a human form in the window anymore.

CHAPTER SEVENTY-TWO

THE FOG OF WAR

Wednesday, March 15, 1978

At about midnight, Israel demonstrated that they'd had enough of Yassir Arafat's killers.

The cloudy night above the village of Khiam in southern Lebanon was illuminated by flares fired from Israeli artillery stationed on Israel's northern border. Thus began Israel's response, code-named "Stone of Wisdom." The flares were followed by a devastating artillery barrage, as two tank columns poured north and Israeli fighter-bombers, including F-15's fresh from Lockheed's St. Louis factory, pummeled the village from above. This was just one of four major thrusts into Lebanon, in Israel's effort to create a buffer between its own people and the terrorists who made Lebanon their base.

The Palestinian fighters, vastly outnumbered and out-gunned, fled, as well as the residents of the villages unfortunate enough to be located too close to Israel: Naqura, Bint Jubail, Marun al Ras, Uzai, Yarin, and others. Tyre's port facilities were bombed. The coastal highway was ravaged by Israeli gunboats just offshore, discouraging any attempt to reinforce the PLO from the north.

Within seventeen hours, Israel would control six miles and more of Lebanon's southern border, 400 square miles in all, despite the 30,000 Arab League's peacekeeping forces (mostly Syrian) that preferred to watch the carnage from a safe distance, north of the Litani River. Syrian jets provided air cover for the retreating Palestinians but made no effort to engage the superior

Israeli planes. People fled from beleaguered Beirut. 400 people died overall, 130 of them civilians, 14 of them Israeli soldiers. And the "peace process," of which the previous Christmas Day had been a pivotal accomplishment, seemed to be buried in the rubble of places like Khaim.

Israel would achieve its objective: a buffer zone on her North. Yassir Arafat also would win; he had brought the peace process to a halt, if only temporarily. The only losses, it seemed, would be the Palestinians, the Lebanese farmers and the shopkeepers who now had no shops to keep.

Kathryn Rossberg, the first Mrs. Robert Alan Eastland, was nervous and confused at the abrupt change in plans, but she was glad to be leaving Lebanon without her husband. It had been an ugly confrontation, every bit as horrible as she'd feared, which was why she had put it off so long. It hadn't been her intention to address his behavior while away from home, but she couldn't hold it back any longer. What Eastland had done to Monica disgusted Kathryn. She had made it clear that, once she returned to the States, their marriage was over. And if she had anything to say about it, so was his political career.

Peter Scott heard the whole story, including her threat. Threat? Her promise. In her mind, so what if Scott knew? She'd never liked him, and he'd never liked her. Anyway, soon the whole country would know.

That had been the previous day, before they found themselves in the middle of a war. But even with hostilities almost within sight of their hotel, there was something strange in Scott's insistence that she and her daughter take this late flight out of Beirut to Amman, while her husband flew separately to Cairo to take a reading on Egyptian intentions. Especially strange, since it was neither a military nor a commercial flight but a private charter, while a war was going on. However, she would get out of Lebanon. Feelings about Scott aside, *he's doing the right thing for us*, she thought.

Monica Eastland was simply too tired to care, physically and emotionally. She had endured the shame of what her father had done for three of her fourteen years, and now, having told her mother and confronted her father, she'd faced his rage and denials and veiled threats in return. She knew that she was paying a dreadful price for the truth—the disintegration of her family. She had lost her dignity and her sense of safety in her own home. She was losing her relationship with her father in a desperate attempt to regain it. Above all, she was desperate to be free of carrying the weight of it all.

As the Cessna climbed on its easterly heading, it passed through 2,500 feet, tripping a pressure-sensitive switch inside a satchel of explosives in the rear of the plane. The tail of the aircraft was severed and fell away, spiraling awkwardly to earth.

The charge had been carefully and expertly measured; it was designed to do its work as discretely as an explosive can, arousing a minimum of suspicion on the ground.

The blast was not enough to kill the plane's three occupants outright. Mercifully, Monica was knocked unconscious, and spared the experience of the final plunge. But Kathryn Rossberg Eastland's last moments of life were filled with rage at her fate. She was no fool. She knew how she and her daughter were dying, along with an innocent Lebanese pilot. And she knew why.

Peter Scott lingered at the airfield long enough to hear that radio contact had been lost over a Palestinian area not particularly safe for anyone with a U.S. passport. Return of the bodies could likely be negotiated. But the wreckage would never be seen by officials of the U.S. government. Nor, his government would assume, would it need to. A war was going on. Things happen. Innocent people get hurt, and unidentified airplanes are sometimes caught in the crossfire. Assured of that, ex-Special Forces veteran Peter Scott slept surprisingly well.

CHAPTER SEVENTY-THREE

THROUGH SHATTERED GLASS

4:06 a.m. Light was visible in the clearings but still absent in the thick growth and windfall. Even a Navy SEAL is no match for a fallen twenty-four inch tree trunk that a few hours before had been a sixty-year-old birch standing in the forest. Rushing toward the cabin, without the luxury of time for caution, his right knee found it, sending him sprawling, his face landing hard on the wet ground, his knee shattered and the pain almost unbearable.

4:08 a.m. "Shannon: What exactly did you tell your young friend?"

"I told him everything. Every detail. Did you know that you work for a monster?"

Seconds counted. The agents were moving, weapons ready, toward the cabin. Erickson hoped someone would arrive in time to resolve the crisis that was developing before his eyes.

4:09 a.m. "Shannon, do you have any idea what you've done to your father?"

"Mr. Scott, I know exactly what my father has done to *me*! My body is nobody's toy, Mr. Scott."

Looking at the motionless form of Agent Barker, Erickson was confused by the questions Scott was posing, and the young woman's defiant replies. *She is gutsy, talking like that to a loaded gun.* But still, he sensed he was listening in on a much more complicated conversation that left him on the sidelines. And with a gun pointed his way, he wanted to know why. "I don't understand."

Scott calmly, coldly, explained. "Simple. Let me tell you what the newspapers will say tomorrow. A clearly unbalanced, hostile lumberjack, unable to get to the President, goes after his daughter instead."

"And why would I do that?"

"Mr. Erickson, we both know why you'd love to settle an old grudge from Cambodia."

Erickson didn't respond. *Scott knows?* Scott continued. "Friendly fire's a horrible thing, isn't it, soldier? It's hard to lose your buddies that way. Kind of sticks with you. Wakes you up at night. Makes you think of ways to right the wrong. Makes you … *crazy*, even."

Now it was Shannon's turn to be confused. "What's this about?"

"Shut up, Shannon. You have bigger problems right now."

Michael asked, "You knew. How?"

Scott smiled. "Eastland has no idea how much I know about his military service. My job is to know what is there, and decide what to keep locked away. I'm amazed, frankly, that you ever found out.

"In any case, here's the morning news you won't be here to read. You're hell-bent on kidnapping, and then killing this poor young kid, despite our best efforts to rescue her. Sadly, a brave agent dies in a vain attempt to protect his charge. I'll arrive and be forced to take you out. Unfortunately, I'll be too late to save her. But when you die, so does your memory, and the president has nothing to worry about.

Michael understood. *Scott will kill the agent and the girl with my gun, then kill me with his, and no one will doubt his story. A perfect crime. And he's likely to pull it off. No—I have one option.*

"And when you die, Shannon, so does your dirty little secret. Don't worry about Aaron. I can keep him quiet too. So I suggest you say your little prayers. And don't bother begging for your life. It's over."

Shannon was shaking. But she was also clear: *If I die, I die with the dignity my father never respected.* "I don't beg. I won't give you the satisfaction."

"I don't care, kid. You've got about a minute of life left anyway, so why don't you—"

"You're on Dad's side in this, aren't you? You're protecting a rapist! Proud of yourself, Mister Scott? I have hated you from the day I met you. I'd rather die than see either one of you again."

4:11 a.m. The injured SEAL crawled toward the west side of the cabin. His injury slowed him by several critical minutes, but he arrived in time to witness a terrifying scene.

In the dim light, Scott's profile could be seen silhouetted in the window. From a distance, the SEAL couldn't hear the conversation, but Charlie Mann plainly saw Scott's hand coming up, leveling a long gun. There was the loud, angry voice of a young female, the weapon pointed directly at someone. What happened next consumed less than four seconds.

Mann brought his rifle up as swiftly as he could, clicking off the safety. His target centered in the gun sight.

Michael was unarmed, his rifle now in Scott's hands. At that moment he longed for a weapon more than at any time in his life. But he was not without options. *Maybe I can buy just a few seconds ...* It wasn't a conscious thought; just the act of a man who had risked his life for others before, and was willing to pay the ultimate price one more time. Erickson lunged into the line of fire. There was the blast of Erickson's rifle; Michael twisted from the impact and fell to the floor. Shannon screamed.

As Scott, enraged at Erickson's move, raised the rifle toward Shannon, there was the shattering of glass, the thud of impact on human flesh. Only then did one hear the crack of a rifle about forty yards distant, echoing through the forest.

It was not like the movies. There was no gasping breath, flailing arms, body pirouetting in an agonizing dance. At the moment of impact the body went simply, instantly, limp. The neurological signals that had guided Peter Scott since infancy, ceased. He dropped almost vertically to the floor, falling slightly to his left, driven by the momentum of the projectile that entered just above the right ear. The eyes, which a moment before had been focused and piercing, were now expressionless, seeing nothing.

There had been no time to prepare. Peter Scott had no idea that in an instant, he would pass from intense determination, perfect health, and immense power, into eternity—in a flash of incredible pain that ended the moment it was perceived. One moment he was squeezing the trigger that would protect his protégé. The next moment …

And at that same moment, a Navy SEAL closed his eyes. His trained instincts, his pride at always fulfilling his mission, vanished in revulsion at what he had been forced to do.

⁜

Everyone at the end of the driveway jolted upright at the sound of one, then two, gunshots. Tony dissolved into tears, his mother held him closely, trying to calm him while trying to contain her own emotions as well. *Oh, God, please ...*

⁜

A quarter mile from the manor, three journalists were frustrated. The thanks they felt they deserved had instead been a cold and threatening demand: *Leave. Now.* As they drove, Chief Benson's vehicle followed them to make sure they did in fact retreat to the village.

The windows in the van where closed. They heard a strange crack, followed by another—this time much louder. Strobe jumped. "What was that?" To Bates, it sounded like gunfire. He decided not to introduce that possibility into an already-unnerving night. "Just a tree falling."

⁜

For a moment, Shannon stood motionless, not breathing, eyes blankly staring at the space where her would-be executioner had been raising the weapon that should have ended her. She brought her hands to her face, blocking what she knew lay on the floor before her. She felt suddenly alone. For a moment she wished that if she opened her eyes, the sun would have risen, the room would be empty, and all would be well. But when she did, she saw only the same varying shades of shadow around her. Perhaps that was best; on the floor were the bodies of three men; one unconscious, one dead, his blood spreading— but one, she realized, was moving, and gasping in pain. Mercifully, it brought her mind back to the pared-down First Aid class she'd taken last winter. Refusing to look past the reclusive islander, Shannon knelt next to Erickson. "He shot you?"

"Yes."

He's so calm, she thought, unaware that this was a man who had felt violence before. "I'm bleeding, and need something to stop it. Can you find a towel or something?" Still in shock, Shannon got up, felt around the counter to her right, and found something soft. *A towel? Wash cloth? Shirt? Doesn't matter.* She knelt again, followed Michael's arm down to his hand. "Let me hold this on you." Michael complied; she pressed the unseen object as firmly as she could onto Erickson's side. There was no time to realize what she would ponder an hour later: *He saved me; maybe I can save him.*

⁜

Agents Nguyen and Cooper arrived less than a minute after the gunshot, expecting to find something horrible. What they found was horror enough: an unconscious agent and Peter Scott's body, blood flowing from a gruesome wound.

But what they did not expect was to see the president's daughter—on the floor with Michael Erickson, her blooded hands pressed against his side.

They called for backup and medical assistance. Michael still lay on the floor, bleeding. The agent in charge turned to Nguyen.

"Call the Command Post—clarify that Shannon is unharmed."

She stepped outside, radioed her message, and saw a shadowy form slowly coming her way. Before she reached for her weapon, Lt. Mann identified himself. She helped him onto the porch. Only then did she take Shannon's arm and led her away.

CHAPTER SEVENTY-FOUR

UNCOMMON VALOR

When the message that Shannon was safe and unharmed reached the manor, the First Lady and First Son knew all they needed to know. Ms. Eastland demanded and was given a car and driver, and headed toward the command post.

Time and distance are the enemy on Madeline Island when the need for medical attention is urgent. The nearest hospital is twenty miles by land—after the ferry ride. It could take an hour before arrival at the emergency room. With the island's roads choked with debris, it could take that long just to get a well-equipped ambulance to the scene. Michael Erickson didn't have that much time.

No one had the equipment to perform more than the most perfunctory first aid, which was sufficient for Agent Barker and Lt. Mann, but far less than this patient needed. There was no need to hurry in attending to Peter Scott. But Michael Erickson was still alive. Agent Cooper placed a call to whoever was listening. With every kind of emergency radio in action during those turbulent early morning hours, he knew he'd have a substantial audience.

And for that reason, he chose not to disclose Scott's death publicly.

"We need a helicopter. We have three male subjects down, one with a bullet wound; two with lesser injuries. The wounded male is conscious but needs help immediately. Please respond."

Ten seconds passed. He was ready to repeat the message when the radio crackled. "This is U. S. Coast Guard, Bayfield

Station, responding to the medical emergency. Please verify."
A minute later, a Coast Guard helicopter, on station for the presidential visit, was warming up, and would land on the nearest open ground. It would bring an EMT from the mainland and two Coast Guardsmen with a stretcher.

⌗

In the first light of morning, Agent Nguyen was seen escorting the president's daughter out of the forest. By this time, the First Lady and her son had arrived. An embrace sealed the reunion of Mary Lee, Aaron, and Shannon. They were ushered toward the Suburban that the agent in charge had used as his command post. "We need to get you folk out of here."

"Not until I see the man who saved my girl's life."

"I understand, Ms. Eastland. But our orders are clear: to get you to safety. Besides—he needs to get on that helo, right away."

"Fine. Obey your orders. Just not yet."

Two stretchers emerged from the direction of the cabin, headed toward the waiting island ambulance. They would be transported to a nearby clearing near the airport, where the Coast Guard's helicopter could already be heard as it settled onto the grass a quarter mile away. Barker's stretcher-bearers and those attending to the injured SEAL were directed by the agent in charge toward the helicopter, but Erickson's was steered toward the vehicle that held the Eastland's. Mary Lee walked toward Michael Erickson fully aware the encounter needed to be brief.

His eyes were closed; at first she wondered if he were conscious. But when she spoke his name, he opened his eyes, and turned his head toward her.

"Thank you. Thank you for saving my baby girl's life."

Erickson smiled weakly. "Is she okay?"

She smiled back. "Yes, thanks to you. I don't know how we can ever repay you."

"No need." He took a deep breath and tried to shift his position on the stretcher. He winced as pain shot through his abdomen, and gave up the effort. He turned to look at the First Lady again. The paramedic holding the IV bag said, "We need to get going."

Erickson, without talking his eyes off Mary Lee Eastland, said. "Ms. Eastland: tell me—does your husband ever talk about his experiences in Vietnam?"

Mary Eastland looked puzzled. "Yes, why?"

"Has he ever mentioned anything about being in action over Cambodia?"

"No, I don't think he served there. Why do you ask?"

Michael closed his eyes. "Just curious. It's not important now."

Within minutes, a barely conscious man, a Navy sniper and a downed agent would be aboard, and as the first light of dawn on July 4th filtered through the trees on Madeline Island, the helicopter was rotating away from the shattered forest and toward Ashland, the nearest town with a medical team ready to receive them.

CHAPTER SEVENTY-FIVE

HOPE, IN SPITE OF

The media van had carried Gary, Samantha and Strobe back toward the village. They had work to do, and needed each other to do it. The experienced Bates could sift through the night's events and distill the essentials into a coherent story for Samantha's time-conscious medium. Strobe's footage wouldn't serve Bates' newspaper directly, but it gave Gary an excellent tool for reviewing the events he'd soon be emailing to Washington. Hopefully, landline connection wasn't a casualty of the storm. If so, he's seek a satellite link. None of them would know the fate of Peter Scott until the nation did, and it would be days before that was known.

After a frantic hour of reviewing, editing and brainstorming, both had their stories. Samantha even convinced Bates to give an on-camera interview, his reputation adding gravitas to the rookie's report.

Bates, with nothing to go on apart from the mysterious sound he heard while bouncing over storm-generated debris, decided to focus on what he did know.

Samantha left Strobe to finish editing and uploading her report. Gary would send his later in the morning.

⁘

The 3rd of July had become the 4th virtually unnoticed. Impromptu teams of islanders were clearing roads and securing damaged properties, especially around La Pointe; the village took the brunt of the storm's wrath. Farther east on the island, heavy forest cover had softened the blow. The overnight cleanup was driven by the need to move first responders. It was still ongoing when a cloud-filtered sun brought light to the effort.

Two exhausted journalists walked toward the island's business area, hoping someone, even without electricity, had something resembling breakfast. By now, word was sketchy, but what they had learned was dramatic: Shannon was safe. Three injured parties were airlifted off the island. Someone named Erickson, a reclusive local, had rescued Shannon Eastland.

"Slow down, Samantha."

"Why?"

"I want to talk to you." Gary's hands were in his back pockets; his eyes focused on the debris-covered gravel road at their feet. He shook his head. "This has been quite an experience for me, Sam."

"Not every day you get this close to the president."

"I've gotten close to a few. But that's not what I'm talking about."

Samantha looked toward Gary; he lifted his head, his eyes meeting hers. "My best experience this week was … Well, this remarkable rookie from that other news medium."

Sam smiled. She had any number of comebacks in her arsenal, but used none of them. "Thank you, Gary. I'm grateful I met you too." She slowed to a stop; Gary turned, and they stood face to face. "Gary, what is it about me that you find so interesting?"

"Hey—I've got seniority, kid. I'm supposed to ask the tough questions."

"You're not used to talking about yourself, are you?"

"I'm from Washington, remember? Transparency can kill you in that town. People ask you questions for ammunition, not information."

"So?"

"So, when someone asks me how I feel, all my walls go up. And I like my walls. Let my guard down, and I feel like I'm walking down Pennsylvania Avenue buck naked."

Samantha grinned. "That's an image I can do without, Mr. Bates. You want to make progress with *this* woman, you'll need to class up your act."

"Sorry."

"Back to my question: what did you see in me?"

"You have the qualities I seek in a woman. And yes, my dear Samantha, I am attracted to you. There. I said it.

"But there's something different about you. Something you are. Depth. Confidence. More than I've seen from rookies— from a lot of people in this business. And your faith—I mean, your God-faith intrigues me, but in light of what we've experienced, I am in awe of your faith in humanity. You're not cynical yet. I don't know if that comes from inexperience, or— well, does something require you to give people the benefit of the doubt—I mean, after what we've been reporting in the last 72 hours, what's to be hopeful about?"

CHAPTER SEVENTY-SIX

SEIZE THE DAY

Samantha looked out on the lake—now calm, but carrying broken branches, odd pieces of lumber, abundant evidence of the storm.

"I'm not required to be naïve, if that's your concern. In fact, I think I can be a realist about the world as it is, and not run from reality when it's … " She shrugs. "horrible. Like hearing what sounded like a gunshot, and thinking: *Did someone just die?*" The young journalist relived that moment, and fought to restrain the shaking in her voice.

"But I'm a hopeful realist. What I believe, and how I practice that, gives my life its form. I have as many questions as you have about how the death and mayhem we just witnessed goes on and on."

"Well—how *does* your God allow that? There's tons of 'god' figures out there. Looks like people can pick one they like off a menu."

Samantha paused; *An abstract conversation here will die a well-deserved death.* A thought was forming. "Maybe God is a lot like this Michael guy."

Bates' eyes widened. "Listen, Rookie—I've had enough shock tonight for a lifetime. How the hell— Sorry. Let me put it nicely: Have you gone over the edge? God is a weird lumberjack who lives off the grid?"

"What did he just do?"

"God—or Michael Erickson? He's God incognito? You're not making this easy."

"Slow down. What did Michael just do?"

"Okay. Somehow, he found a lost kid in a thunderstorm."

"Yes! Went the second mile, right? I can only hope I'd be like that 'lumberjack'. He's more Jesus-like than most church people I know."

It would be several days before they, or anyone, knew the full extent of Michael Erickson's role in Shannon's rescue.

They turned towards town again, walking slowly. Gary spoke next. "Samantha: be honest with me. Could I ever court you? It's important. I need to know."

"Gary, I can't quite comprehend the world-famous Gary Bates courting little, young Samantha Wells. I know my mother would be thrilled."

Gary grinned. "Oh yeah? She a fan of mine?"

"Sorry. Probably never read a word of yours. But she's always wanted me to succeed, and to her, dating a successful someone is good enough to be hopeful."

"Well, if I get the chance, I'd like to make her proud of her daughter."

"Gary: what's good enough for Mom is not good enough for me. I'm not riding anyone's coattails. I will succeed with or without being on someone's arm—just so you know."

"I wouldn't date you if I didn't believe that already. By the way: how about your Dad? Would I be his kind of guy?"

"That's the tough one. He's a Republican by birth with a very short list of acceptable newspapers, and the *Post* isn't on it. Unless there's a George Will column somewhere.

"Your question has become important to me too. A relationship that doesn't respect my spiritual journey simply won't go very far. But regardless of what happens between us, you've been courting me for the past few days, and I've loved every minute of it, Gary. Honestly, I hope this continues. And I promise I won't preach at you."

"Good. I'm not quite ready to fall on my knees, Kid."

"*Carpe diem,* Gary. Seize the day."

The village grocery store had set up an impromptu breakfast counter, selling juices, pastries, and a few hot meals cooked on a camp stove. They got in line behind about two dozen other members of the media. A truly private conversation was out of the question, but a few indirect comments could be risked. Gary turned to Samantha.

"If I 'seized the day'—would it improve my love life?"

She smiled and took his hands. And there, with members of the national media watching, she leaned over and kissed him on the cheek, amid applause and good-natured jabs from colleagues who knew the reputation of this eligible but rough-edged bachelor. Gary Bates, senior correspondent for the *Washington Post*, blushed for the first time in years, while Samantha Wells of WLOW-TV whispered in his ear:

"I actually like you, Mr. Bates."

CHAPTER SEVENTY-SEVEN

AFTER THE STORM

The crisis officially passed, as far as the nation was concerned, at 5:30 a.m. Central Daylight Time, when a weary and unusually meek secretary of the interior was tasked with addressing an impromptu press conference outside the manor. The morning's light was muted. The rain had stopped, the wind had ceased, and the lake was calm, except for a storm-generated surge that alternately raised and lowered the western end of Lake Superior by nearly a foot. After the violence that shredded the manor's grounds just hours before, the island was eerily quiet. The only sound came from generators powering the media vans—those not damaged in the storm—and the ever-present chain saws.

With the press secretary already en route to Washington, it fell to Secretary Malone to announce to the world that the president's daughter had been found, that she appeared in good health and would return later that morning to Washington with her mother and brother. They had assurance from doctors that she had survived her ordeal and was now safe and sound. There would be a statement from the White House following the family's reunion, but no details would be released until a full investigation had been conducted. There would be no comment on the rumors of kidnapping, nor would there be any speculation regarding casualties. Peter Scott's death was not public knowledge, and wouldn't be until the White House could craft a suitable news release. His body was discretely evacuated along with government equipment on a Coast Guard helicopter.

Malone raced through an obviously uncomfortable speech without entertaining any questions—at a time when the world had plenty to ask. He left the podium and returned to his room at the Bed and Breakfast. Only now had he gotten his moment before the national press corps, not to strut his stuff before potential clients but to face unanswerable questions about a catastrophe that might be catastrophic for his ambitions too, but for which he held no blame. The last of the president's staff gathered their belongings and headed toward the island's airport for the short helicopter ride to Duluth, then back to the nation's capital by military transport.

An hour earlier, Mary Lee Eastland had stood on the gravel driveway in the storm-shattered forest near the Neale cabin. She, her daughter and her son had embraced without words, watched by a cadre of well-trained government professionals who had not been trained for such a moment.

The First Lady had looked through tear-clouded eyes around the circle of onlookers and mouthed a silent *Thank you* knowing that three of the participants in her daughter's rescue were at that moment being airlifted toward a mainland hospital. As roads were cleared, she and her children were driven toward the village by vehicles with U.S. government plates. One would carry Franklin, Mark, Debra, and Tony, on the orders of a female Secret Service agent. But before they left the now-emptying command post, Agent Nguyen, who had played a critical role during the last six hours, walked toward the Neales.

"I want you to know that in my reports, each of you will be commended for your cooperation in finding Miss Eastland. Dr. Neale, you will also be named in my report for your courage in this emergency.

"And personally ... thank you, from the bottom of my heart." She turned, and walked away.

No one else would die in the early morning hours of July 4th. There had been, an hour earlier and years before, enough of that.

But there were casualties. A host of careers were mortally wounded. A prominent family was shattered, the nation itself would be shaken, but not as much as two young men and a younger woman.

The Neales, spent and tired, would long for respite on a day when the interviews—interrogations, really—consumed them. For Franklin, Mark, Debra, and Tony every detail, every memory, every word, was dissected, until they were finally released. They could return to the cottage only under federal escort, and only to gather some clothing and personal items—the cottage was now a crime scene. None of them had any desire to stay there anyway. Following a few discrete conversations with people they trusted, a rental property far from town—mercifully far—could be theirs for a while.

⁂

Within a day, the roads would be cleared of windfall, although it took two more before power was fully restored. Life on Madeline Island was attempting to recapture the rhythms it had known before the First Family's invasion. Flags still flew along Main Street, some now tattered, thanks to a brief but violent storm. The signs welcoming the visitors would be taken down, one by one. Lots that once held vans belonging to the government and to the news media were empty again.

The ferries would resume their normal schedules—though they would be somewhat more crowded now, packed with those wanting to see the place that had been so prominently in the news. Damaged buildings were boarded up until windows could be replaced, and those with more severe damage would soon be attended to by an army of trades people who followed the insurance adjusters to La Pointe. The marina was busy, and its storage lot unusually full for July, as more than a dozen boats were hauled out for inspection and repair. Several would never sail again. Nothing would ever be the same.

As the euphoria of the president's visit faded, questions emerged that no one seemed willing to answer about the disappearance of the First Daughter during the storm. About Michael Erickson's mysterious involvement, or strange radio messages following the storm. About the absence of Peter Scott. The island was frustrated: so many questions, everyone with the answers locked in stony silence. Something had happened. Something had changed. *What happened to the First Family on the 3rd and 4th of July?*

CHAPTER SEVENTY-EIGHT

THE SOUND OF SHEER SILENCE

The Neales arrived late at a rented cabin seven miles east of the village, set back in trees that had escaped the storm's wrath, providing respite for an exhausted family. They dined by lantern and candlelight on a simple meal: salads, burgers, sodas and cake, provided by a sympathetic islander. Then they slept, restlessly, and rose on the 5th to a calm, clouded morning.

In their seclusion, it would be some time before they learn that, in the early hours of Independence Day, the Rev. Shelly Griggs had given birth to a baby girl, weighing seven pounds, six ounces, and in perfect health.

Shelly and her husband David named her, their first child, Madeline.

The previous two days were marked by commotion, tension, terror, and noise, but they will look back on July 5th as unforgettable for different reasons. On this day, no one spoke, except for an occasional *okay* or *Thank you*. After the fury, it was deathly quiet, a sound of sheer silence, as it needed to be.

Franklin was angry. So was Mark, who knew the work of the past two years had been undone in a day.

Or was it? With this new "chapter" it could be his most successful book yet. After what his family had endured and was enduring still, Mark wondered: *Could that be sweet revenge?*

But for Franklin, his family had been unalterably scarred, burdened by knowledge they could not un-know. From this day forward, stripped of the privacy and tranquility they had come here to find, the lives they had known until the 3rd of July in the Year 2000 had been taken from them, and *What do we do now? Our lives are still at the mercy of a child molester with the power to destroy us.*

⁜

On July 6th, Mark's phone rang at 6:45 a.m. He instinctively groped for the phone and pulled it to his ear.

"Mr. Neale?"

"Yes."

"Good morning, Mr. Neale. Sorry to call so early. This is Rebecca Mathers; I'm on staff at the White House. May I speak to your father, Doctor Franklin Neale? It's very important."

"Ah … let me find him." Mark found his father, already drinking coffee, sitting on the covered porch.

"Dad?"

"Heard the phone. Who was it?"

"The White House."

"Son, that would have been funny a week ago."

"Seriously, Dad. It's the White House, and they want to talk to you."

Franklin got up and reached for the phone in Mark's hand, worrying about why he was of interest to Washington. "Hello— this is Franklin Neale."

"Doctor Neale: I'm Rebecca Mathers, President Eastland's personal secretary. The president has asked me to arrange a telephone conversation with you this morning at seven o'clock your time. Please understand, he will require the strictest confidentiality. Will you accept his call under those conditions?"

The still-groggy professor tried to clear his head, long enough for Ms. Mathers to ask, "Are you still there?"

"Yes, I'm still here. And yes, I'll accept."

Realizing that "confidential" probably excludes his family, he clarifies—"Yes. As you described it. For privacy, can you call on my cellphone?" "Of course," she said.

After taking back his phone, Mark looked at his father. Both of them were puzzled, and not a little worried. "So, who—what was that about?"

His father slowly sat down at the kitchen table, eyes fixed on the opposite wall. "I'm not sure I can tell you."

Franklin was torn between wanting to clear the air—and wanting it all to just go away. The previous days haunted them. Franklin, Mark, Debra, and Tony carried knowledge that if— no, *when* it became known, would strip their lives of peace, and drown them in reluctant fame—or infamy—as those who exposed the President of the United States to political ruin.

He knew that the president had to make the first move. Finally, the president made that move. Good. *But why this? Why am I—why are we—being approached? Is he wondering what kind of risk we pose? Will he try to buy our silence? Will he threaten us? Will this be a truly private conversation?*

And under the best of circumstances: what can possibly be said that won't blow up on us?

What is Eastland's agenda? Terrifying questions, no good answers.

⁜

Debra heard Franklin's cellphone ring, and saw her father-in-law in the back yard. The phone rang only once, before her father-in-law answered.

"Hello."

"Doctor Neale." It was a statement rather than a question, from the secretary.

"Yes."

"One moment," followed by a click, a pause, and a voice.

"Good morning, Doctor Neale. Thank you for taking my call."

"Good morning, Mr. President. How can I be of service?"

There was a pause. Then, the leader of the free world sighed, and began.

"I need to know what to do."

CHAPTER SEVENTY-NINE

THE CALL

Dr. Neale wanted no part in this call. *I'm not trained for this—and I'm not clear about what "this" is. What are his expectations; and why am I suddenly counselor to a dangerous man? One hasty word, and I could unleash some terrible outcomes.*

"I am surprised that you called me, Mr. President. May I ask why you are not talking to someone in Washington?"

"Fair question. I need advice from someone that isn't connected to this town. Most people around here don't know my … situation. I'm not ready to reveal publicly what you already know. The fact is that beyond my family—and yours, of course—I'm not ready to tell my staff, or *anyone*. So far, it hasn't hit the press—is that because you haven't talked about it with anyone?"

"I haven't, Mr. President. Neither has Mark, Debra, or Tony."

The president paused. Then said, "This is not easy for me to admit, Doctor Neale. But I haven't slept since I got home. I've hardly eaten. I'm hiding from my staff. *Hiding.* They are floundering because I'm floundering. People around me are scared. *I'm* scared. You are the only person I've said that to."

"May I ask why I'm that person? We hardly know each other—"

"I know. And I'm taking a risk here."

"So am I, Sir."

"I get that. I'm sorry. But Dr. Neale—here I am."

Franklin's mind was racing. *He is fragile. Any blunder could turn all hell loose—especially for anyone named Neale.*

Or, by some miracle, I could salvage something less terrible than this. That's my task. Not a miracle—just a soft landing, some breathing room, draining some of the tension that's tearing this man apart. That will be difficult enough.

But it might be enough.

"Mr. President, how has it been for you and your family?"

"I've apologized to them. Frankly, 'apologize' is too weak a word."

"Can you tell me what that was like?"

"Hardest conversations I've ever had. We talked as soon as we were together. They were more than angry, and held nothing back. I had to let them. I had no defense.

"Sir, I pray I'm never in that kind of conversation."

"I hope you aren't either, Dr. Neale. I didn't beg. I made no excuses, no pie-in-the-sky promises. If there is a future for this family, it will be their call."

The president continued. "Shannon was—is—broken. I'm still trying to absorb her response. She said, 'Don't ask me to forgive you, because I won't.' Dr. Neale, she experienced things no one should, especially …" The president's voice broke, and after a long silence he continued. "… Especially a child."

Dr. Neale waited, giving the president time, and time for this ordinary citizen to frame his words for a president in crisis; this was no ordinary chat between friends. In the professor's mind, time had stopped, and the world was populated only by two men bound by a firestorm of destruction, cruelty and death. They could, in this fragile moment, begin a long road to healing. But the outcome would depend, almost entirely, on the words this eighty-year-old teacher of theology would now dare to speak.

"Mr. President, you asked me what you should do. Your family, especially your daughter, will need help, and that will take time—maybe a lifetime. Shannon especially needs and deserves your confession—you've begun to do that, and I commend you. That took courage. But there are as well things you *cannot* do and should *not* attempt."

"Such as …"

"Knowing how you hurt Shannon, you may feel you need to fix this. Maybe the 'Dad' in you is finally emerging, which is good. But you can't play the Dad Card right now. Shannon may not be willing to restore your relationship. Perhaps never. That is her right.

"I suspect that even your presence, Mr. President, feels like a threat to her. Above all, you can *not* be alone with her. Your only option, Mr. President, is *distance*—guardrails, between you and your daughter. Your family, if necessary your staff as well, need to know and protect those guardrails.

"Frankly, the White House is a terrible place for a deeply traumatized young woman. I urge you to do whatever it takes to provide her as father-free a sanctuary as you can. Even if it means finding that sanctuary away from such an intrusive environment.

"And Sir, I think this will be very hard for you."

Eastland did not respond, leaving the two men locked in tortured silence.

Finally, the president spoke—and changed the subject.

"I have a question I've wanted to ask ever since, well—you'll understand it better than most: What about Peter Scott? He nearly killed my daughter.

"Here's why I'm asking, and I need this held in confidence. This is for your ears only, Dr. Neale: During the standoff in your cabin, Peter Scott was trying to kill Shannon, and was shot by a federal agent before he could."

Dr. Neale was in shock. *Why is he telling me this? What I knew was bad enough.*

"Again, Dr. Neale, we are not ready to reveal this. But my concern is: If he was that ruthless, did he deserve what happened to him? Actually, I've been thinking that he got what *I* deserved."

Doctor Neale was sifting through possible responses, but the president did not wait for them.

"Dammit, I'm responsible for that man's death, and I almost got you and that Erickson guy killed—*and my own daughter*! This can't be fixed with prayer and hugs. So what do I do with that? I need your opinion, Dr. Neale—what do I do in the here and now? Resign? Surrender to the Attorney General? Crawl on broken glass up a mountain?"

CHAPTER EIGHTY

TRYING TO COME HOME AGAIN

Franklin chose his words carefully.

"Frankly, sir, we all deserve the consequences of what we do. But—despite what he did and tried to do, I grieve his death. From what I know, I also grieve his life. It seems to have been empty, devoid of grace; just a grim battle against whatever got in his way. I pray he's finding grace now."

Franklin paused, gathering his thoughts, struggling to hold back. *So much I want to say about the nightmare we live in because of you.* Franklin couldn't risk a blowup that ended the conversation in disaster—and yet, it was time to speak hard, irreversible words.

"Mr. President, I don't speak with malice toward you, but I will be honest. If I may speak bluntly, Sir?"

"Of course."

"I'm honor-bound to tell you that you must face justice. I mean that, Sir; you must embrace the consequences that would befall any other citizen. You have hurt the country as well as your precious family, and if what you have done becomes known, as I suspect it will, that hurt will be substantial.

The harm you've inflicted on your family also applies to … well, 'we, the people.' We as a *nation* are wounded. The people who put you in office may soon want your head on a platter if and when they find out—for a while recently, so did I. Frankly, forgiveness will be almost impossible for many of us to give.

"Even so: you are not beyond hope—"

The president interrupted. "That's easy to say, Dr. Neale. But my world is built on cause and effect, the blind forces of nature. Right now, I calculate the odds of any good coming out of this—politically, legally, or with my family, to be zero. Be careful talking about hope in this. Where's the substance?"

"You're a stubborn man, Mr. President. With all due respect, I am equally stubborn. I will not abandon three core principles that ground my life: justice, hope—beginning with *grace*. Grace humbles us, Mr. President; it reminds us that beneath our title and power, our successes and failings, we are at the core still just children, loved by God. And the most important of those words is: *loved*.

"Forget law or politics, Mr. President. Despite how angry I am toward you right now, I'll tell you what my preacher-father would tell you: the God of the universe specializes in the impossible, and has already vetoed our judgments, including mine about you, and yours about yourself. And yes, there is substance to that. Such as: despite your 'calculation' … you called for help."

Eastland was silent again, caught off guard. Spirituality was not his native tongue, and in an either/or, zero-sum world, "grace" was a myth anyway. Too many slick and smooth would-be saviors had offered easy formulas for salvation that had contributed to thick callouses on his heart. Once again, he changes the subject.

"I have an ugly question, Dr. Neale: Aren't you obligated to report what you know, and—are you going to fulfill that obligation?"

He's right. I should, Franklin thought. But —"Mr. President, I'm not the one who should report it."

"Then who, if not you, should report what I did?"

"You should."

Another long silence. When the president finally spoke, he was defiant.

"You want me to turn myself over to my own government, with the virtual certainty that I'd wind up in prison by Inauguration Day?"

"Mr. President, we need to back up for a moment."

"I'm not sure where you're going with this."

"My question is this, and I don't expect an immediate answer: Have you told the truth of your actions to *yourself*? Have you truly owned all this?"

The president was still defiant. "Don't you think that this has dogged me every minute of every day, for years?"

"Sir, you tried to claim your public persona as the true Robert Eastland. You were running from the *you* that could do such things, but you knew that you had lost your innocence. Because nothing, ever, just goes away. If you do not fully own what you did, it will own *you*, for the rest of your life.

"You've hidden what you've done long enough to become accustomed to a *lie*—and the fear of being found out. Now that's happened. But you do not yet have the skills to live in the light of day."

Dr. Neale took a breath, horrified at what he'd just said to the world's most powerful—and at the moment, most fragile—person. It was frightening, releasing his family's fate to someone gifted in deceit and evasion, and powerful enough to destroy them.

The President paused. "Back to my concern: is there any chance you will honor any legal obligation to turn me in? I think I should know."

The Doctor's mind was screaming. *There's no way we do the right thing—or do nothing at all—without it destroying us. I look at our future knowing what we know, and I don't see an upside.* Part of him wanted to threaten his president: *It's not fair to put that burden on us! If you don't, <u>we</u> will disclose everything we know!*

"Sir, I'm aware of the consequences if I report—and, if I don't and am found out as having withheld this. There is no way we respond without our lives blowing up. I think you know that.

"Still, Mr. President, we've made the decision to remain silent. We have chosen to trust you.

"So, again: what do you do? You start by re-orienting yourself around grace. Don't over-think it, Mr. President. That love, that grace, makes it possible to own what you did, to repair what you can without shame, and to live without being tyrannized by what you cannot repair. You can't change history, Sir. Still, you can reconstruct your integrity, which I suspect you've often traded for power. Mr. President: make a better trade this time. It may take the rest of your life, but after all that's happened, why would you want to spend your life in any other pursuit?"

Neale's words haunted Eastland. *Nice words, but he doesn't know ... What would he do if he knew about Kathryn and Monica?* In the president's tortured mind, any talk of grace for the sin Neale knew was canceled by the sins the good doctor knew nothing about. When Eastland spoke, his tone was no longer angry and defiant, but softer, weary, resigned.

"I hope that can happen. I just don't know. Dr. Neale, there's a piece of this that goes back a long time, and, believe it or not, it's a lot worse."

As if what I've learned isn't bad enough, the Doctor mused. "Mr. President, is there something else I need to hear about?"

"No! It's a burden that you don't want to carry. What I will say is that I remain doubtful, and with all due respect, I don't need another self-appointed holy man telling me that God loves me."

Dr. Neale sensed that the president had heard all he was willing to hear, and it was now up to that tortured man on the other side of the phone.

"Mr. President, you called, desperate for answers. It has been an honor to speak so personally with you. I will never forget it, and I hope I have been helpful. The Neale family will protect what we know about your family's trauma, trusting that you will own up to your actions. I believe you will. And I hope you find what you are seeking. I will pray that you do. Thank you, Mr. President."

"Good bye, Doctor Neale."

The line clicked off, and the dial tone reminds a weary, emotionally-drained man that the caller is no longer there. Franklin is spent, overwhelmed. *He just ... hung up. I have no way of knowing if anything I said reached him. I don't know if he will do the right thing—the pressure to evade the truth must be overwhelming. None of his advisors, his cabinet, his legal representation, will support a confession.*

That leaves us holding the truth—and we are at risk because we hold it. If he fails to come clean, will we wind up as collateral damage? Now I have Peter Scott's violent death to carry as well. I did not ask for this!

Even so: may something positive ... anything at all ... come out of all this.

May I have been guided by a Power beyond myself.

"Dad—" It was Debra—"who was that?"

"Sorry—I can't—"

"I know. But this wasn't the usual chat with your golfing buddies, was it?"

Franklin smiled. So did she, with a look that said: *It's all right; you don't have to say a word.* "You're not going to tell me, are you?"

"Not this time, honey."

She pulled him close, kissed him on the cheek. Then she whispered in his ear.

"The way you're acting, Dad, you'd think it was the president."

Franklin smiled. "Just a lost soul finding their way home, Debra. One a lot like me."

CHAPTER EIGHTY-ONE

LONG ISLAND

The seventh of July began with the Neales at breakfast, each one quiet, deep in their own thoughts. Two words broke the silence as Mark Neale looked at his wife and son.

"Long Island." Franklin knew that he would not be present for this conversation.

Two hours later, Mark, Debra and Tony anchored off a forested strip of sand that shares its name with a larger, more famous island hundreds of miles to the east. Their solitude was guarded by a lighthouse, a steel tower that had raised a beacon over the water for generations.

This time, they could see the hills surrounding Bayfield to the northwest, the open waters of Lake Superior to the northeast. Due north, Madeline Island's southern flank extended almost to the horizon.

Here, they were alone. Mark and Debra walked a beach much like this years before, pondering Mark's decision to leave academia for a risky venture: distilling a mountain of research and lectures into book form. They had a child on the way, and conventional wisdom dictated stability over risk. But their fears were balanced by the conviction that Mark had something to say about the presidency that needed to be heard. Their risk was generously rewarded.

Mark was pondering a new question now: *Has the presidency in which I've had invested my intellectual life betrayed me? Was the highest office in the land irreparably poisoned? Has the current president fractured it beyond repair?*

Even more was haunting the scholar-writer: Had the third of July tarnished the magnificent city they called home, and should they escape what felt increasingly toxic?

"Deb … Tony …"

"I know what you're going to say," Debra said.

"Which is—"

"You're thinking of leaving the District."

"Dad—why?"

Mark was surprised. "Tony—you want to stay?"

"It's where my friends are. Besides—if we leave, what about Grandpa?"

Debra responded. "He's still healthy, active, and doesn't mind being alone. Grandpa has always said we shouldn't worry about him. He would be furious if he was our reason to stay."

There were tears, especially from Tony, who had grown up around the gritty, complicated, vibrant capital city at the center of his universe. He also knew that his parents made no capricious decisions, and while he would advocate for staying, he would follow their lead.

Debra read her husband well, and understood his special relationship with the city and people who had filled his life with purpose. She smiled.

Leaving was attractive partly because of the events that surrounded the Eastland visit. People would guess he was holding information that everyone wanted. But no matter where they lived, that would be true; they could escape Washington, but not it's history, nor their part in it.

"I'm not sure, Deb. No easy answers."

Indeed, no easy answers. Years later, Mark Neale would retire, still wondering and still writing in (and about) a city he would fail to stop loving.

CHAPTER EIGHTY-TWO

THE PRESENT, AND THE FUTURE

A week in the hospital (and months of rehab) brought Sally Crane back to health. She still loves the water, and keeps in touch with two men who, on the worst night of her life, saved it, and gave her new purpose. With her husband Mike she sails the Apostle Islands again, now trained as an EMT. And when she's not saving someone else's life, the big lake remains their happy place.

⌗

A simple cabin shelters a solitary figure. Eyes closed, the crisp bite of early fall brings a smile to his face. A breeze at sunrise coaxes the first leaves from their branches, as multicolored autumn falls softly to earth. This autumn, he feels truly at peace. The nightmares of three decades ago are fading, and the midsummer violence done to his body is healing. In his hand is a medal, bestowed in a private meeting between two once-hardened hearts, but not recorded in the White House schedule. He suspected, but did not know, that an island neighbor, a retired professor, had set the table for this moment, a quarter century after their paths first crossed. The President of the United States, in a step toward the truth that would set him free, honored this veteran who served with uncommon valor, in a battle his nation denies.

Michael will miss the fall hunt; he would have chosen to abstain this year in any case. By Christmas, he'll be strong enough to practice his trade once more, and furniture—

exceptional quality, unapologetically expensive, of wood salvaged from the storm—will find its way into homes again.

⁂

Madeline Island would gain a more robust tourist trade, but lose, for a while, some of its innocence. Many who came that summer and fall brought their expectations with them, and that was unfortunate. The spirit of the place is peace, which requires attentiveness that only a slower pace provides. Dark skies reveal every star; silence—an endangered species—is abundant. One comes to such a community to restore, not to check off a "point of interest." This same community grieved what they lost for a time, but a new narrative of resilience formed. They had watched heroes rise among them.

⁂

A new face appeared on a Duluth TV station that autumn, a rookie beginning her journalistic career. Her predecessor was Samantha Wells, now of Washington, D.C., who cited "personal reasons" for her departure, causing speculation in the newsroom: How did this rookie move so fast to such a strong market? She had let it slip that a "friend" in Washington had paved the way for a successful interview.

The news director, when accepting Samantha's resignation, noted the sparkle in her eye.

⁂

A lengthy phone conversation that fall linked one sixteen-year-old boy with another who was beginning a less public life in New England. Since the events that brought them together, it would be their first conversation, but not their last. A decade later, one would stand just to the right of a woman who had won his heart, while his best friend—a former First Son—stood as witness in a simple outdoor ceremony at a place called Big Bay, a former First Daughter in attendance.

❖

On a spring day in 2001, on a quiet hill in Virginia where the faithful gather to pray, they join in the presence of God to witness the union of Missy Jackson to Charlie Mann, former member of the Navy's elite. The people will rejoice as two of their own become one.

The preacher will pronounce them husband and wife— they will kiss and embrace to the unrestrained cheers, tears and applause of those who love them. Charlie will beam as he walks with his bride down the aisle. Trained for battle, taught to kill, he was considered one of the nation's finest. Yes, he killed. And yes, he walks with a bit of a limp that will make tending his small farm a bit more difficult. But today he begins new memories, as a husband, eventually as a father, and in the work of his childhood dreams, tilling the soil and harvesting the fruits of his labor. After service to his country, Charlie Mann will finally be home again.

❖

For Tom Malone, being Eastland's interior secretary had been a tough ride. *I won't miss it*, Malone thought. But knowing that now-President Gray would be vetting Malone's replacement—his mind was at work. *If I'm lucky I'll be asked to step aside. Or he'll just fire me. But for now, I'm still here. I can still leave a legacy, on my terms.*

A week later, Chief Wade Sanders opened a letter from the Department of the Interior. He saw the name on the letterhead, and laughed. *You're still "Secretary," Mr. Malone? It must be lonely there, in the Short Timer's Club.*

But after two pages of words like "Whereas" and "Therefore be it Resolved"—bureaucratic pretentiousness at its best—a declaration: a small but important acreage adjacent to Wisconsin's Red Cliff Reservation would be "preserved in perpetuity in its natural state." There was the usual sign-off: "Sincerely, Thomas Malone, Secretary, Department of the

Interior." But there was more—a hand-written note: *Chief Sanders: This is your accomplishment. You are a force to be reckoned with. I am honored to know you, and the community you so ably serve.*

The chief neither knew nor cared what kind of deal-making had persuaded Wisconsin to surrender its Marsh-era policy. What he was certain of: two men, a thousand miles and worlds apart, shared a smile that said: Well done.

⁜

The most painful consequences fell on the Neale family. Notoriety, much of it unwelcome, followed the third and fourth of July, forcing a heartbreaking choice: to sell their island retreat. Violence had stolen its serenity. Terror and death happened there—too many painful memories. But the flood of curious and intrusive citizens destroyed its once-treasured seclusion, and sealed its fate. It could no longer be their refuge.

Still, the Neales would return every year to a rented cottage hidden on the island's eastern shore, away from the maddening crowds. In the years that would follow, they would lay Dr. Franklin Neale to rest beside his wife, on this island, on an inland sea.

⁜

But before all these things:

A presidential campaign rages, and conventions will soon select their candidates. But on a late summer morning in the Year of Our Lord 2000, far from any hint of political intrigue, Matthew Harris is awakened by the sound of tires on a gravel road.

CHAPTER EIGHTY-THREE

EPILOGUE

Matthew and his friends had pitched their tent in a hillside clearing. Their shelter faced west toward a rock-encircled fire pit, then a small spring-fed pond, then the rolling grassland of the Harris family ranch. Behind the tent and to the east, the hill abruptly dropped toward the road running north and south. Beyond the road, a cemetery.

His buddies are sound sleepers. Matt slips quietly into the first light of morning and walks toward the sound. He stops at the crest of the rise, looking past the now-familiar stream and the road on its far bank. What he sees is puzzling: here in the middle of nowhere is a State Trooper, her car idling as she stands by its open door, its police radio chattering. Matthew stays low, motionless, peering through the grass and brush, seeing but not wanting to be seen, waiting for … something.

Five minutes later, more road noise, as a three-vehicle parade stops, just outside the cemetery gate. Matt is mesmerized.

Robert Alan Eastland, President of the United States for a few hours more, rides in the back of a gray government SUV through the Sand Hills that once were his home. *Air Force One* had made an unpublished landing at Offutt Air Force Base in Omaha in the predawn hours; *Marine One* had whisked the president westward to a remote location north and west of North Platte, far from inquisitive eyes. He was escorted by two unmarked cars carrying the requisite Secret Service agents, as the long shadows of first light filter through trees that have shaded this quiet place for generations.

An election looms that means nothing to him. In fact, he chose this time, while the eyes of the world are elsewhere. A modest security detail is at his insistence, and while his staff worries, they understand. This is a difficult day for all of them.

It is difficult as well for the passenger in the president's SUV. Mark Neale, Robert Eastland's biographer, was invited to witness this morning's pilgrimage. Before leaving Washington, he had heard from the president the reason why two graves in a rural cemetery are this morning's destination. This too, the president insisted, must become part of Neale's narrative, including the consequences this soon-to-be former president would receive.

Trying a former occupant of the White House had never happened. The consequences would test the limits of American justice: What does conviction and punishment do to the institution of the presidency? There was a practical question: where and how to incarcerate a former president who has, even in prison, lifetime Secret Service protection? And this: never had a defendant been so eager to assist his own prosecution and persuade the court of his guilt.

The next occupant of the Oval Office will float the idea of a pardon, but Robert Alan Eastland will publicly reject it. He would, the pundits predicted, spend about a decade, maybe more, as a prisoner. But in an act of mercy, he will be released after seven years into the care of his family, as he battles the cancer that will claim him.

The road climbs to the right, away from the stream and around a low hill. Just before the road drops again to rejoin the stream, a wrought-iron arch marks the entrance to the small gathering of headstones, barely two acres in size, covering the rounded crest of the knoll. The date, 1869, stands atop an arch formed by an anonymous 19th Century blacksmith. Though pocked by decades of rust, it stands erect and true now, held in a new concrete base and bearing a fresh coat of glossy black, applied by Matthew Harris and his father. The picket fence around the cemetery is immaculately painted in white. The grass is green and manicured, in stark contrast to the coarse vegetation of the surrounding hills.

It is almost too perfect. The century-old headstones have been re-set, standing in straight rows across the knoll, as plumb as the day they were first raised over many whose lives had begun and ended within a day's walk of their resting place.

Hundreds of rural cemeteries languish, left behind as communities died and people moved on. But this particular cemetery on this particular hill has been loved, a tribute by, and to, the people of this region. One of their own had risen to prominence; his ancestors lay interred on this hill. He now returns, not to visit old friends—indeed, only Matthew Harris would know he was here—but to acknowledge his past.

The small procession is met by the State Trooper, who remains at the end of the driveway. This is a private affair, except for an unseen, almost teen-aged, boy.

Later that morning, the secretary of state will open a letter from her president, the contents of which she anticipates. At about the same time, the attorney general will open another, acknowledging in detail the president's role, indirect but real nonetheless, in the deaths of four people: a Lebanese pilot, a political giant, and two of his own beloved. This letter was written with the full knowledge—and horror—of his personal attorney. The president knew full well the consequences of this letter, and in his writing, he held nothing back.

More immediate consequences are already under way. An unmarked van will soon carry the worldly goods of private citizens Robert Alan, Mary Lee, Shannon, and Aaron Eastland from the White House, after the shattering of their public lives. At noon in a solemn ceremony, Vice President Richard Gray will be sworn in as the new president, his burning goal tarnished by how he reached it. And with that oath of office, Robert Alan Eastland's public career will be, mercifully in his eyes, over.

The vehicles raised very little dust on the dew-covered road and stopped alongside the drive that bisected the small rural cemetery. As always, the agents get out first, scan the area in all directions, and with nods more than words assure each other that all is clear. Indeed, at this hour and in this place, there should be no other humans for miles in any direction. Young Matthew remains unseen. The right rear door of the Suburban is opened, and out steps the president of the United States, the most powerful man in the world, dressed in loafers, slacks, and a sweater.

The president? Matthew Harris shakes, simultaneously fearing the consequences should he be seen—and wondering if anyone will believe him when (and if) he tells the story.

The Suburban's left rear door opens, and the writer emerges who stands silently, lost in his own struggle to make sense of it all.

No words are exchanged; only the president walks the forty paces past headstones of no public consequence to those with his surname engraved in rose-colored granite.

It is a strange feeling, Agent Barry Lindhurst thinks. He would not have reached this proximity to a sitting president without the ability to detach, focus, and remain professional. Yet in this moment, knowing that this tour of duty is ending in something other than triumph, he longs to know the mind and heart of the man forty paces away. For the first time in his adult life, his eyes moisten. He sees not the power and energy of a powerful man at the top of his game, but an ordinary man bearing incredible pain.

That ordinary man had set in motion a series of events that would place before the people he had served the truth about events he had almost succeeded in obscuring. Truth that includes his sins against his wife, daughter, and son, and the family that had been murdered so many years before. They will lead to consequences that he was ready to accept.

He had sought and was receiving a different consequence from Aaron and Mary Lee. The healing would take longer for Shannon, and scars would remain. But the healing will, with time and compassionate counsel, continue. It will involve facing the pain time and time again until finding wholeness, in a subdued sense of family, a husband and father humbled, purged of ambitions that nearly destroyed him, and grateful for the peace he would find.

And now this—an act symbolic but essential, and heartfelt. He kneels, his eyes closed, at the graves of those he had loved too little. The man known for eloquence says nothing. He holds two red roses, not purchased in the usual way from a Washington florist. At the president's request, they were cut from the garden surrounding the church in which he and the woman he now honors had said their wedding vows. One is placed, slowly, reverently, atop each headstone.

The gesture is touching, but his presence is the fullest symbol of penitence; one step on a long and painful path toward closure, liberation … and grace.

ACKNOWLEDGEMENTS:

Writing can be a solitary exercise, but publishing is emphatically a team sport. I wrote, re-wrote, and re-re-wrote *Firestorm* at the upper limits of my writing ability, but along the way I received loving but at times brutal honesty from my beta readers and my editor-publisher. They are the sole reason I'm proud to see my name on the cover. So thank you, Kitty, Anna, Mark, and Mike, from the bottom of my heart. In addition, I thank many of you who, having read *Fifty-Three Weeks*, affirmed and encouraged me to keep telling stories. I set this novel in a real and wonderful place: Madeline Island, part of Lake Superior's Apostle Islands National Lakeshore. I love this place and its people. And while the people I describe are fictional, I hope that I have honored their dignity, resourcefulness and the extravagant love they have showered on my family for almost four decades. The principal characters have a voice. The longer I lived with them, the more they told me about themselves, which challenged my writing: *No, I wouldn't have said it that way. Try this.* I didn't always like what they self-revealed. But while a closer look soiled some, heroes emerged, rising to challenges they never expected to face. Because this story echoes some of the political dynamics in 2024's election drama, I offer this disclaimer: *Firestorm*'s issues and characters emerged more than two decades ago, and that original story remains intact, even in the names of primary characters. Historical figures and events are depicted as accurately as possible. This includes the weather, drawing on a particular storm that I witnessed as it impacted the novel's setting. I did not attempt a happy ending, and these stories of flawed yet precious people continue past the last page.

Though I don't envision a sequel, the reader (and perhaps the author) have permission to imagine what the final chapter could be.

REFERENCES:

The US Secret Service: Walter S. Bowen & Harry Edward Neal: Chilton, Phila/NY, 1960

Protecting the President: Dennis VN McCarthy w/Philip W. Smith; Wm Morrow & Co. 1985 Secret Service Chief: U.E. Baughman w/Leonard Wallace Robinson: NY, Harper Bros.,1961 & 1962

Daily Weather Maps: June 24-30, 1991 (NOAA/NWS, National Meteorological Center)

War Without End; Anton La Guardia: St. Martin's, 2001

The Hundred Years' War on Palestine; Rashid Khalidi: Metropolitan Books, 2020

ABOUT THE AUTHOR

Dale Stohre served six congregations as their pastor, and founded The Anchorage, an innovative program in and for the marketplace, where through small groups, seminars, radio and print media, he was a "pastor-at-large" for working people in his hometown of Duluth, Minnesota. A junior college writing class in the mid-1960s sparked a love for the written word that continues into this, his second published novel. Social justice is one of his passions; part of his love for life, God, mountains, the Great Lakes, his wife Beth, and their shared families. When he's not writing novels, he and Beth can be found walking in the neighborhood around their home in Franklin, Wisconsin, or hiking a secluded trail somewhere.